Cooper

NO SHADE

A Hood Rat Novel
by K'wan

NO SHADE

A Hood Rat Novel

PROLOGUE

It was a slow day in the hood. It had rained off and on throughout the night leaving the air humid and the benches wet so people were deterred from hanging out that early in the day. For the first time in a long time, everything was in slow motion and that suited Ms. Pat just fine.

Ms. Pat was an older woman of undetermined age and quick wit who everyone either loved or despised, but she didn't care either way. She was who she was and made no excuses for it. Dressed in a faded housecoat and tattered fuzzy slippers with hard cardboard soles, she shuffled into the living room of her project apartment. There were empty beer bottles, overflowing ashtrays on the coffee table, and someone had left a greasy bag on one of her orange, plastic covered sofas. When she saw the mess it was in, all she could do was shake her head, as she knew it was the work of her son Mookie and his crime partner Fish.

Mookie was almost forty years old but still lived at home and expected his mother to clean up behind him as if he was a child. Of all her children, he had always been the most dependent on her and the most troublesome.

Ms. Pat stood there with her hands on her wide hips trying to figure out where to start when the front door swung open. Moving with reflexes born of decades in the streets, she immediately dropped to one knee and dipped her hand in the front pocket of her housecoat. By the time the first figure bent the corner into the living room, she already had her .38 cocked and ready to bang on the intruder. Her

I

finger had just brushed the trigger when she realized the intruder was her great granddaughter, Jalen. Without giving her gun-wielding elder a second look, Jalen tossed her knapsack on the floor and picked the television remote up off the coffee table.

"Girl what in the T.D. Jakes is wrong with you, coming in here unannounced like that!" Ms. Pat barked. She hurriedly put the .38 back in her housecoat and adjusted her wig that had slid to the side when she dropped to one knee.

Jalen turned her eyes from the television long enough to roll them at Ms. Pat then capped, "It ain't my fault, blame her."

Ms. Pat shuffled over to Jalen and snatched the remote control. "Little girl, who in the hell is her, and ain't you got manners enough to know to speak to your elders when you walk into a room?"

"Hi," Jalen said reluctantly, rolling her eyes again.

Ms. Pat grabbed Jalen by the arm and yanked her to her feet. "Little Ms. Thang, if you roll them hateful eyes at me again, I promise you I will slap you blinder than Ray Charles."

"Ouch, why you manhandling me like that?" Jalen squirmed.

"Because that's what you do with animals, you handle them and right now you're acting like the unruliest critter I ever laid eyes on. Now where is ya mama?"

"She's outside talking to Mr. Happy," Jalen flopped on the couch and folded her arms.

Ms. Pat stormed over to her living room window, which faced the back of the building. She stuck her head out and scanned the parking lot for her granddaughter. Sure enough, Jada was leaning against Happy's truck listening while he spewed a bunch of nothing

II

in her ear. The chicks in the neighborhood flocked to Happy like flies on shit because of what they saw on the outside, but Ms. Pat knew what was in his heart, and she didn't like it.

"Jada Butler," she called her granddaughter by her full name, "you better quit playing in the pig pen and bring yo' ass in here."

Jada frowned at her grandmother and held up her hand signaling to give her five minutes.

"That's the same hand you need to be using to tan these kids' hides instead of taking bribes," Ms. Pat shouted. "Jada, you need to come and tend to this trump-mouthed child before I have to lay hands on her."

"I wish you would," Jalen mumbled. It was barely above a whisper but Ms. Pat had super keen hearing.

Without turning from the window, Ms. Pat removed one of the slippers she wore and threw it at Jalen. The shoe spiraled like a Frisbee, slapping Jalen square in the forehead. "Jada," she continued screaming, "if I got to call yo' ass one more time then you're gonna be next on my shit list. You better ask these niggaz about me!" Ms. Pat slammed the window closed.

Jalen was sitting on the couch with her hand over her forehead and staring daggers at Ms. Pat. Her lip was trembling but she wouldn't give Ms. Pat the satisfaction of seeing her cry. Of all Jada's kids, Jalen was the coldest. She was a Butler through and through.

"I know that look," Ms. Pat said, taking off her glasses and wiping them on her housecoat. "You're probably thinking if you were a little bigger you would kick my ass, ain't you? Well I got a newsflash for you little girl; you ain't bigger than me, and I'll be

III

dead and in the ground by the time you are. I don't know or care what yo' mama teaches you at home, but in here we practice respect and you will learn to respect me, do you understand?"

"Yea, Grandma," Jalen sniffled. A few tears managed to escape and they softened Ms. Pat.

"Stop crying baby," Ms. Pat rubbed her back affectionately, "I ain't trying to hurt you, I'm just trying to teach you better than I did ya mama and yo' grandmama."

"But it hurts," Jalen cried, pointing at the knot that was forming on her head.

"Life is pain, baby girl," Ms. Pat kissed the knot tenderly. After she got Jalen to stop crying she turned the television to one of her favorite daytime talk shows. It was already forty-five minutes into the show, but Ms. Pat figured she could catch the last fifteen minutes of foolery.

As usual, the slightly graying host sat cross-legged with his easy smile and sarcastically caring eyes, as a ratchet young girl confessed her darkest secrets to her boyfriend and the rest of America. She had slept around town like a dog in heat and wasn't sure if her boyfriend was the father of their youngest child. The fact that the host had managed to line up another young black couple to come on the show to embarrass themselves was nothing new, but it was who his guests that day, happened to be, that had Ms. Pat glued to the television. The host addressed them as Kareem and Coco, but Ms. Pat knew them as Boots and Bernie. They went through the routine cursing and pleading session, which was common with the guests on the

IV

show before they got to the meat and potatoes of the show, the paternity results.

The host's build up was dramatic. He peeled open the envelope, scanned the contents, and a smile tickled the corners of his mouth. "Kareem, in the case of two year old Hassan, you are…NOT the father!" the host announced with his usual flair.

The confession seemed to suck all of the wind out of Bernie and his eyes watered up. Some of the audience seemed to have sympathy for him, but Ms. Pat felt none. He was finally hearing from the horse's mouth what people had been trying to tell him for year, Boots was a whore.

Bernie broke down and started sobbing uncontrollably, not caring that he was on television. The host rubbed Bernie's back and tried his best to console him. Of all the men he'd seen get hit with the deathblow on his stage, Bernie had taken it the worst. Boots watched from a distance with unapologetic eyes, occasionally turning her attention to the audience to curse at someone who had insulted her. She seemed more relieved to have gotten the secret off her chest than bothered at the fact that she had no idea who the father of her child was.

The host had finally gotten Bernie to stop crying and brought them all together for a group huddle while he whispered to them about working things out with the help of his show's counselors. As soon as everyone relaxed, Boots moved within arm's reach of Bernie, and he did something he should've done years ago; he pounced on Boots. By the time security made it to the altercation, Bernie had already socked Boots in the eye and was in the process of strangling her. Security managed to pry Bernie's hands from around Boots' neck and escorted him backstage, where he was taken into custody by the local police and the cameras caught it all.

One camera managed to get a close up of Bernie's face as he was being handcuffed and he was actually smiling. He had whipped Boots out in front of millions of witnesses and would surely go to jail because of it, but at the end of the day, it was all worth it. Boots had been making a fool out of Bernie for years and that black eye he'd given her on daytime television made them even.

Ms. Pat had seen enough. She turned off the television and looked to her great granddaughter. "Baby, hand me the classified section outta that newspaper next to you."

Jalen handed Ms. Pat the section she requested and watched curiously, as she thumbed through the real estate section. "Grandma, how come you're looking at apartments when you already have one?"

"Because when trash like that falls this close to your doorstep that means it's time to move on. There goes the damn neighborhood...again."

VI

PART I

WELCOME BACK

NO SHADE: A Hood Rat Novel

CHAPTER 1

"I don't know why we didn't take my car," Billy said with an attitude from the passenger seat. She wore her signature scowl, and her hair was pulled back into a ponytail. What little she had tried to do with it, had started to sweat out in the hot ass car. Billy tried her best to remain still because every time she moved, she burned her arm on the imitation leather upholstery. It was a balmy ninety-degrees outside, the air conditioning in Reese's piece of shit car was busted, and Billy didn't find this out until they were already off the block. She was already late and going back would make her tardier.

"Why you always complaining about something? I'd have thought you'd have been happy we're taking my car since you always complain about your truck being a gas guzzler whenever we need to go somewhere," Reese pointed out. Though she wouldn't admit it, she too was hot. She glanced up in the rearview and the sweat on her forehead had begun to make her foundation run. She tried to fix it with her thumb, but it didn't help. Reese was always conscious about her make-up being correct because she had slightly bad skin.

"Filling my tank up is a small price to pay instead of burning up in here," Billy fanned herself. She rolled the window down, but it didn't help. The air outside was almost as humid as the air inside. "Jesus, I can't take it!"

Reese sucked her teeth. "I'll be glad when we get back so I can get you the hell out of my ride, with your complaining ass."

"Well that makes two of us, jail bird," Billy capped. "I'm still trying to figure out how your ass managed to get arrested twice in less than seventy-two hours."

Reese gave her a look. "Don't even try it, Billy. I'll wear the first one, but the second arrest was all on you. I got locked up for holding you down, remember?"

"Well you wouldn't have had to hold me down if you hadn't have put that nut ass idea in my head," Billy shot back.

"I wish you could've seen yourself out there going Rambo in front of all them white people," Reese laughed, reliving the moment in her head.

"It's not funny, Reese. I could've ended up with a record behind that and lost my job. You know they don't play that when you work for the State," Billy said seriously.

"Billy ain't nobody trying to put you on 'America's Most Wanted' for no street fight. And as far as your job goes, Marcus got her to drop the charges so your job isn't gonna find out. Even if they did, it'd be a fool's move to fire you. Nobody looks out for those kids the way you do."

For the last few years, Billy had been working for the Department of Child Services as a social worker. Billy came from the same background as most of the kids she worked with, so she connected with them in ways that most couldn't. The pay wasn't great, but she had full benefits and for the first time in her life, was doing something she enjoyed for a living. Billy couldn't save every kid who passed through her caseload, but the ones she could, made her feel like she was doing her part.

2

"How much further?" Billy asked, changing the subject.

Reese looked down at the GPS. She had to balance it on her lap because the crack head she had bought it from didn't sell her the window mount with it. "Should be just up ahead."

"Why the hell did she fly into Newark instead of JFK or LaGuardia? It would've been a lot more convenient."

"Because she got a buddy pass hook up from one of her homeboys," Reese made air quotations with her fingers. "You know that bitch is cheap and ain't trying to spend it if she ain't got to."

Billy shook her head. "You would have thought she'd have learned some damn class living in Hollywood all this time. I guess you can take a chick out of the ghetto, but can't take the ghetto out of a chick."

Reese drove in silence for a few minutes before asking. "So, how did she sound when you spoke to her?"

Billy shrugged. "She sounded like herself I guess. How was she supposed to sound?"

"I dunno; I'm just trying to make sure everything is kosher. I don't want no shit, Billy."

Billy sucked her teeth. "Reese, calm your ass down. She and I talked in great length about it and she's cool, at least for the time being. If you had kept your inner-hoe in check, you wouldn't have to be concerned."

"Billy, I wish you would stop saying it like I did it on purpose," Reese said.

3

K'WAN

"Sure, people slip and fall on random dicks by accident all the time," Billy replied sarcastically. "Look, don't worry about it. Everything will be fine."

Reese pulled off the 1 & 9 South and followed the airport terminal signs for American Airlines arriving flights. She weaved in and out of airport traffic with the grace and disrespect of a native New York driver, pissing off the other motorists. She scanned the sea of faces waiting for curbside pick-up, but none of them belonged to her friend. Reese was about to circle back around when Billy spotted her, two terminals down from where she was supposed to meet them.

Billy took a minute to take in the measure of her friend. The California sun had added a rich tan to her skin, bringing the African American side of her more to the forefront than usual. Her signature weave was gone and she now wore her hair in a short curly style that fit her round face. She had put on a bit of weight since they had last seen her, but it seemed to have been distributed in all the right places. From the way her jeans hugged her thighs and lack of stomach, you could tell that hitting the gym was one of the habits she had picked up while living in L.A. From the way the butterscotch colored young man in the flight attendant's uniform was hanging on her every word, it was obvious that no matter how much she might have changed physically, at heart, she was still Yoshi.

Having seen enough, Reese started beeping the horn.

Yoshi flashed a look that said hating bitch, before holding up one finger signaling for them to give her a second. She exchanged a few more words with the flight attendant before he grabbed the

4

majority of her bags and struggled with them to the car, while Yoshi watched with an amused expression on her face. She hadn't lost her killer's instincts.

"Still the same old Yoshi," Billy remarked as soon as she got into the car.

"Ain't shit changed about me but my area code. Now shut up and give me some love," Yoshi leaned forward and hugged Billy over the front seat. "I missed you, mami," she kissed her on the cheek.

"I missed you too," Billy replied.

"So, you just gonna get in my whip and not speak?" Reese asked, noticing that Yoshi hadn't so much as looked at her the whole time.

"Hi Reese," Yoshi said dryly.

"This bitch," Reese mumbled under her breath.

"Look, this is supposed to be about me and not y'all petty ass shit, so knock it off," Billy interjected.

"You're one hundred percent right, Billy. I apologize," Yoshi said.

"Me too," Reese added.

"But bump all that, we haven't seen you in like ten years, heifer. How's life in California treating you?" Billy changed the subject.

"Knock it off, Billy. It's only been two years since I've been home, so stop exaggerating. As far as California, I love it. It never snows and the weed is always on hit. I don't know why I waited so long to get out of the Big Apple."

"And how's business?" Billy asked. She had been hearing good things about Yoshi's new venture through the grapevine and was anxious to get the scoop from the horse's mouth.

"Business is great, now. In the beginning, it was slow, but once I was able to get my name out there things began to pick up. I mostly do videos and fashion shows, but I did manage to land some work on a few movies last year. One of the girl's I did hair and make-up for on a video plugged me with somebody she knew in the glam department on a film they were shooting out in Hollywood. Once they saw me work my sorcery and turn them tired looking hos into beauty queens, word got out, and more gigs started coming in. I even had to hire a small staff."

Yoshi was a former video girl and exotic dancer who had applied the money she'd made and the things she'd learned and started her own company. She did styling and make-up for various entertainment companies. Yoshi had started her business out of a roll-on she kept in the trunk of her car, but was now starting to flourish.

"Listen to you sounding all business-like," Billy teased.

"Everybody has to grow up and grow out at some point, Billy. You're the one who taught me that. It's crazy because it took me leaving New York to really get focused on doing what I had to do."

"Sometimes change is good, ma," Billy said. "On another note, I really appreciate you making this trip on such short notice. I know with getting your business off the ground and dealing with life in general, it wasn't the most convenient time for you."

6

NO SHADE: A Hood Rat Novel

"Knock it off, Billy. You think I wouldn't show up for my best friend's wedding? Now, spill. I wanna hear exactly how this miracle came about and don't leave out any of the details."

CHAPTER 2

Several weeks earlier:

Getting across the waiting room was like trying to make it through the club. It was as hot as the devil and crowded with people, mostly women and children, but there were a few men scattered about also. They were from all walks of life, from the working class who needed a little help, to the scam artists who were trying to beat the system, to those who had hit rock bottom with nowhere else to turn. On any given day, you could find the most predictable to the most unlikely people passing through the musty halls and waiting rooms of 55 W. 125th Street, also known as the welfare building.

"Can I help you?" the fortyish looking woman behind the counter asked. She was plump, wearing old-fashioned brown glasses, and her hair was pulled back into a ponytail.

"I sure hope so because I been here for three hours and ain't nobody tried to help me yet," Claudette said, hand on her hip and clicking her gum. She was dressed a pair of hundred dollar jeans, two hundred dollar sneakers, but wearing a ten dollar graphic T-shirt. She reached up and scratched her fuzzy braids with blue acrylic nails that needed filling. Claudette was only eighteen, but she had the worn eyes of a woman who had lived hard and fast far too early.

"Who are you here to see, honey?" the woman behind the desk asked, trying to keep her tone even. She saw hundreds of Claudette's on a weekly basis — young, belligerent, and clueless— so she already knew what to expect.

"The same thing I wanted when I came in here this morning, to talk to my case worker, Mrs. Lee." Claudette rolled her eyes.

The woman behind the desk felt her finger tightening around the ink pen she was holding. For a brief instant, she had a flash of stabbing the smart mouthed young girl with the pen, but she valued her job and her freedom. "One moment." She picked up the phone on the desk and punched in an extension. "What was your name?"

"Claudette...Jenkins." She drug her name out slowly as if the woman couldn't speak English.

The woman gave Claudette her back while she spoke to someone on the phone, presumably Mrs. Lee. This earned her another eye roll from Claudette. After a conversation, which lasted less than sixty seconds, the woman hung up the phone and faced Claudette. "Have a seat and wait for your name to be called."

"This is some bullshit," Claudette said in a raised voice. "What the fuck is the sense of giving out appointments if y'all gonna make us wait all these damn hours? I hate this fucking place!"

"Yet you continue bringing your ass back looking for assistance," the woman said, letting her temper slip.

"What the hell did you just say to me?" Claudette snapped.

"Listen," the woman behind the desk said, calming herself, realizing she was about to go over the top on Claudette. "I don't know you personally, so I don't know your story, and I'm not judging you. You hate this place, right? I don't blame you. It's always crowded; they make you jump through hoops for little to no money, and it takes forever to get anything done. I was on public assistance for six years because I needed help feeding my kids, so I

9

get it. Some people come here and deal with this shit because they don't have a choice. Ain't no shame in needing help, but have you ever considered looking for work, so you won't have to deal with this?"

"I know you ain't up in here trying to read nobody?" Claudette was defensive.

"No, I'm just asking you a question. You look healthy enough to work or maybe even go to school. You're young, and there are a bunch of grants and things that you may qualify for if you're continuing your education. I'm telling you this so you won't have to come down here and deal with this."

Claudette's face twisted as if she had just smelled something foul. "What the fuck do you mean 'get a job'? If I could get a job, I wouldn't be down at this raggedy muthafucka going through the motions for one hundred and ten dollars in cash and two hundred and fifty dollars in food stamps. What the hell am I supposed to do with that? Don't be trying to give me no fucking advice like you know me!"

"You're right, ma'am. I don't know you, and I apologize," the woman said, mad at herself for even opening her mouth and trying to encourage the young girl.

"Damn right you don't know me." Claudette flipped her hair and walked away.

Claudette picked her way back across the room, stepping on toys and narrowly avoiding a collision with a group of unattended kids who'd decided to start a game of tag in the waiting room. Holding their seats alongside Claudette's kids was a girl named Rocky.

Rocky was cute young girl with a bright smile. After she'd had her son, she'd put on a little weight, but still had a fair shape. She was holding up for the time being, but a rib platter or two would push her over the line. A few months prior, Rocky had been laid off from her job, and, when the unemployment checks ran out and she was still unemployed, she had to do what she had to do for her and her son.

It was her first time in life applying for public assistance, and she was a bit confused about the whole process. She looked around like a lost puppy, trying to figure out what was going on and where she should be standing when she bumped into a familiar face—Claudette. She and Claudette weren't close friends, but they lived in the same building and occasionally shared a blunt sponsored by a mutual friend. Claudette, even at eighteen, was a vet, so she offered to show Rocky the ropes.

"What'd she say?" Rocky asked, cradling Claudette's four-year-old daughter, Ranique.

"The same shit they've been saying since I got here this morning…Nothing!" Claudette plopped down on the hard plastic chair next to Rocky. "These bitches down here be getting on my last fucking nerve. They constantly have you running back and forth then waiting for hours, just to ask you a bunch of personal-ass questions, and then send you on your way with a few funky hundred dollars and a few food stamps."

"Damn! Sounds like we'd be better off getting jobs," Rocky said.

Claudette sucked her teeth. "I'm gonna pass on that job shit, boo. Right now, I got a two-bedroom apartment in the projects, and my rent is only one hundred and eighty-eight dollars because I'm unemployed and on public assistance. Do you know how much I'd be paying for a two-bedroom somewhere else with no assistance? The cost of living in New York is too damn high to get by without some type of government assistance. Even if I worked a forty-hour week like a square, I'd probably be giving up my whole monthly paycheck just to pay rent on a shoebox apartment that's barely big enough for me and my kids."

"Mommy, I'm hungry," Claudette's two-year-old son Raymond hugged her leg. He was a chubby lad who was few shades lighter than Ranique, with curly hair, on account of his father being Puerto Rican.

"Boy, your ass is always hungry. Didn't I feed you this morning before we left?" Claudette said, sounding irritated.

"But that was only cereal, Mommy. I'm still hungry," Raymond whined.

"You're always hungry. That's why your ass is so fat now." Claudette shoved him away. It was only a slight push, but Raymond dramatically fell on the floor and started crying. "Boy, get your ass up. You're in here embarrassing me," she told him. Raymond ignored her and continued crying, kicking his feet against a lady's chair. "Ray-Ray, you better get up before I give you something to cry for."

"No! I'm hungry!" Raymond yelled and began kicking the chair of the lady in front of him really hard.

12

Raymond's show was attracting the attention of everyone in the waiting room, especially the woman whose chair he was kicking. She looked at Claudette, wondering if she was going to do anything, but the teenager just sat there with her arms folded.

"Excuse me. Could you please make your son stop kicking my chair?" the woman asked. She was brown-skinned and in her mid to late twenties. She was neatly dressed in tan Capri pants, a brown V-neck blouse, matching sandals, and was sporting a beautiful gold necklace.

"Does it look like this little muthafucka is listening to me?" Claudette asked with an attitude. Tired of people staring at her, Claudette snatched Raymond from the floor roughly and shook him. "You better quit clowning before you end up the cause of me fucking a snooty bitch up," she said loud enough for the woman to hear her.

"Did you just call me a bitch?" the woman asked.

"Wasn't nobody talking to you. I was talking to my son, lady," Claudette said.

"Little girl, you need to be more mindful of how you talk to people. That mouth of yours is gonna land you in trouble," the woman warned.

"I ain't no little girl. I'm grown so what comes outta my mouth ain't none of your damn business," Claudette got loud.

"Y'all keep it down back there," a security guard yelled from the front.

"Mind your business, Barney Miller," Claudette shot back.

13

"Claudette, just chill out," Rocky whispered. People were looking at them, and she was feeling embarrassed.

"It ain't me who needs to chill. It's these muthafuckas in here. I swear, if this lady don't call me soon so I can take care of my business, I'm going the fuck to jail." Claudette was speaking to Rocky, but looking at the woman who she'd been arguing with.

"If I didn't know any better, I'd say you had a problem from the way you're looking over here at me," the woman said.

"If you want a problem, there can be a problem." Claudette got to her feet and started taking her earrings off.

The woman also stood. She didn't want to fight, but she wasn't going to allow Claudette to snuff her either. "It ain't that serious, but you ain't gonna keep bumping your gums and thinking I'm going to take it. I'll fuck around and go to jail for putting my hands on you."

"Claudette…" Rocky reached for her, but Claudette slapped her hand away.

"Fuck that! This bitch is acting like she wants it. I dare you to put your fucking hands on me," Claudette challenged. She knew the woman was reluctant because of the age difference and was playing on that.

"Like I said, I might go to jail for putting my hands on you," the woman repeated.

"But I won't," a voice called from behind Claudette. She found herself confronted with a younger version of the woman she was arguing with. Without saying another word, the girl punched Claudette in the face and sat her on her ass. "Bitch, you trying to

14

stunt on my sister?" She jumped on Claudette's chest and started wailing on her.

"Sharon, chill out," the woman tried to pull her little sister off Claudette.

"Fuck that, Reese. I'm gonna teach these hos about their mouths," Sharon kept tagging Claudette.

The waiting room was thrown into chaos. Claudette rolled around on the floor with Sharon, trying to get her off while her children wailed. Security rushed the scene and started manhandling the girls. Sharon was trying to get to Claudette, but accidentally punched one of the security guards, and he started hitting her like she was a man.

"That's my baby sister!" Reese screamed and jumped on his back. She had damn near clawed his eyes out before his partner was able to pull her off. When it was all sorted out, Claudette, Sharon, and Reese were taken into custody, and Rocky was left with Claudette's kids.

Rocky looked down at Ranique, who had now joined her brother in a fit of crying, and let out a deep sigh. "Fuck my life."

CHAPTER 3

"Life!" Quanna said, slapping her comb on the edge of her workstation. Her booth was closest to the door of the salon, so she always got the tea the moment it came through the door. She had one girl in the chair, whose hair she was braiding to prepare for a sew-in weave. Two more girls sat around them, on folding chairs, leaning in to make sure they heard every bit of the latest neighborhood dirt. Being that it was the first of the month, the beauty salon was popping, and there was a sea of nappy heads waiting to be addressed, but Quanna was more focused on spreading the gossip than the logjam in the hair salon.

"Damn! He mad young. Why they give him so much time?" one of the girls in the folding chairs asked. She had a shower cap over her heard, waiting for the conditioner in her head to settle so she could get rolled up and go under the dryer.

"Probably because he's shot, at least twenty cats, and that's just in Harlem," Quanna said. "I didn't know him personally, but I seen him at a few spots, and he was always on some thug shit, so I can't say I'm surprised."

"That's a damn shame, because I was trying to see about that one there," the girl in the second folding chair said, seemingly genuinely saddened by the news. She wasn't getting her hair done, just keeping her friend company and getting caught up on the gossip. She was wearing a one-piece spandex suit that only drew attention to her beer belly, and a pair of green plastic earrings that didn't match anything she had on.

16

NO SHADE: A Hood Rat Novel

"You know you'd go straight to hell for putting your old-ass pussy on little Ashanti," Quanna told her.

"I don't give a fuck. They said he was the next up and coming hood star and a bitch like me is looking for a come up. That young girl he was running around with wasn't fucking his little ass properly, and that's why he stayed in trouble. I would've put this mouth on him so good that he wouldn't have even wanted to leave the house, let alone go to prison. My head game still ringing in the hood." She popped her lips for emphasis.

"Well, bitch, unless you're going to mail your pussy to him in a care package, it doesn't sound like it's gonna happen," the girl with the shower cap said.

"You know, it never ceases to amaze me how bitches try to make legends out of lies," a voice called from the far end of the salon. A girl sat in the chair, while the Dominican chick in the pink smock brushed her long black hair out. She was light- skinned with pink pouty lips. The girl had been listening to the women cackle but waited until the right time to make her presence known. After the Dominican woman, finished brushing her hair out, she rose slowly from the chair and turned her cold eyes on the gossipmongers.

"Who the fuck is you?" the girl with the shower cap asked, wondering who the busybody was who'd interrupted their dish.

"Let y'all washed up bitches tell it, I'm the young girl who ain't fucking Ashanti properly, but my name is Fatima," she said with a chill to her voice. From the look on some of their faces, she knew that they knew who she was, and what she was about. "Where do I

17

know y'all from for y'all to be having mine or my man's names in ya mouths?"

Quanna and the girl with the shower cap remained silent, knowing they were wrong and feeling embarrassed for getting caught dishing the dirt, with her sitting a few feet away. The girl with the plastic earrings knew no such humility.

"Slow your roll, little girl. We was just down here talking shit. It ain't that serious," the girl with the plastic earrings said.

"It's serious enough for you to be down here having wet dreams about a piece of dick you'll never touch," Fatima capped.

"Fatima, don't start no shit in my spot," Madi called out to her from behind the register where she was ringing a customer up. She was the plump Puerto Rican girl who owned the salon. She and Fatima had history because, back in the day, Madi dated Fatima's father, Cutty, who was an old-school gangster known to be about that murder work. Rumor had it that it was Cutty's blood money that helped Madi get the shop off the ground.

"Nah, it ain't like that. You're family, Madi, so I'd never disrespect your joint like that," Fatima said over her shoulder, but she kept her eyes on the girl with the plastic earrings. "I understand. Trust me, I do. Bitches that spend their lives looking in the window of a restaurant will always be left to wonder if the food is any good."

She looked the girl with the plastic earrings up and down like she was little more than a stone caught in her shoe. The chattering in the salon suddenly ceased and all was silent, save for the low hum of the hair dryers.

NO SHADE: A Hood Rat Novel

"Take them thirsty hos to church!" someone shouted from the far end of the hair salon, her lone voice seeming to bounce off every wall.

The girl with the plastic earrings rose to her feet, and stood eye to eye with Fatima. Fatima was slightly taller than she was, but the girl with the plastic earrings was at least twenty pounds heavier. Matching Fatima's cold stare, she said, "I ain't trying to sit down for a meal, boo, but I hear that take-out menu is something special." She grinned.

Someone snickered, but Fatima didn't bother to look and see who it was. She turned to Madi, who was trying to close the register and hustle over to her and then back to the girl with the plastic earrings, who was smirking at her mockingly.

"Fatima, don't!" Madi screamed, but it was already too late.

By the time, the girl with the plastic earrings realized Fatima had swung; she was bouncing off the salon door and stumbling forward for another helping of her knuckle sandwich. This time, Fatima hooked her twice in the gut, knocking the wind out of her, but she wouldn't let her opponent fall. Fatima grabbed the girl with the plastic earrings by her hair, only to have it come off in her hands, exposing the thin braids that had been hidden beneath the laced-front wig.

The girl with the shower cap sprang to her feet with intentions of helping her friend, but her rescue mission was a short one. Two fists connected with the side of her head, sending her chin-first to the ground. Fatima's home girl, Pam, danced in place like a boxer, eyes sweeping the room and daring anyone else to jump in. She had been

19

sitting quietly among the girls, listening to their gossip and waiting to see how Fatima would react before she made her move. Pam was an old head from the projects and known for her knuckle game.

Fatima grabbed the girl with the plastic earrings by the back of her one-piece jumpsuit, swung her around, and delivered vicious blows to her face and head. The girl's one-piece ripped, spilling forth her saggy titties and gut as she crashed to the floor.

"See, I told y'all not to start no shit in my place!" Madi yelled. She slapped her hand on a button behind the counter, and, within seconds, the door to the office swung open and two burly Spanish dudes rushed out. One was older with salt and pepper hair, the other a younger version of him with thick black hair. "Victor, Macho, see these broads out, please."

"Let's go, ladies," Victor, who was the older of the two men, said. He scooped the girl wearing the shower cap off the floor and threw her over his shoulder like a sack of potatoes while grabbing the girl with the plastic earrings roughly by her arm. She was still dazed from her beating, and her legs barely supported her, so Victor had to half-drag her. On his way out, he almost knocked over two women coming in. One was average height, wearing a sweat suit and her hair in a ponytail, the other was tall and dark, in full glam mode, heels, and heavy makeup, even though it was the middle of the day.

"Excuse you," the one in the sweat suit rolled her eyes.

Victor mumbled something in the way of an apology and kept going.

"Y'all gotta go, too," Macho told Fatima and Pam. He wasn't happy about it, because he had been trying to fuck Pam, and throwing her out of the shop wouldn't win him any points, but he had a job to do.

Pam cut her eyes at everyone in the shop, including Macho, before storming out. Fatima followed a few paces behind. When she got to the door, she turned to Madi. "I apologize for this, Madi."

"Just go, Fatima," Madi said through clenched teeth. She was too heated to talk.

"Excuse me," Fatima said as she passed between the two girls who had just walked in, on her way out.

"Damn! What happened in here?" the girl with the sweat suit looked around the shop in astonishment.

Chairs were overturned, and loose rollers littered the floor. On the wall, Madi's favorite autographed picture of Celia Cruz hung at a funny angle on the wall. The glass in the frame was cracked in a web across her face.

"Billy, you just missed some shit, girl!" Quanna said excitedly. She couldn't wait to bring Billy up to speed on the fight.

"Quanna, if I were you, I'd be more worried about taking care of hair instead of spreading gossip. This is my place of business, not the stoop," Madi said sharply.

Quanna rolled her eyes at Madi but was smart enough not to open her mouth for fear of being fired. Madi was cool with all the girls in the salon, but she wouldn't hesitate to throw them out on their ass if they messed with her money. "What are you getting, Billy, your usual?"

"Nah, not today. I don't have time to sit up in here all day getting my hair braided, so I'm just gonna get a quick wash," Billy told her, taking a seat along the wall.

"You getting something done, too?" Quanna asked the tall dark-skinned girl who had come in with Billy.

"No, I'm good, sweetie. I have a stylist who I keep on retainer," Kat told her. She had a deep, sultry voice that matched her sinfully proportioned body. Kat was six feet of hips, ass, and attitude.

"Well, excuse the hell out of me," a woman who had been eavesdropping from the next chair said.

"Kat, why don't you sit your ass down?" Billy pulled Kat down into the seat next to her. "You do the most sometimes."

"It ain't that I do the most. It's that you don't do enough, honey." Kat crossed her thick, chocolate legs. The tight skirt she wore slid up so far that you could almost see her goodies, but Kat didn't seem to notice or care. "Why do you run around dressed like a hobo all the time?" she teased, tugging at the zipper of Billy's sweat jacket playfully.

"I dress comfortably, Kat. Not everybody is comfortable running around in stilettos before noon." She kicked the heel of one of Kat's tall black shoes. The heels were so sharp that she could've killed a man with them.

"Most bitches can't navigate the world in these pumps, but that doesn't mean they don't want to. I'm a part of a rare breed, boo." Kat flipped her long, heavy weave, hitting a little boy in the next seat in the face, almost knocking him out of the chair. Kat didn't even seem to notice. "You clean up nice, Billy, and you need to flaunt that shit."

Billy had heard that speech a million times, be it from Kat or her friends. She had deep caramel skin, and long black hair that was all hers, and a body that would put some video vixens to shame without even trying, but Billy carried herself like one of the fellas. When other little girls were playing with dolls, you could find Billy on the basketball court with the boys. Growing up, Billy had always been teased about being a dyke, and for a time in her life, she wasn't totally sure which way she wanted to go, but that changed when she met Kat's brother Marcus. In him, she found a man who awakened everything in her that being a woman was about.

"So, when you gonna make my brother make an honest woman of you?" Kat asked, changing the subject.

"Your brother has got his hands too full to be thinking about marriage. I thought I would see him more when he took over ownership of Shooters, but it seems like he spends more time there now than when he was managing it."

Shooters was a club that Marcus had inherited from the previous owner who also happened to be his mentor when he was in the streets. Marcus loved that club more than anything, and sometimes Billy wondered if he loved it more than her.

"Yes, my brother is definitely the workaholic of the family. It only took him one time to get into some serious trouble to make him get his shit together," Kat recalled the close brush Marcus had had with prison when they were younger. He was looking at an asshole full of time for being in the wrong place with the wrong people, but, through God's mercies, he managed to walk away with only probation. For a while, he still towed the line of the lawless, but he focused the majority of his attention on legitimate ventures.

"Yeah, let him tell it, he's trying to build something for us, but I don't see why he has to stay out until all hours of the night, especially lately. He's been moving real funny."

"Funny how?" Kat asked.

"Well, you know me and Marcus been together for a long time, so I know all his habits, and he knows mine. Anyhow, he crept into the crib on some late night shit, and tried to ease into the bed. I played like I was sleep and let him think he got it off. When he went to sleep, I smelled his balls."

"No, you didn't!" Kat gasped.

"Kat, you know I'm not a jealous chick, so I don't know what made me do it, but I had a funny feeling in the pit of my stomach. So, I tipped my head down and sniffed his balls, and they smelled like soap."

Kat stared at her blankly. "You're tripping because your man had clean balls?"

"Kat, if you leave the house at seven AM and come back nearly twenty-four hours later, are your private parts gonna smell fresh?" Billy asked.

The realization of what Billy was trying to say had finally sunk in. "You don't think he's cheating, do you?" she asked.

"I don't know what to think, Kat. I just know I don't like how your brother has been moving lately," Billy said.

Kat laid her hand over Billy's reassuringly. "Listen, ma, my brother isn't the most forthcoming when it comes to his whereabouts, but he ain't a grease ball. I've never known Marcus to cheat on any of his girlfriends."

"There's a first time for everything," Billy shot back. "I don't know what's going on, Kat, but I plan to confront him about it. If it feels like he's lying, I'm leaving his ass."

"I'm ready for you, Billy," Quanna called from the chair.

Billy got up and prepared to sit in the chair, when her cell phone rang. The caller ID said Unknown. Normally, she wouldn't have picked up, but something told her it might be important. "Yeah," she answered.

"Billy, this is Reese," the caller said.

"Reese, why the hell are you calling me from an unknown number?" Billy asked suspiciously.

"Because I'm in jail!" Reese announced, loud enough for people to hear through the cell phone. "Now stop asking so many questions and come get a bitch out!"

CHAPTER 4

It was almost dark by the time Rocky got back to the block. As a result of the scuffle in the waiting room, the police got involved, and Claudette and the girls she had been fighting with were arrested. Rocky took the kids and left before the police started asking questions that might've landed them in the system.

The kids were hysterical after Claudette was arrested, but a quick trip to McDonald's soothed them. Rocky sat and listened as the little girl told her about the last time Claudette had been arrested. That time it was for drinking in public, and she had had her kids with her then, too. As it turned out, the kids had seen Mommy get arrested a few times. It was always for something petty, and she never stayed away more than a day or two, if that.

When Little Raymond asked if Rocky was going to keep him and his sister, Ranique, until their mother was released, she suddenly realized she had a problem on her hands. She was stuck with someone else's kids and had no idea what to do with them. Claudette had family in the neighborhood, but Rocky didn't know them well enough to know exactly where they lived. She would see Claudette's mother from time to time, but it was mostly while she was lurking in and out of the shadows looking for a blast. There was no way Rocky was going to scour the hood knocking on random dope houses to find her, so she decided to let the kids spend the night at her place and hoped for their mother's speedy release.

With the setting sun, the projects began to stir. Young men and women lined the avenue in clusters, shooting the breeze or plotting.

NO SHADE: A Hood Rat Novel

There was always something going down on the strip, especially on the first of the month. On the first, everybody came out. Dope boys came out to relieve the addicts of their checks in exchange for drugs, and hood rats came out to spend their paper on whatever they couldn't afford the other thirty days of each month. It was the one day that nobody in the hood felt poor.

Rocky kept her head and down as she passed the different groups. She could feel their eyes on her as she passed. Rocky was still fairly new to the hood but was beginning to develop a name for herself because of the company she kept. Rocky could see the walkway into the projects a few feet away, so she added haste to her steps, pulling Raymond and Ranique behind her. She wanted to get off the block as quickly as possible without bumping into anyone she knew. She had almost made it, when her luck turned. Standing at the mouth of the project entrance were two knuckleheads named Wise and Dolla.

Wise and Dolla were a part of the Big Dawg Entertainment crew, led by drug dealer turned multi-platinum album selling mogul, Don B. Big Dawg. He was like hood royalty, and even though Wise and Dolla weren't rappers, they were affiliated, and they wore the affiliation like badges of honor. When they weren't off doing dirty deeds for Don B., you could find them in the hood, trolling for victims aka thirsty groupies.

Rocky barely knew Wise and Dolla, but she couldn't stand them. Wise was cool when his brother wasn't around to put the battery in him, but Dolla was in full asshole mode 24/7. When Rocky had first moved into the projects, Dolla tried to get with her, but she shot him down. She didn't have anything against him, but she wasn't interested in getting into another relationship so soon, after what happened with her baby daddy. Dolla took it way personal and gave Rocky grief whenever he saw her. From the way Dolla was smacking his lips and rubbing his hands together, Rocky knew her already bad day was about to become worse.

"What's popping, ma?" Dolla asked, looking Rocky up and down. The street light caught his bald head, where he had his sunglasses propped. He was dressed in blue jeans, a black t-shirt, and wore his company chain, which was a gold medallion with a Rottweiler head etched into it. The rubies in the eyes of the dog's head looked like they were glaring at Rocky.

"Nothing," Rocky said dryly. "How you doing, Wise?" she addressed his brother.

"Chilling," Wise said coolly. He was a few years younger than Dolla and slightly less talkative. He mostly sat back and watched things play out. Like Dolla, he was rocking a Big Dawg chain, too, but his was a bit smaller and without the gaudy rubies. He was the more conservative of the two.

"Where ya mama at, lil' nigga?" Dolla asked Raymond.

"Locked up," Raymond replied as if it was normal.

"Claudette stays getting locked up," Wise said from the sidelines.

"Well, good seeing y'all." Rocky tried to cut it short and walk away, but Dolla blocked her path.

"Why don't you stick around for a minute? I got some bomb-ass weed that I was about to twist up." Dolla pulled two Dutch Masters from his pocket and dangled them in front of her. "Get rid of them crumb crushers, and let's go to the moon."

Rocky looked at the cigars and frowned. "Nah, I'm gonna pass. I smoke that shit with you and the next thing you know, I'll be on a pissy mattress in some basement while y'all thirsty niggas take turns groping me. I heard how y'all Big Dawg guys do."

Dolla sucked his teeth. "That ain't nothing but lies and hate."

"Pure hate," Wise co-signed.

"Shorty, we getting money at Big Dawg. What the fuck do we look like having to drug a bitch for the pussy? My team is top shelf while the rest of these clowns are bottom feeders."

"Well, I'm gonna go with the bottom feeders on this one," Rocky told him and brushed past Dolla.

Wise laughed, which made Dolla angry.

"See, I tried to let you ride shotgun with a real nigga, but your ass is too high on your shoulders to touch the seat," he spat, but Rocky kept walking. "That's a'ight, bitch. Didn't nobody want that uptight-ass pussy anyhow. Bourgeois ho!"

Rocky threw her middle finger up over her shoulder and kept walking. Dolla's insults had gotten under her skin, but she wouldn't give him the satisfaction of showing it. She was glad her friends hadn't been around to let them hear him talking about her like that, especially Wanda. She would've cut Dolla's ass too short to shit and then went in on Rocky for not being about that life. Wanda had no patience for weak people, and didn't mind telling you as much. She was so caught up in her thoughts that she literally bumped into someone hard enough to lose her balance. She almost fell flat on her face, but a pair of strong hands grabbed her by the waist to steady her.

"My fault. Are you okay?" he asked.

Rocky opened her mouth to speak, but no words came out. He was younger than Rocky, this much she could tell, but there was an air about him that made him seem much older. Around his neck hung a thirty-inch gold chain with small diamonds between the links. On his arm was a large tattoo of a bloody meat cleaver, slashing through the words Dead Men Tell No Tales. He wore his hair low, but not so low, where you couldn't see the wavy brown curls sprouting from his skull. His skin was the color of wet sand drying in the morning sun. Eyes like melted caramel drank her in, almost larcenously. He cracked a faint smile, showing off two rows of perfect white teeth.

Rocky had never seen him in the hood, but she knew he was somebody from the way the passing crack addicts kept looking at him. It was as if they would drop to their knees and praise him at any given second. He was clearly a street cat, and Rocky didn't go for street cats, but he was still the finest specimen of a man she had ever seen.

"I asked if you were okay?" he repeated.

"Oh...I'm fine," Rocky stammered. "It was my fault. I should've been watching where I was going."

"No harm done, sweetie," he told her and kept walking.

Rocky stood there in awe, watching the young dude as he ambled down the street. As he was passing the corner where Dolla and Wise were standing, she saw Dolla stop him, and the two began talking. Seeing him talking to Dolla's greasy ass killed any fantasies that she might've been having about him.

"What's a bourgeois ho?" Ranique asked unexpectedly.

Rocky blinked twice in shock before thinking of an acceptable answer. "Something bad people say, and, if I were you, I wouldn't repeat it in front of your mother."

"Mama says ho all the time, especially when she's on the phone talking to her friends," Raymond offered.

"Well, it's a bad word, and kids shouldn't say it," Rocky explained.

Rocky continued through the projects toward her building. She was already two hours later than she had told the babysitter she would be, and knew she would be pissed. Rocky would shoot her a few extra dollars in hopes of appeasing her enough to where she didn't give her grief if she needed to use her again.

Rocky was about to pull out her cell phone to call and let the babysitter know that she was in the neighborhood, when she heard someone calling her name. From the deep southern drawl, and the way the voice seemed to echo throughout the whole projects, Rocky knew who it was before she even turned around.

Ms. Pat was a legend in the projects, having been there since they were first built, and raising three generations of criminals and misfits. They ranged from the beautiful and larcenous to the ugly and cold-blooded. There was no shortage of stories attached to the Butler clan, but no one dared whisper about them within earshot of Ms. Pat. Her children and grandchildren were a rotten lot, but they were her family, and she loved them as only a mother could.

Normally, Rocky looked forward to seeing Ms. Pat, especially when she needed to get her head right, but Ms. Pat was as notorious for her long conversations as she was for her exotic weed. Rocky wasn't much in the talking mood that night, so she tried to give a simple, "Hello," and keep it moving, but she would have no such luck.

"Rocky, c'mere for a second child," Ms. Pat called to her from the bench. She was flanked by two of her cronies, Earnestine and Rita.

With a deep sigh, Rocky headed in Ms. Pat's direction, with the children in tow. "How y'all doing tonight?"

"Can't complain," Rita said, her lips gently pulled back like she would burst into a smile at any second. Behind her tinted glasses, her eyes hung low and dreamy. She was an older woman with a genuine spirit and a deep love for quality marijuana. On any given day, you could come to her for a piece of advice or a joint from her stash when you were in need.

Earnestine was less vocal in her reply. She raised the tall can of Lime-O-Rita, which was wrapped in a brown paper bag, and tipped it in salute. Earnestine wasn't as old as Ms. Pat and Rita, but she was up there. She had held together better than most women her age. She was the mother of three teenage kids and grandmother to a newborn, but every so often, you could find her in a neighborhood bar or after-hours joint, trolling for supple young men.

"Ain't seen you out here on the bench talking about people with your crew lately. How you been, sugar?" Ms. Pat asked, from her perch on the far end of the bench. Her hair was done up in big silver curls, with bifocal frames of the same shade sitting on her nose. Draped across her shoulders was a blue nylon jacket with the letters N.Y.C.H.A etched across the breast and the back. Sitting behind her ear was a loose cigarette.

"I've been okay, just busy," Rocky said.

"Apparently so, because the last time I seen you, you only had one baby and now you've got two more," Ms. Pat looked at Claudette's children over the rim of her glasses.

"Oh, I'm just babysitting for Claudette for a few hours," Rocky lied.

"Umm hmm," Ms. Pat twisted her lips disbelievingly. "What they get her for this time?"

"Fighting," Rocky admitted shamefully.

"I wish I could say I was surprised. That girl spends so much time in the precinct you'd think she had time shares," Ms. Pat said with a chuckle.

"Well, let me get these kids upstairs. I left my son with the babysitter, and I was supposed to be back hours ago," Rocky said, starting to walk off.

"Oh, that reminds me. I saw your son heading to the avenue with Boots," Rita told her.

"To the avenue?" Rocky asked in shock. When she had left her child in Boots' care, she was specific about not wanting him to go any further than the playground.

"Yeah, she strutted by here about twenty or thirty minutes ago, mumbling something about she had moves to make," Rita filled her in, while passing the joint she was smoking to Earnestine.

"I told her that I didn't want my son on the avenue!" Rocky said heatedly. The avenue was hot, and there was never any telling when something might go down, which was why she hated walking that way to get home. Sometimes she would go all the way around the block just to avoid it.

"Shit! It's the first of the month. You know all these lil' heifers running around like they got ants in they pants, trying to spend that good government check. Lazy bitches." Earnestine took a deep pull off the joint, holding the smoke, and washing it down with a sip of her Lime-O-Rita.

"Earnestine, you need to quit throwing shade like your ass doesn't get a check every month, too," Ms. Pat said.

"Yeah, but I had over twenty years in on my job. I earned that money, sweetie," Earnestine boasted. She raised the joint to take a pull, and Ms. Pat snatched it from her unsuspecting fingers.

"Snatchies!" Ms. Pat yelled when she took the joint. She inhaled deep, and turned her attention back to Rocky. "Let me ask you something," she said with smoke rolling from her mouth as she spoke. "Why would you leave your child in the care of somebody who doesn't half take care of their own kids?"

"What do you mean? Whenever I see Boots' kids, they look clean and happy," Rocky said.

"Yeah, the ones who ain't in the system," Ms. Pat fired back. "Boots got more kids than me and Earnestine put together, but they broken up and here and there."

"Don't forget most of 'em got different daddies," Rita added. She was licking the edges of a sheet of bamboo paper, rolling another joint.

"Hush," Ms. Pat told Rita and turned back to Rocky. "Look, I ain't saying nothing about Boots behind her back that I wouldn't say to her face, so it ain't like I'm talking bad about her; I'm just pulling your coat. You seem like a nice girl and actually wanna do something for yourself, so don't fall into keeping time with the wrong people."

"Too late for that," Earnestine added.

Ms. Pat shot Earnestine a look, but didn't say anything. "Rocky," she turned back to the girl. "Don't worry too much about Boots having your son up on the avenue. She's trifling as hell, but she wouldn't let anything happen to your baby. I'll give her that. She'll be back before a time."

Rita stopped her joint rolling and fixed her eyes on something in the distance. "One time!" she shouted when she saw the two beat walkers running through the projects. Moving as swift as the wind, Rita threw her weed in the grass and hurried away from the bench.

Before Rocky even realized what was going on, all three of the old heads had vanished, leaving her and the kids standing in a midst of weed smoke and empty Lime-O-Rita cans.

CHAPTER 5

"Bro, why do you feel the need to give Rocky grief every time you see her?" Wise asked once Rocky had gone.

"Fuck that uppity bitch," Dolla said. "When you see her by herself, she all quiet and innocent, but once she get around them ratchet-ass bitches from down the block, she gets on some other shit, like she's all that. Bitch, be one way with me or don't be no way at all."

"I think you're just tight because you tried to fuck and she shut you down," Wise told him.

"Man, that wasn't about nothing. I got a hundred bitches that would drop their drawers for me in a New York minute. What make Rocky so different?" Dolla asked.

"The fact that you were sweet on her," Wise replied. "You can front for the rest of these niggas, but I'm your brother, so you can't lie to me, duke."

"Shut up, lil' nigga. You always shooting your mouth off like you know something," Dolla said sharply.

The partial truth in Wise's words struck a nerve in Dolla. It was true. When he first started seeing Rocky around, he took a liking to her. She was a new face and didn't carry herself like the rest of the hood rats. Dolla was drawn to Rocky like a fly to a sugar cube, and, in the beginning, she seemed to like him, too, but the sugar turned to shit when Rocky got settled in and started hanging with a chick named Wanda and her cronies. At one point, Wanda and Dolla were fuck-buddies, but she got caught up and tried to force Dolla into a

36

relationship, but he already had a girlfriend. When Dolla rejected her, Wanda tried to get back at him by spreading a rumor about him having a small penis. He trumped her rumor by posting pussy pictures she had sent to him to Facebook. Wanda hated Dolla and decreed anybody in her circle had to hate him too, or be branded disloyal. This included Rocky. Wanda's decree ended Dolla and Rocky's budding romance, and put Rocky on Dolla's shit list with the rest of them.

"Yo! Check it out." Wise tapped Dolla and nodded in the direction Rocky had walked in. They spied her talking to a pretty dude with curly hair. The way Rocky was smiling from ear to ear at whatever the young man was saying, irritated Dolla.

"Thirsty-ass broad," Dolla grumbled.

Wise kept watching the kid as he broke off from Rocky and headed in their direction. As he got closer and his face was illuminated by the streetlights, Wise realized that he knew him. "Oh, shit! That's the Turk!"

"The who?" Dolla asked, as the name wasn't familiar to him.

"His name is Turk, but some people call him the Butcher's Boy," Wise explained.

The Butcher's Boy was a name that Dolla was familiar with. He was supposed to be a real head case, partial to solving disputes with a meat cleaver. He was a part of Shai Clark's new regime. From the stories, Dolla had heard about him, he'd always expected him to be much bigger and uglier.

"How the hell do you know one of Shai's people?" Dolla asked suspiciously.

37

His brother wasn't an angel, but he wasn't a street dude, so Dolla found it curious that he would be familiar with anyone in Shai's organization.

"I met him once or twice through a friend of mine, when I was going to college in upstate New York. The Turk attended a private high school a few towns over called Saint Anthony's. It was one of those exclusive joints where all the kids who attended came from old money families. He was one of the founders of a crew that called themselves the Billionaire Boys Club," Wise explained.

"So why you all open off the male version of 'The Facts of Life'?" Dolla asked, not really getting where Wise was going with the story.

"Dolla, for as much as you claim to know about what's going down on the streets, you mean to tell me you've never heard of the Billionaire Boys Club?" Wise asked. Dolla just shrugged his shoulders. Wise shook his head sadly. "Because a lot of the little niggas who went to Saint Anthony's came from criminal families, they tried to play the role of thugs, but when the Turk arrived on campus, he showed them what a thug was really about. He hooked up with Baby Doc, Nickels, and a few other kids and formed the Billionaire Boys Club. Any law that was broken within a twenty-mile radius, BBC either did it or put it together. Nothing moved without them getting a taste. They were an underage criminal organization. By the time the police in that hick town even got hipped to what was going on right under their noses, those little bastards had already licked for over a million. Them country-ass cops wanted to hang the Turk's half-breed ass, but Shai stepped in and pulled a few strings."

"Must've cost Shai an asshole full of favors to sweep that under the rug," Dolla said.

"It did, and he was pissed about it. Nickels is his cousin Gator's son, and Baby Doc is his right hand man's only kid, so they got off with a beat down by the big homies, but Turk was an outsider and had to pay a heavier price. Swann put a few of the young boys on him to teach him a lesson. They put Turk in the hospital, but he took two of them to the emergency room with him. When he got out, Swann brought him onboard to work off the debt, as payment for Shai saving his little ass from the slammer."

"Oh, my! This Turk cat sounds like someone we need to get friendly with." Dolla rubbed his hands together. It was something he always did when he was up to no good. "Holla at the nigga, Wise."

"Me? You're the one who wants to get to know him. You holla at him," Wise protested.

"Man, stop being a bitch and get him over here." Dolla pushed Wise in Turk's path as he was passing.

Wise stood there with a dumbfounded look on his face, confronted with the Turk. The way his copper eyes looked at him made Wise's mouth dry. Finally, he found his tongue and said, "What's good, Turk?" He extended his hand.

Turk looked at Wise's hand like it had shit on it. "We know each other?" he asked.

Wise looked over his shoulder at Dolla, who was watching him intently, before turning back to Turk. "It's me, Wise. We met at that

39

party in Binghamton when you and ya BBC crew came through and turned it up, remember?"

"Oh, word?" Turk's face softened as a light of recognition went off in his eyes. Just when Wise thought Turk was about to embrace him, his face hardened again. "Nah, I don't remember you, money. Pardon yourself." He brushed past Wise, leaving him standing there with a dumb expression on his face.

"You got played, son!" Dolla laughed and pointed his finger in Wise's face.

"Fuck you," Wise slapped Dolla's hand away angrily. "You're the one who wanted to get all cozy with him, and I tried to tell you he was bad news."

"I was just trying to see where his head was at. I thought maybe the lil' nigga might've been worthy of fucking with the Big Dawg crew, but apparently, he ain't. Ol' pretty-ass nigga better hope he don't get tossed up, walking on this strip like he from around these parts," Dolla spat, watching the Turk walk down the street.

He stopped on the corner where three or four older heads were standing around shooting the shit. They were old school gangsters in the hood who no longer had any real power, but they were still dangerous. Turk said something to one of them, which prompted a response, but Dolla was too far away to hear what they were saying. Whatever it was couldn't have been nice, because he saw Turk's face sour. One of the dudes got off the gate and shoved Turk, but, before it could go any further, it was broken up.

NO SHADE: A Hood Rat Novel

"Now this should be interesting." Dolla rubbed his hands together. "Come on, son." He started in the direction of the disturbance.

"Where the hell are we going?" Wise asked.

"Hopefully to see this pretty nigga get his shit pushed in," Dolla called over his shoulder.

*

Turk hadn't meant to be so short with the kid Wise. He actually did remember him from the party in Binghamton, because Wise and his people had bought a few ounces of weed off one of Turk's boys, but it wasn't the time or place to be strolling down memory lane with a dude he doubted he'd ever see again. Turk's mind was elsewhere.

Once again, Swann had sent Turk off on what he called a dummy mission. Since he had been working with the Clarks, he always found himself stuck doing grunt work— debt collections, delivering messages that couldn't be sent over the phone, running errands. They made him do everything that he felt was beneath him. When he was with the Billionaire Boys Club, he was a boss...a man of respect, but, when he became a part of the Clark family, it was as if someone had hit the reset button on his career and he was demoted to the rank of foot soldier. This was the big leagues, no more nickel and dime capers.

The Clarks played for higher stakes than he could've imagined. Shai made it clear from day one, that if Turk wanted respect and prestige, he would have to earn it in the trenches. Turk understood, but he didn't like it. He'd often thought about telling the Clarks to go fuck themselves, but two things kept him from doing so; the fact that he still owed Shai for keeping him out of prison, and Swann's promises that it would get greater later. He and Swann hadn't met on the best terms, but over time they got close, and Turk looked up to him like the big brother he never had. It was his faith in Swann that kept him going.

"Spare a dollar for a pint of whiskey?" Turk heard someone ask from behind him. He turned and found himself staring at a messily dressed man wearing a large hoodie. For the most part, his face was obscured by the hood, but Turk could make out the nest of shaggy hair lining his jaw and dark eyes.

Turk dug around in his pocket and handed the man a five-dollar bill. "Try not to drink it all up in one sitting, old timer," he told him.

The man examined the bill and smiled, showing off a mouth full of gold teeth. "Much obliged," he said and staggered off towards the liquor store.

"Should've pawned that gold in your mouth instead of out here begging," Turk said to no one in particular, and continued on his way.

Turk spotted the dude he'd been sent to speak with, standing in a group on the corner. They were passing around plastic cups and cat calling at young girls who walked past. Turk knew the type, dudes who had once been holding weight but were now washed and trying to hold onto their glory through the re-telling of war stories. He'd dealt with their type before. If Turk didn't handle the situation tactfully, egos would get bruised, and examples would have to be set. He hated Swann for sending him down there to talk to the old head, but orders were orders, so he sucked it up and stepped to his business.

"What's good, fellas?" Turk greeted all the men respectfully, before turning his attention to the person he'd come to see. "Carl, can I holla at you for a minute?" he asked the slim man, who was sitting on a milk crate.

Carl looked up at him. "You know me from somewhere?" he asked aggressively.

"We've met once or twice, but I'm here on behalf of a mutual friend. You know Swann, don't you?"

At the mention of Swann's name, Carl's face went slack, but he quickly recovered and went back to scowling. He looked Turk up and down. "Swann must be getting desperate if he's sending kids to handle his affairs."

"I'm nineteen," Turk informed him, "but that's beside the point. I'm just here to collect the compensation you owe from the car you hit."

Carl had been drunk one night and hit the car of a woman Swann was dealing with. Carl didn't have insurance, so in exchange for her not calling the police, he agreed to pay for the damages in cash. Once Carl was in the clear, he disregarded the debt. It was only a few hundred dollars, but to Swann, it was a matter of principal.

"All the money the Clarks getting, I know Swann ain't stunting no punk-ass few dollars." Carl sucked his teeth. "Look, tell him that the next time I see him in the club, bottles on me all night." He went back to his drinking and ignored Turk.

43

Turk frowned because he knew where this was about to go and he was trying to avoid it. "Carl, I'm not trying to break your balls here, but you know how Swann is. If I go back to him empty handed, what do you think he's going to do?"

Carl took a slow sip from his cup. "That sounds like a problem for you and him to work out. Now get the fuck from around me before I get mad."

Turk sighed. "Carl, let's not do it like this. If I have to come back here, it's not going to be good for anybody."

Carl sat his cup on the ground and stood toe to toe with Turk. "You must be hard of hearing." He shoved Turk. "I said get the fuck out of here." By then, Carl's buddy had grabbed him and was holding him back.

Turk just smiled. "Okay, you got it, Carl. Enjoy the rest of your night, fellas," he told the men and walked off.

"And don't bring your bitch ass back around here no more!" Carl yelled after him.

"Carl, that was some fool shit you did," one of the men he'd been drinking with said. His name was Steve. "You think it was wise to blow shorty off like that if Swann sent him?"

"Fuck that lil' nigga! If Swann wanna see me, then he needs to come check me like a man. I ain't answering to no snot-nosed kid," Carl said.

"You think he gonna come back?" Steve asked.

Carl snorted. "If he knows like I know, he won't," he capped and went back to his drinking.

NO SHADE: A Hood Rat Novel

*

A few feet away, Dolla and Wise were watching the exchange. Dolla got excited when he thought it was about to go down between Carl and Turk. Sadly, it ended without incident.

Dolla shook his head. "See, Wise, you out here praising these niggas like they're somebody, but they really pussies. Turk came over here trying to be tough and got ran off the block!"

"I wouldn't speak so soon," Wise pointed to the corner.

Turk had indeed come back, and, this time, he was wearing gloves, and he was no longer smiling. When he raised his gloved hand, the streetlights reflected off the meat cleaver he was wielding.

*

Turk moved so swiftly that they didn't even see him until he was already on top of them. He swung the meat cleaver, bringing the dull end across the bridge of the nose of the man standing closest to him, breaking it. Seeing their fallen comrade and the cleaver wielding mad man, everybody scattered, except for Carl. Turk had him cornered like a rat.

In desperation, Carl threw his drink in Turk's eyes; temporarily blinding him, then took off running. It only took Turk a few seconds to recover and take off after Carl. Carl was just about to cross the avenue, when Turk hurled the meat cleaver at him. The heavy blade flipped end over end and came to rest in Carl's back. Carl fell in the middle of the street, almost getting hit by a taxi.

People looked on in horror as Turk walked up on the bleeding man, ripping the cleaver violently from his back. Using his foot, he flipped Carl over and straddled him. A small crowd had gathered, watching the two men in the middle of the street, but Turk continued about his business as if he didn't have an audience. When he was in one of his fits, as his therapist called them, he blacked out and couldn't focus on anything but his tools and the meat on his cutting table.

"I tried to be a gentleman about this, but you wanted to be a savage, so here we are." Turk used his knee to pin Carl's shoulder to the ground and stretched his arm out with his free hand. "Swann told me that, if I left here empty handed, I might as well not come back, so I have to take him something."

"I'm sorry, man. I'll pay…please, tell Swann I'll pay!" Carl pleaded.

Turk smiled. "I gave you a chance to pay in cash, but now you'll pay in pounds…and I don't mean European money, I mean pounds of flesh." He brought the cleaver down and cut off Carl's hand.

NO SHADE: A Hood Rat Novel

CHAPTER 6

Billy was mad as hell that she had to cut her hair appointment short to get Sharon and Reese's asses out of jail. When she found out what they had been arrested for, it made her even angrier. Sharon was a young knucklehead, so nothing she did surprised Billy, but she expected more from Reese. Of all of their friends, Reese was the only one still living in her second childhood. They dropped Sharon off at her mother's apartment and then headed for Reese's place.

"That's word to everything I love. That little bitch is lucky I didn't kill her in there," Reese fumed.

"And your ass is lucky that it was written up as disorderly conduct instead of assault!" Billy shot back. "Reese, what the hell are you doing fighting in the welfare office?"

"That heifer started it, and I finished it, so don't come at me like it's all my fault," Reese retorted.

"Reese, that fighting shit was cool when we were young and running up and down Lenox Avenue, but you're too grown for it now. You're somebody's mother for Christ's sake."

"And I'm also a woman who won't be disrespected," Reese countered. "Billy, if you had been in my shoes, you would've done the same thing."

"The difference between me and you is that I wouldn't put myself in that situation in the first place. You're out here moving like a real fucking chicken head, and that's why none of these men you get with take you seriously," Billy said, a bit sharper than she

47

intended. She saw that her words had hurt Reese, and she felt bad. "Reese, I'm sorry. You know I didn't mean it like that."

"Nah, you meant it like you said it. It's cool, Billy," Reese told her, hiding the hurt in her voice. "You know, I know that I'm not perfect, but I'm trying. You're right, I've made some poor choices in men, and I'll probably make some more before it's all said and done, but I'm not ashamed to be out there looking for a good man. You can't knock me because I wasn't blessed with a fairytale romance like you and Marcus."

Billy laughed. "A fairytale? Maybe at one time, but now I'm not so sure. I've got my fair share of problems, too, Reese, so I apologize for throwing stones when I live in a glass house."

Reese looked at Billy, and for the first time she saw uncertainty in her face. Of their whole circle of friends, Billy had always been the strongest and most confident.

"Is everything okay, ma?" Reese asked, immediately forgetting that they had just been arguing.

"I don't even know, Reese," Billy admitted. She went on to give her the short version about her suspicions about Marcus.

"Nah, I can't see Marcus cheating on you. That dude loves you," Reese assured her.

"I know he does, Reese, but just because he'll never give another woman his heart doesn't mean he'll never give them the dick."

"You're right about that," Reese had to admit. "So what are you going to do about it?"

48

"I don't know. I guess I'll just wait to see what's going to happen and hope for the best," Billy said.

"That ain't the Willamina Jefferson I know," Reese said, calling Billy by her government name. "If your gut is telling you that something is going on, you move on it. Don't wait around for the other shoe to drop. You either confront him or catch him in the act. Where is Marcus now?"

"He said he was meeting with some potential investors at Shooters," Billy told her.

"Then, that's where we need to be. Let's see if he's really where he says he is."

*

Billy let Reese talk her into swinging by Shooters Gentleman's club. It was a business her boyfriend Marcus had helped build and eventually inherited from the owner, Shooter. Billy had stood by Marcus as he built it from a hole in the wall strip club to one of the hottest spots in the city.

With Reese leading the way, Billy went inside the club. It was still early, so the crowd was light, but there was still a nice sprinkling of people inside. Some were sipping drinks and watching the show while others got lap dances. Across the room, Billy spotted Marcus's friend and the manager of the spot, Bear. They called him Bear because he was big and hairy with a nasty temper.

"What up, Bear?" Billy greeted him.

Bear hugged her and smiled. "Hey, boss lady. What brings you here tonight?"

"Just looking for my man. Is he upstairs in the office?"

"Nah, I haven't seen Marcus all day," Bear told her. When he saw Billy's facial expression change, he realized that he'd fucked up. "Billy, he might've come in earlier and gone before I got here. My shift didn't start until a half hour ago." He tried to clean it up, but it was too late.

"It's all good, Bear. When I leave here and you call him to warn him about my popping up, because I know you will, tell him that if I catch him foul, I'm gonna bust his shit," Billy snapped and left the club, trailing a major attitude behind her.

*

"I can't believe he lied to me," Billy said once she and Reese were back in the car.

"All niggas lie, even the good ones," Reese told her. "If he isn't at Shooters, where could he be?"

"I have no idea," Billy said, scrolling through the text messages on her phone.

When Reese noticed that Billy had an iPhone, it gave her an idea. "Are your phones on the same account?"

"Yes, why?" Billy couldn't see where she was going with it.

"Track his phone. All you have to do is log into your Cloud account, and as long as his phone is on, it'll tell you exactly where he is. The Cloud knows everything."

Billy could've slapped herself for not thinking of that. She had always trusted Marcus, so there was no need to question his whereabouts. Leave it to Reese's larcenous ass to give her a sneaky solution to her problem. Billy quickly pulled up the app and tracked Marcus's phone. To her surprise, he wasn't even in New York. It had him somewhere in Jersey City. "Reese, you down to take a ride?"

Reese grinned devilishly. "When am I not?"

*

The tracker had led them to restaurant in downtown Jersey City. Billy spotted Marcus's car parked in the parking lot. The sight of it immediately filled her heart with dread, and she was no longer sure if she wanted answers to her questions. She was about to suggest that they go back, but Reese was already out of the car and on the case.

"Come on. Let's go see if we can see him through the window," Reese called to Billy, heading toward the restaurant. With her heart in her chest, Reese followed.

It only took them a few seconds to spot him. Marcus was sitting at a table near the window with an attractive blonde. Billy watched speechlessly as they smiled at each other over wine glasses. When she saw Marcus reach over and touch the blonde's hand tenderly, she wanted to vomit. She went from shock to surprise to rage. She tried to rush the restaurant, but Reese stopped her.

"Nah, don't do it like that, ma." She held her back. "We can't go storming into this restaurant handing out ass whippings. We gotta

51

be ladies about it. Let's wait for the bitch in the parking lot then whip her ofay ass."

*

Billy could barely contain herself, sitting in her car and waiting for Marcus and his date to come out. She was beyond hurt. Marcus had promised to always protect her heart, but he had betrayed her. She had invested years of her life into their relationship only to find out that he was no better than the rest. Billy was so mad that she fully intended on going to prison that night.

Marcus came walking into the parking lot, arm in arm with the blonde. She was tall and pretty, dressed in an expensive skirt suit and carrying a leather briefcase. Billy figured she could use the thick leather case to bludgeon both of them to death. She waited until Marcus and the blonde had gotten to his car before pouncing.

Marcus and the blonde were caught totally by surprise when Billy came out of the shadows and commenced beating the blonde's ass. Billy tore into the blonde like a prizefighter, hitting her in every part of her exposed body. Reese was right there with her, getting her kicks and stomps in where she could. Marcus tried to grab Billy, but that only turned her rage on him. She cracked Marcus in the face three times, before he was able to grab her in a bear hug.

"Billy, what the fuck are you doing here?" Marcus asked in total shock.

"I catch you creeping with another bitch, and that's all you can think to say to me?" Billy struggled in his arms. "Word to Jah, may his soul rest in peace, I'm gonna kill you and this home wrecking cracker!"

"Billy, you need to calm down. This isn't what it looks like," Marcus held her at arm's length.

"Then what the fuck is it, Marcus?" Billy raged. She was now crying and shaking violently. "I gave you my heart, and you stepped on it. You couldn't even do me the courtesy of stepping out on me with a black bitch; you had to chase a white one, not that it makes it any better, but damn! And you," Billy turned to the blonde, who was on her hands and knees picking up the small velvet pouches that had spilled from her case. "I should kill you for breaking up my relationship, you whore...you tramp...you—"

"Jeweler," Marcus cut her off. He walked over to the white girl and helped her to her feet. "I apologize for this, Inga, and I promise to make it right. I'll throw a few grand extra on top of what I already spent for your troubles," he promised.

"Marcus, what the fuck is going on?" Billy asked, now totally confused.

When Marcus turned back to her, he was furious. "If you had listened instead of jumping out the window, I could've explained to you who Inga is. She's my jeweler, not my mistress."

"Marcus, why have you been sneaking around acting all suspicious if there's nothing going on?" Billy demanded an explanation.

"I haven't been sneaking around. I was making some moves with my old crew, so I could afford to get this made for you." He pulled a small box from his pocket and popped it open, revealing a flawless diamond in a platinum setting. Around the band were smaller diamonds. It was the most beautiful ring Billy had ever seen. Marcus got down on one knee in the parking lot and looked up at Billy. "Since the day I met you, I've only had eyes for you. Willamina Jefferson, will your crazy ass spend the rest of your life with me?"

PART II

BAD INTENTIONS

NO SHADE: A Hood Rat Novel

CHAPTER 7

Present Day:

"Now that was straight out of a ghetto fairytale," Yoshi said after Billy had finished her story.

"Tell me about it. I got a ring and fingerprinted all in the same night," Billy joked.

"I'm really happy for you and Marcus, ma. After all the bullshit we've been through, if anyone deserves their shot at happiness it's you two, real talk," Yoshi said.

"We've definitely been through some shit," Billy recalled some of the rougher times in their lives. As a group and individually the girls had been through some rough patches.

"Out of curiosity, why are you guys getting married so fast?" Yoshi asked. "Most people take at least a year to plan their weddings, but you guys aren't wasting any time. What's the big rush? You pregnant or something?"

"No, I'm not pregnant, dumb ass," Billy laughed. "It was Marcus's idea. I tried to tell him we don't have to hurry, but he says he doesn't want to wait. He says he doesn't want to waste any more time than he has to before making me his forever lady."

"Aww that is so sweet," Yoshi said. "Marcus always was a good guy like that, even though he was always trying to play gangsta back in the day. Even with all that tough shit, you managed to break him down and I'm proud of you, girl," she gave Billy a high five.

"Yeah, I know I was a bitch to him in the beginning, but anything worth having is worth working for and I worked that nigga like a dog," Billy joked. "But on the real, Marcus has been a blessing to me. Love like ours comes along once in a lifetime."

"You know I know," Yoshi said, thinking of her one true love and his fate.

When Billy realized she had re-opened an old wound she covered her mouth in embarrassment. "Oh my God, Yoshi, I'm so sorry."

"It's cool, Billy. It's been a few years now so I don't break down at the mention of Jah anymore," Yoshi said as if it was no big deal.

Jah had been Yoshi's one true love and the scourge of Harlem. Back then, Yoshi had been a wild child herself so she and Jah's souls connected like missing pieces to a puzzle. His love for her and wanting better for them is what had made Jah decided to hang up his guns. He was ready to divorce the streets to be with Yoshi, but the streets weren't quite ready to let him go. When Jah was murdered, he took with him the part of Yoshi that was capable of love. She had been with other men after Jah, but none of them were ever worthy of her heart.

"Let's not ruin my visit by talking about depressing shit. We've got to keep our focus on planning your wedding."

"Yes, my wedding," Billy let the words roll around. "It's less than two weeks away, but it still doesn't feel real to me."

"It will when you're walking down that aisle," Reese said.

"God I hope I don't pass out from nervousness," Billy said.

"If you do, we'll carry your ass the rest of the way. You're going to marry that man, and your whole crew will be there for you, just like old times."

"Everybody except Rhonda," Reese said, unwittingly darkening the mood. Rhonda had been the fourth member of their group, and by far the most outspoken. She could be abrasive, rude, and downright ghetto, but she was still one of them. A few years prior, she had been murdered by the man she'd led to believe was her son's father.

"What do you think Rhonda would say if she were here?" Billy asked.

"Make sure you get him to put a baby in you too so if y'all split you can get child support on top of alimony," Yoshi imitated Rhonda's voice.

Billy and Reese both busted out laughing. "Yeah, that girl always was about her paper. You know, not a day goes by when I don't think of her crazy ass. I could always call Rhonda if I was dealing with some shit that I couldn't figure out. She had a solution for everything, even though most of the time; her solutions were outlandish as hell."

"You ain't never lied," Reese added. "Do you remember the time when I thought I was pregnant and was scared to tell my mother? Rhonda to the rescue. She told me that if I drank a whole bunch of Matla and sat in a warm tub I could give myself a homemade abortion."

"Oh shit! I remember that!" Yoshi exclaimed.

"I don't know who was a bigger idiot, her for suggesting it or me for listening," Reese laughed.

"Reese your ass was on the toilet for days after drinking all those nasty ass Maltas," Billy recalled.

"I might not have been pregnant, but it sure felt like I was gonna give birth the way my stomach was hurting," Reese recalled. "I miss those days...I miss us."

"I think we all miss our sisterhood, but some of us are more reluctant to admit it than others." Billy cut her eyes at Yoshi.

Yoshi threw up her middle finger. Since they were young, Billy had always been the one trying to play peacemaker between the girls. Yoshi understood where she was coming from, but wasn't sure if she was ready to make her peace with Reese. A few years had passed since the incident, but every time Yoshi thought about it, she wanted to pop-off. In time, they would squash it, but it would be on her terms. To avoid getting pulled further into a conversation she wasn't ready to have, Yoshi busied herself looking out the window.

It had been a long time since she had been back in Harlem, and it had changed a bit but was still familiar to her. The sights, the sounds, the smell, she felt like she was home. Yoshi loved her new life in L.A. She lived in a nice house, the weather was always beautiful, and she was getting money doing something that she enjoyed. California was definitely easy to fall in love with, but her heart would always be in Harlem.

Yoshi snapped out of her daze when she felt the car coming to a stop. She looked up and saw the familiar looming brick buildings of the projects. "What are we doing in the hood? I thought we were going to Billy's so I could drop my bags and freshen up?"

"We are. I just had to make a stop to buy some bundles of hair," Reese told her.

Yoshi made a face. "You still buy bootleg hair from the projects?"

"Damn right! And this ain't no bootleg; these are some quality bundles. You know Ms. P don't half-step when it comes to her merchandise."

*

Mrs. Pat stood in her kitchen wearing her favorite floral housecoat and a pair of tattered slippers. Her head was wrapped in a scarf that was damp with sweat. She had been standing over the stove for hours and still wasn't done handling her business. She bounced in place to the tune playing on the small boom box sitting atop the refrigerator. Every few seconds, she would stop to sing out part of the song on the radio, "I'm in love with the coco." Her hand swirled the fork around in the pot with the expertise of a chef making a poached egg, getting a perfect spin on the cocaine. She picked up a measuring cup, holding a small amount of white powder, and began sprinkling it into the pot. "Baking soda...I got baking soda..."

One of the big homies in the neighborhood found himself in need of a chef at the last minute and had called on Ms. Pat to come out of retirement. Even ten years removed from selling hard drugs,

Ms. Pat still had the best whip game in town when it came to cooking coke.

Ms. Pat stopped her whipping when she heard a knock on the door. She turned the fire off on the stove, and dropped a lid on it to make it look like a meal she was simmering instead of a felony. Moving quickly, she gathered the crack she'd already cooked up and threw it all into a false bottom in her refrigerator under the vegetable bin. She wasn't worried about it being the police, because if it had been, they'd have busted her door down instead of knocking, but she still didn't want anybody in her business. The knocking continued as Ms. Pat washed the coke residue off her hands into the sink. With her trusty .22 tucked in the pocket of her duster, she went to answer the door.

"Hold your damn horses!" Ms. Pat yelled as she eased up on the peephole. Once she confirmed the identity of her visitor, she undid the multiple locks and pulled the heavy project door open. "Girl what the hell did I tell you about bringing your ass around here without calling first?"

"I did call, but you weren't answering your phone," Reese said.

Ms. Pat pulled her iPhone from her pocket and checked it. Sure enough, she had five missed calls. "Damn, I forgot to turn my ringer back on," she said more to herself than anyone. "Okay, bring your asses on in here," she stepped aside to let the girls enter. "How y'all doing?"

"Fine, Ms. Pat. How about you?" Billy asked.

"Trying to make it in this white man's world," Ms. Pat told her. "Oh, congratulations on your wedding. That Marcus is fine as wine."

Billy smiled. "Thanks. I guess news travels fast, huh?"

"You know don't nothing go on in the hood without me knowing about it. The whole hood is buzzing about you taking one of its most eligible bachelors off the market. Oh and I'll be expecting an invitation."

"You know I wouldn't leave you out, Ms. Pat," Billy lied. She hadn't planned to invite the whole hood to her wedding, just family and friends, but she knew that if she left Ms. Pat out, she'd likely never hear the end of it.

"Did my order come in?" Reese asked Ms. Pat.

"Yeah, I got you faded. Give me a sec," Ms. Pat told her before disappearing into one of the bedrooms. When she returned, she was holding four packs of hair. "I got the three packs of Remy you asked about, but I wanted to show you this new Malaysian wet and wavy I got in this morning," she held up one of the bundles for the girls to inspect. "Check the quality on that."

The girls took turns stroking the hair.

"Damn, Reese wasn't lying about you having the hook up," Yoshi said, running her fingers through the hair to check the texture.

"You know Ms. Pat don't fuck around," the old woman said, speaking of herself in third person. "I'll tell you what, I planned on letting these go for two-fifty, but since Reese is spending with me already, I'll let you have them for two hundred even."

"I hadn't planned on buying any hair, but I can't pass up on a deal like that. I'll take two," Yoshi said, getting her money from her purse. "Billy, you better get in on this. That wet and wavy would look banging on you at your wedding."

"You know I don't be putting all that fake shit in my head," Billy waved her off.

"Fake?" Ms. Pat scowled at her. "Child, I'll have you know that Ms. Pat don't do fake. Every bundle I sling has grown from someone's head. You can run a DNA test on any of my shit and trace it back to the original owners."

"I know your stuff is official, Ms. Pat. I've just never been big on weaves and extensions," Billy explained.

"Well not all of us can be blessed with such beautiful hair, Billy. But for the ladies who need a little something extra…I got it for the low-low," Ms. Pat bust back into her song. "But seriously, I'm really happy for you Billy. You know for a while a lot of us thought you played for the other team," she stuck her tongue between her fingers and wagged it at her.

"Never, I'm strictly dickly," Billy declared.

"I'll bet you are now. I know a lot of women that would change their sexual preferences and their religious beliefs for a piece of that chocolate candy you're about to marry. I'll bet y'all gonna do it big too."

"I'm fine with a small ceremony, but Marcus wants a big wedding. Since he's paying for it, I'm not complaining," Billy said.

"He still working at that strip joint?" Ms. Pat asked.

"Marcus doesn't work at Shooters anymore, he owns it now," Billy corrected her.

"Well excuse the hell out of me. I'm surprised that sour old bastard Shooter was willing to let it go, but then again, he always did have a soft spot for Marcus. That boy was like a son to him."

62

"Ms. Pat, I didn't know you knew Shooter." Reese was surprised.

"Yeah me and Shooter go way back...as in the back seat of his Cadillac. I swear that man could do some things with his mouth that can still make me weak in the knees just thinking about them," Ms. Pat braced herself against the wall dramatically. "I gots to make sure I wear my good wig for this one. You make sure you have your wedding planner sit me at Shooter's table, ya hear?"

"Oh, we're not using a wedding planner. We're doing it ourselves," Billy told her.

"Child, you have no clue what you signed up for," Ms. Pat shook her head. "Me and my first husband Charles, may God curse his black ass soul, planned our wedding too. That translates to he kicked out the money and I did all the work. Honey, let me tell you, it was a damn nightmare. From it raining on our outdoor ceremony to my ghetto ass relatives throwing hands at the reception, it seemed like everything that could go wrong did. For my second and third weddings, we used a planner. If you want I can refer you to someone."

"Nah, I don't think that'll be necessary Ms. Pat. I've taken care of most of the stuff already and the rest of the odds and ends I got my girls to help me handle," Billy told her.

"That's good that you got reliable friends in your corner. Y'all kind of remind me of me, Earnestine, and Rita...except we was prettier at y'all age, no shade," Ms. Pat chuckled. "So which one of these heifers is the Maid of Honor?"

"I am!" Yoshi and Reese said at the same time.

Reese looked at Yoshi. "And what makes you think you're going to be the Maid of Honor?"

"Because I'm her best friend," Yoshi replied.

"Well so am I, not to mention that I've known her longer," Reese shot back.

"Bullshit, Reese. You weren't even allowed to come outside after dark when me and Billy first started running the streets. I've been her A1 since day-1."

"Well I was the one here with her for the last couple of years while you've been off doing your own shit. Unlike some people, I don't abandon my friends."

Yoshi gave Reese the side-eye. "Bitch, you use the word friend so freely you can't even put stock in it coming out of your mouth. Maybe if my so called friend hadn't totally violated me by fucking the guy I was seeing, I wouldn't have felt like I had to leave!"

And there it was...the elephant that had been in the room since Yoshi stepped off the plane.

CHAPTER 8

"So, you just gonna sit there buried in them papers or address the elephant in the room?" Wayne asked from the chaise lounge on the other side of the office where he had parked himself, nursing a glass of scotch. He had come to the club directly from work so he was still wearing his postal uniform.

Marcus looked up from his paper shuffling. "And what elephant would that be?"

Wayne stopped mid-sip and gave Marcus a disbelieving look. "The fact that you about to drink the Kool Aid, that's what elephant! Jesus, for a man about to go to the electric chair you sure as hell are calm about it."

"Wayne, I'm getting married, not being executed," Marcus said.

"Same shit if you ask me. Marriage, or execution…either way your life is over," Wayne said in a matter-of-fact tone. Wayne was one of Marcus's oldest and dearest friends, but he was also one of the few people who knew how to get under his skin. He knew just what buttons to push.

"And how would you know when you've never been married? Come to think of it, we've known each other since junior high school and I can't remember you ever even having a steady girlfriend," Marcus pointed out.

"That's because I'm smart," Wayne threw his drink back, and made his way across the room. "I don't have to have ever been married to know that it's a sucker's bet," he flopped his two-hundred and fifty pound frame into the chair on the other side of Marcus's desk, and helped himself to another glass of the scotch. He'd filled his glass halfway before Marcus relieved him of the bottle.

"Take it easy, Ned the Wino. You know this aged shit is for special guests," Marcus told him. He had paid a pretty penny for a case of the expensive scotch and only broke it out when he was trying to impress a potential business partner.

"Oh, so I ain't special now?" Wayne faked hurt.

"Yeah, Special Ed," Marcus laughed.

"You ain't shit, Marcus. Anyhow, like I was saying; you name me one nigga we grew up with that can say they're in a happy marriage?"

"What about Lewis? Him and Claudia seem like they got a good thing going," Marcus said. Lewis was another guy who had gone to school with Marcus and Wayne. He'd married his childhood sweetheart and was now living somewhere in New Jersey, working at a big company. They didn't see each other much, but would occasionally get together on weekends when their schedules permitted.

Wayne laughed. "Fool, that Mr. and Mrs. Perfect shit is a Jedi mind trick. That relationship went nuclear years ago and now they can barely stand each other. Lewis cheats on Claudia and she cheats on him, but they'd rather fake it until they make it for appearances. Try again."

Marcus's wheels spun as he went through the mental list of names in his head of friends or even acquaintances, but sadly couldn't think of anyone outside of Lewis and Claudia. It was like the sanctity of marriage had been lost on his generation.

"You see what I mean?" Wayne continued. "Dawg, marriage fucks everything up because in order for it to work, you have to stop being you."

"That's a crock of shit. I'm going to be the same person before and after my vows," Marcus declared.

"Are you trying to convince me or yourself?" Wayne threw his drink back and slammed the glass on the table. "All night poker games on Thursdays…dead. Weekend trips to Miami…dead. Us test driving the girls before you decide if you want to hire them or not…dead-and-stinking!"

"Funny, because everything you just named was more beneficial to you than me," Marcus pointed out.

"Marcus don't front like you don't benefit from the perks of owning a fucking strip club. You ain't no angel," Wayne accused.

"I never said I was, Wayne. I've done a little dirt here and there, but once I take my vows all that shit is behind me. Having your pick of a dozen bitches is cool, but having one who makes your life worth living is a blessing. I ain't gonna fuck that up by trying to prove to you single muthafuckas who ain't got shit to lose that I'm still that nigga."

Wayne shook his head. "See, you're changing already."

"The bottom line is I know I'll have to make adjustments, I get it, but I'm happy to do it because I love Billy. You act like because I'm getting married I'm not going to be the same dude I've always been. Before and after the wedding it'll still be business as usual."

"Not all business," Wayne told him. "The minute you say 'I do' you're agreeing to sacrifice your individuality for the sake of the union. Ain't no more you only y'all. Everything you do from there on out, you'll have to consider Billy first. Can you honestly say you're ready for that?"

Marcus poured himself a healthy shot of scotch. He hadn't planned to drink, but Wayne had his wheels spinning. "Absolutely," he threw the scotch back.

Their conversation was interrupted when the office door swung open unexpectedly, and a well-dressed older gentleman walked in. He was decked out in a green leisure suit and black shoes polished to a high shine. It was rare that you would ever catch the old timer out in public dressed in anything but his best. From his processed hair to the gaudy pinky ring he wore, his whole style was an ode to the gangsters of his generation.

"I guess knocking on a closed door is a lost art," Marcus said.

"Yeah, unless you own those closed doors," Shooter replied.

"A minority owner," Marcus corrected him.

"Minority or majority, it's still my name on the marquee and my blood and sweat in the foundation of this establishment," Shooter reminded him.

"Whatever, old head," Marcus teased him.

"Old or not, I still got enough swag to knock a bitch half my age," Shooter said in his best pimp drawl. "What are you two jokers up to?"

"I'm in here trying to show our boy the error of his ways, trying to talk him out of this marriage shit. Help me talk some sense into him Shooter," Wayne urged.

"Why, so he can be a single and miserable like you?" Shooter asked.

"I am not miserable. I'm happier than a sissy in Dick-Town with my life," Wayne said.

"Horse shit," Shooter scoffed. "You spend your days lugging mail and your nights chasing random pussy. Ain't none of them broads you lay with worth their salt."

"I like a little variety that's all," Wayne said.

"Variety is cool, but consistency is better. Sure, you get a lot of pussy but what do the women you lay with contribute to your life other than a cheap thrill?" Shooter asked. "I'll bet you couldn't tell me the last time you ate a meal that wasn't either delivered or came out of a microwave."

"Shooter, why you hating on me?" Wayne asked.

"I ain't hating on you, young blood. I actually feel kinda sorry for you. You're a handsome young man with a good job, your own place, and a credit score that ain't in the toilet. You might actually make some girl a decent husband one of these days, if you could get off your own dick long enough to see a woman as more than something to be conquered."

"Amen to that," Marcus added.

"Y'all just some haters," Wayne folded his arms and pouted like a child.

"So, I hear in a few nights this joint is gonna be on everybody's to-do list," Shooter said.

"Yeah, hosting the birthday party for Shai Clark's wife is going to bring us a hell of a lot of publicity," Marcus said proudly.

"Indeed it is. Just make sure it's the right kind of publicity. Inviting all them mobsters in here all it once is gonna be a handful to keep under control," Shooter warned.

"Shooter we have gangsters in here every night, this won't be any difference," Marcus said.

"Boy, Shai Clark and his bunch ain't no street corner dope boys. They're Mafioso. There's a big difference. Make sure your security people are on point, young blood."

"Bear and his team have got it under control," Marcus told him, sounding surer than he really was. In truth, he had been so focused on pulling the wedding together that he hadn't really weighed the pros and cons of letting Shai have the party at Shooters. All he saw was the opportunity to host the biggest event in the city and the large cash deposit Shai had one of his people drop off. He wasn't hurting for money yet, but between keeping the club running and kicking out dough for the wedding, he was starting to feel a slight pinch in his pocket and the money generated by the party would be a much-needed blessing.

"Do you hear me talking to you, Marcus?" Shooter asked.

"I'm sorry, what did you say?" Marcus snapped out of his daze.

"I asked if everything is straight with the wedding," Shooter repeated.

"I guess. I left the planning to Billy. I'm just cutting the checks," Marcus said.

"Boy, I ain't gonna envy your bank account when she's done with it. Women go over the top with everything, especially weddings. If you need to hold a few dollars just let me know."

NO SHADE: A Hood Rat Novel

"Thanks, but I'm good Shooter. I got a few irons in the fire bringing some extra income in," Marcus said.

Shooter gave Marcus a look. "What kind of irons?"

"Stop looking at me like that, Shooter. I'm not back hustling if that's what you're thinking," Marcus said, trying his best to sound convincing.

"You damn well better not be. I've invested a lot of time and money into cleaning you up, boy. I didn't give you my club to have you lose it while you're rotting away in some prison cell."

"Don't worry, Shooter. Prison isn't in my future," Marcus assured him.

There was a soft tap on the door.

"Enter," Wayne called out, as if it was his place and not Marcus's.

One of the day shift managers, Tammy, came into the office. Tammy had been working at Shooters for a little under a year and proved to be one of Marcus's most valued employees. Tammy was five-five, light-skinned, with a million dollar smile, and a figure that could've made her rich if she was a dancer and not a manager. That wasn't where Tammy's head was. She was more concerned with getting through college than she was twerking for dollars.

"Hey sweet thang. You must've known I was in the building," Wayne greeted her. "Why don't you sit on Santa's lap and tell him what you want for Christmas," he reached for her, but Tammy slapped his hand away.

"Nigga, you try and touch me uninvited again and you're going to lose that hand," Tammy said seriously. She was normally a sweet girl, but could be quite the firecracker when provoked, which Wayne did every chance he got.

"Wayne, stop harassing my staff," Marcus told him. "I'm kind of in the middle of something. What can I do for you, Tammy?"

"Sorry to disturb you, Marcus, but there's someone here to see you," Tammy said.

"Who is it?" Marcus asked in an annoyed tone. He hated unexpected visitors.

"He wouldn't give me his name, but he says he's an old friend," Tammy told him.

"Everybody's a damn friend or long lost relative when you're on top," Shooter mumbled.

Marcus ignored Shooter. "Send him up, Tammy, but make sure you have Bear pat his ass down first."

"You got it, boss," Tammy said with a playful twang before going to retrieve Marcus's guest.

Wayne's eyes followed Tammy's ass until she disappeared through the door. "Damn, I'd suck a baby outta her pussy!"

"Wayne you know you ain't Tammy's speed. She's not into dudes in uniform," Marcus laughed.

"So I've heard. Tammy likes them clean cut, and engaged," Wayne said suggestively.

"And what's that supposed to mean?"

Wayne twisted his lips. "Come on Marcus, how long are you gonna play this game? I know you're hitting that."

"Nah, you know I stopped mixing business with pleasure a long time ago," Marcus told his friend.

"Marcus you never were a very good liar. You don't think anybody sees the way y'all look at each other when you think no one is paying attention? Even when you think nobody is watching, someone always is so you better wake up and get on point."

"You're tripping, man," Marcus waved him off.

"If that's what you gotta tell yourself so you can keep thinking you're slick, I'm okay with it, but I know you better than anyone else. Who you're fucking is your business; I just wanna know how the pussy tastes?"

"Wayne you need counseling," Shooter said. "And you," he turned to Marcus, "are too damn accessible. You pay them managers too much money for them not to know how to handle strays that come in off the street without bothering you with it. Bosses should only sit with bosses."

"Shooter this ain't the seventies and eighties when you held up in this office like it was a fortress. You can't figure out what the consumer wants unless you're in on the ground floor with the common folks," Marcus explained. "Besides," he opened the desk drawer and produced a Desert Eagle, "if a nigga act crazy, this will make them sane real quick."

Shooter laughed. "At least some of my good business sense rubbed off on you."

A few minutes later, Tammy came back into the office, but this time she wasn't alone. There were two of them; the first was a female who was shaped like a bodybuilder. Her long dreads pulled to the top of her head in a large bun. Her face was a mask of pure stone. Trailing her was a smaller man, but he was equally imposing. His

73

wide shoulders strained against the sleek black leather jacket he was wearing. Diamonds of several colors decorated the heavy chains around his neck, speckling his chiseled jaw. The bald-fade hairstyle he wore made the fact that his head was almost perfectly round stand out. He stood there smirking, while a very stunned Marcus looked on, speechless.

The man's lips parted into a wide smile. "What's the matter, Marcus? You ain't happy to see your old buddy Trap?"

Shooter leaned over to Marcus and whispered, "What was that you were saying about prison not being in your future?"

CHAPTER 9

Of all the people Marcus expected to see walk in the door that day, Trap wasn't one of them. It had been six months since the last time, they'd seen each other, and before that, it had been nearly five years since they'd been in the same room. Trap represented a part of Marcus's past that he had worked extremely hard to bury. Considering the fact that Trap was now standing in his office, Marcus hadn't worked hard enough.

"Well don't all get up at once," Trap strolled into the room.

"Damn, Satan must've forgot to lock the back door to hell again," Shooter capped. He had never particularly liked Trap and never tried to hide it. Trap was bad news and trouble followed him like a shadow.

"Good to see you too, old timer," Trap ignored the insult and greeted Shooter with a respectful handshake. "What it do, Marcus? No love for ya man?"

"Nah, it ain't like that," Marcus got up and came from around his desk to greet him properly. "I just didn't expect to see you," he hugged him, letting his hand absently sweep Trap's back for weapons.

"You know I don't like to announce my movements. People know where you're gonna be they know where to get you," Trap told him.

"So, what brings you this far north?" Shooter asked.

Trap shrugged. "A little bit of this and a little bit of that. I had some business in New York and decided to pay a call on my old running partner."

"Well you know Marcus ain't a participant in that race anymore, don't you?" Wayne asked, moving to stand next to Marcus. He didn't know Trap well enough for his dislike for Trap to run as deep as Shooter's went, but he had spent enough time around him to know what he represented to Marcus.

"Big Wayne, you wound me," Trap placed his hand over his heart dramatically. "I'd never track mud into my friend's home. It's good to know that you still got the homie's back though. You're a square, but you never been a sucker and I've always respected that about you."

Wayne didn't reply to the acknowledgement, he simply nodded.

"But dig," Trap continued, "I know you're a super busy cat and I don't wanna hold you no longer than I have to, but I need a few minutes with you in private," he glanced from Shooter to Wayne.

Wayne glanced at his friend to see how he wanted to play it, as did Shooter. At a moment's notice, they'd have been ready to ride out for Marcus. After a few tense moments, Marcus gave them the signal that he had it under control.

"So be it," Shooter got to his feet. "Me and Wayne will be downstairs at the bar if you need us." He led Wayne towards the office door. As he passed the woman, Trap's sister Moochie, she gave him a respectful nod. Shooter returned the gesture. Moochie was good people, but blindly loyal to Trap.

Trap watched Shooter and Wayne until they'd left the office and the door closed behind them. "They've always been protective of you. Good friends like that are hard to come by."

"Indeed," Marcus agreed. "When we find good friends…loyal friends, we appreciate those relationships enough to never compromise them. So to what do I owe the pleasure of your unannounced visit?"

"As I was saying earlier, I had some business out this way…a bit of a dilemma more than anything," Trap explained. "But before we get to that, how come I gotta hear through the grapevine that you're getting married?"

"I wasn't really putting it out there because we're not having a big wedding, just something intimate with a few close friends and family," Marcus downplayed it.

"Are we not family?" Trap asked.

"Of course we are, Trap. I didn't mean it like that," Marcus said.

"I'm just fucking with you, dawg. Mixing your street family with your real family is never a recipe for a successful evening. Those two worlds overlapping can lead to you having to answer some very uncomfortable questions. I can dig it, and I respect it. I wish you and your lady nothing but happiness. Make sure you shoot me an address so I can send you a wedding gift," Trap told him.

"No doubt," Marcus said, before glancing at his watch. "Trap, I ain't trying to rush you off, but I gotta meet wifey in a while and you know how women get when you're late."

"Don't I," Trap laughed. "Moochie hates the fact that I'm always late. Ain't that right?" he asked his sister.

"Whatever, Trap. Get to the point so we can dip. We still got other stops to make, ya heard?" Moochie said in a rough voice. She was all business all the time, and one of the people who kept Trap on point.

"Right, right…my dilemma." Trap got serious. "Big bro, I got a situation that I think you and your squeaky clean reputation can help me with."

"Trap, before you go any further, let me remind you that I don't taint my blessings. I got a legit thing going here and I really can't afford to fuck it up by getting caught up in some street shit," Marcus told him.

Trap's face darkened. "Marcus, I think I'm starting to feel a little disrespected by how your wet nurses, and now you, have been coming at me since I been here. You've been blessed with a second chance homie, it would be some hater shit on my part to try and jam you, and I ain't never been no fuck-nigga. I'm happy for your success, dawg. As far as you not tainting your blessings," he made air quotes with his fingers, "you can miss me with that shit. You tainted this the minute you decided to step out of your element to feed your dreams, or have you forgotten who opened up that pipeline for you when you needed it?"

The truth in Trap's words stung like a slap. Once upon a time, Marcus and Trap had been in business together moving drugs. Marcus found his way down the straight and narrow when he came under Shooter's wing and Trap found success in the music industry, but Trap always kept one foot in the streets.

A few months ago, Marcus found himself having some financial trouble. The club needed renovations, which was eating into the bulk of his money, and maintaining the lifestyle he had become accustomed to was getting harder and harder. His pride wouldn't allow him to tell anyone, not even Billy, about his difficulties. When things looked bleakest, Marcus reluctantly played a trump card he had been holding and called in a favor from an old running buddy. Trap had his people flip some money on the street for Marcus to help him out. Marcus had reservations about getting back in bed with Trap, but he was in a bind. He reasoned that since he wasn't officially back in the game that the rules didn't apply, but he should've known better. Once you allowed a demon like Trap to stick its claws in you, it would hold on for dear life rather than let you go.

Marcus sighed. "What do you want from me, Trap?"

"Just a little courtesy, that's all," Trap said sincerely. "You know I been doing this independent music thing real heavy for the last few years. I've been doing my thing, and I'm almost to the point where I can go legit, but in the meantime, I still got one foot in and one foot out, if you get my meaning?"

"And what does that have to do with me?" Marcus asked.

"I was getting to that. See, it's come to my attention that the good state of Florida is trying to build a case against me for some of my past misdeeds. Now I ain't no angel, but I ain't no John Gotti either, which is what they're trying to say."

"So, what do you need from me? A lawyer?" Marcus asked.

"Nah, I got one of the best defense attorneys in the county on the case. What I need from you is a bit more sensitive."

Marcus didn't like the way he phrased it.

"You see, in the midst of all this criminal investigation shit, they're also looking into my finances. As we both know, mine is a cash and carry business so I don't exactly have any pay stubs I can produce to prove how I make my bread," Trap explained.

"Okay, shouldn't be too hard for me to have the bookkeeper doctor hook you up with some paystubs. I can say you're one of our seasonal managers or something," Marcus offered.

Trap laughed. "Marcus, I own a condo in South Beach and a townhouse in North Carolina. No way in the hell the government is gonna believe I was able to pull all that off from managing no strip club. I was thinking of something on a slightly grander scale."

"Such as?"

"I was thinking we convince them that we're partners here at Shooters," Trap said.

"Trap, you must've fell and bumped your fucking head. Why the fuck would I tell them you own my spot?" Marcus snapped.

"Calm down, Marcus. You and I both know that this is your shit, but the government doesn't. All we need to do is provide them with the phony paperwork."

"I don't know about this, Trap. What if they double check it with the state filing office?" Marcus asked.

"I already thought of that. Most likely when we show them the paperwork, along with you vouching for me, it won't go that far, but in the event that it does, I put some assurances in place."

"What kind of assurances?" Marcus asked suspiciously.

"Best you don't know, homie. The main thing is that when or if an inquiry happens to go through, it'll get overlooked. All I need is for you to give me the go ahead and we straight," Trap said as if it was just that simple.

"Trap, I'd really like to help you, but this shit could end badly. I could lose my club. I can't get involved," Marcus told him.

Trap's face soured. "Well listen at you trying to play Mr. Straight and Narrow. You wasn't talking that shit when we was getting down for a cause that suited you. Where was this Good Samaritan talk when we were banging hammers at niggas trying to protect what was ours? I got blood on my hands in your name, and you gonna leave me for dead in a time of need?"

It was a low blow and they both knew it. Every bit of Marcus's common sense told him that this was a bad idea, but his sense of loyalty and owing Trap a debt, outweighed his good judgment. "A'ight nigga, but if this shit goes bad…"

"Don't sweat it, Marcus. Everything is gonna be cool," Trap smiled. "And to show that I'm a good sport about it, I got one hundred large for you."

"You ain't gotta give me no money, Trap."

"I ain't giving you shit. Fifty of it will go into the salary you're going to pay me over the course of the rest of the year in case they double back and fifty goes in your pocket for your troubles. I'll bring the bread by tomorrow night."

"Nah, that ain't gonna work. I've got a private party going on here tonight and the client has already dropped the bread for it so I can't cancel," Marcus said, thinking on Shai Clark's bag of money.

"Even better, I'll come through and take the stage as a bonus," Trap offered.

"That won't be necessary. I got Big Dawg performing."

Trap's eyes lit up. "As in Don B's crew?"

"Yeah, you know him?"

"Our paths have crossed a few times," Trap said slyly. "Look, I won't hang around. I'll come through, pop a few bottles, and drop your money. After that, I'm gone. Deal?" he extended his hand.

"Okay," Marcus shook his hand, "but after this, my debt to you is paid in full."

NO SHADE: A Hood Rat Novel

CHAPTER 10

It had been days since Rocky had left the house and she was starting to feel like a prisoner. Her son had been staying with her mother so she could move around more freely while looking for work. After what had happened with Claudette at the welfare office, she'd decided a job was less hazardous than Public Assistance.

Finding a job had been trickier than Rocky had expected. She had been filling out applications and emailing her resume around, but still hadn't found anything to suit her. She'd been on a couple of interviews, but it seemed like she kept hearing the same things: "We'll be in touch," or "You're overqualified for the position." She never thought she'd see the day when having a college degree would be more of a hindrance than help.

Being unemployed was just one of many problems Rocky was having. Her bathtub had been clogged for over a week, and Housing still hadn't sent anyone to fix it. She'd put in a ticket for it and even went by the management office twice, but all she was getting for her troubles were excuses. She was getting tired of taking ho-baths in her sink or going all the way to her mother's for a hot shower. For as thankful as Rocky was to have a roof over her head, she was sick and tired of living in the projects.

Rocky was stressed and it was becoming harder and harder to cope with, especially on her own. Rocky's life was too cluttered to try and squeeze a boyfriend in, but there were other perks to having a man around besides the stability of a relationship. At the very least, if she were getting the occasional side of dick, it would help to alleviate the stress in her life, but as it stood, it had been nearly a year since she'd had an orgasm that wasn't self-induced.

Mourning her deceased sex life made her think of the encounter she'd had with the tattooed cutie with the nice eyes. Their meeting had been a brief one, but it was long enough for him to leave am impression on Rocky. It wasn't just because he was fine as hell; it was the way he carried himself. She had around enough gangsters to know one when she saw one, but he didn't strike her as the average. He carried himself with an air about himself that intrigued Rocky. On more than one night, the mystery man had provided the visuals for Rocky's self-pleasure sessions. A part of her felt dirty for thinking of a man she didn't know in that way, but then again, that's what fantasies were all about, visualizing things you were likely to never have.

"Get it together girl," Rocky said to herself, pushing the dirty thoughts from her mind. She felt like the walls of her apartment and her problems were closing in on her, and she needed to do something to break up the sad ass routine of her life so she decided to get slithered.

Rocky dipped into her emergency stash and took out a few dollars for a bottle and some chronic. The liquor store was only a few blocks up so she had that covered, but what she didn't have was a weed connect. The knuckleheads who hung out in the lobby sold weed, but it was mostly dirt. If she was going to do it, she wanted to smoke something exotic, and she knew just who to call to get it for her.

NO SHADE: A Hood Rat Novel

*

"You know, I was surprised when you called me," Boots said, sitting across Rocky's dining room table where she was putting the finishing touches on a blunt of Sour.

"So was I, because I don't really fuck with you like that," was what Rocky wanted to say, but instead she opted for, "You know I don't fuck with too many people in this neighborhood to have them all in my business."

"You smart," Boots said, licking the ends of the blunt to seal it. "These bitches around here ain't about shit. All they do is chat you up all friendly like then put all your business out in the streets. You gotta watch these project hos, Rocky."

"So I've noticed," Rocky said giving her the side-eye. As expected, when she offered Boots the opportunity to get high and drunk for free in exchange for procuring the weed, she was all for it. Rocky copped a pint of Hennessey and Boots called some dude she knew who sold nickel bags of Sour Diesel and got them a four-for-fifteen play. She'd cuffed the five dollars change from the twenty, but Rocky let it slide.

"So," Boots sipped from her plastic cup, "I heard you and Claudette started a riot at the welfare office."

"I didn't start anything, it was Claudette who kicked all that craziness off," Rocky clarified.

Boots shook her head. "That girl is always in some shit. You better watch yourself running with her, Rocky."

85

"On another note," Rocky changed the subject, "I been meaning to ask you something. Was that you I saw on that paternity test show a couple of weeks ago?"

The question caught Boots so off guard that she nearly choked on her Hennessy. "Girl, hell no that wasn't me," she lied.

"Really? Then you must have a twin out there in the world because the girl on the show sure looked like you," Rocky said.

"I get that all the time, Rocky. People always mistake me for someone they've seen on TV. If life had played out different, I would've probably been an actress. God knows I've got the looks," Boots tightened the faded green scarf on her head.

The two girls sat around for a while longer, sipping, smoking, and shooting the breeze until the munchies eventually kicked in. Rocky's fridge was running on vapors so they decided to walk up the street to the Chinese restaurant. It wasn't until Rocky got outside and the sun hit her that she realized she was slightly tipsier than she thought. If she didn't get some food in her system soon, she was going to have a situation.

Boots was the only person Rocky knew who could turn a five-minute walk into a journey that lasted nearly forty minutes. It seemed like they couldn't make it a half block without Boots stopping to talk to someone, she knew. Rocky lingered off to the side, fighting the pangs in her stomach while Boots ran her mouth. Eventually, they made it to the avenue and were making tracks for the Chinese restaurant when Rocky spotted someone that made her pull up short. Heading in her direction was one of the girls Claudette had fought in the welfare office, with two other girls she didn't know. They seemed to be locked in a heated conversation.

As they neared Rocky and Boots, Rocky's heart pounded in her chest. She wasn't sure what to expect when they crossed paths. Rocky hadn't had anything to do with the fight, but she was with Claudette and guilt by association was sometimes good enough to get you an ass whipping. Rocky wasn't a big fighter when she was sober, so she was sure she wouldn't stand a chance drunk. She only hoped that if the girl decided she wanted to go another round that Boots would have her back.

When the girls were right on top of them, Rocky braced herself for the inevitable. To her surprise and relief, the girl didn't give her so much as a second look. One of them gave Boots a half ass, "Hello," and they kept it pushing. Apparently, whatever they were arguing about was more important than Rocky.

"What the hell is wrong with you?" Boots asked Rocky, noticing that all the color had drained from her face.

"Nothing, I just need to get something to eat," Rocky lied.

*

When they reached the Chinese restaurant, they were surprised to find Claudette outside. The scratches on her face from the fight were starting to fade, but there was still some slight bruising under her eye. Claudette leaned against a Mercedes SUV talking to the driver through the window. From the way she was cheesing they were obviously telling her everything she wanted to hear.

"Look at this thirsty bitch," Boots said to Rocky.

When they reached Claudette, she was just finishing her conversation with the driver of the SUV. Rocky saw him hand Claudette a few dollars before pulling off into traffic.

"Hey boo," Boots greeted Claudette happily as if she hadn't just been throwing shade at her.

"What up though, Boots? I'm glad I bumped into you because I've been meaning to ask you about something," Claudette told her.

"What's good?" Boots asked excitedly, thinking she was about to get the opportunity to spill or sip some tea. She loved gossip.

"Little Nae from the other side said you and Bernie were on TV, is that true?" Claudette asked.

Rocky snickered.

"Oh my God, I wish people would stop asking me that," Boots said in a frustrated tone. "I know who my baby daddy is, so what the fuck would I look like going on a show to try and find out?"

"You'd look like the bitch who was on the show," Claudette laughed. "I'm just fucking with you. Where y'all coming from?"

"Shit, me and Rocky was at the crib getting faded. We just came out to grab something to eat," Boots told her.

"Damn, y'all had a session and couldn't even call a bitch? That's shady as hell," Claudette said.

"It wasn't my smoke, Rocky lit me up," Boots threw her under the bus.

"Is that right?" Claudette turned her attention to Rocky. "And since when did Ms. Goodie-Two-Shoes become a pot head? Every time I try to get you to smoke with me you be acting funny."

"Stop lying Claudette. We've smoked together before, but you know I don't indulge like that. I just do it when the mood strikes me," Rocky told her.

"From the way your eyes are all low the mood must've hit you like a muthafucka today," Claudette capped. "So what up, what y'all got on the next bag? I'll throw in on it."

"All I got on me is three dollars to get some wings and fries, but I think we got a little Henny left," Rocky said.

"You know I ain't got it," Boots turned the pockets of her sweatpants out showing there was nothing in them but lint and loose cigarette tobacco.

Claudette sucked her teeth. "Boots how the hell are you broke when you and two of your kids just got your checks on the first?"

"Once I paid all my bills and my rent I didn't have too much of nothing left," Boots said.

"But your rent is only four hundred dollars!"

Boots shrugged. "Social Security checks don't go as far as they used to."

Claudette shook her head. "I swear you get on my nerves with that cheap shit. Luckily, I came into some good fortune. I'll spring for a blunt, but I ain't making the trip to get it."

"Say no more, I'll go holla at Scrams and them down the block. Just give me the bread," Boots extended her hand.

"And bring my change back too," Claudette placed a twenty in her hand. Boots mumbled something under her breath and went off in search of the weed man. "That is one janky ass broad," she said once she was out of earshot.

"Boots is okay," Rocky said.

"You feel like that now, but wait until you really get to know her. That chick is pure slime and everybody in the hood knows it. She out here fronting like that wasn't her ho ass on the show. I ain't surprised that she don't know who her baby daddy is because she'll fuck anything with a pulse. If you got a man, don't bring that nigga around Boots."

"Well I'm single so I don't have to worry about that. Oh, before I forget, you'll never guess who I saw a while ago."

"Who?" Claudette asked.

"One of the girls we got into it with the other day at the welfare office."

"You mean that I got into it with while your ass laid in the cut?" Claudette corrected her. "Anyway, where did you see the ho?"

"On the Ave."

"On the Ave? What Ave, this Ave?" Claudette motioned towards the strip.

"Yeah, she was with two chicks but I don't know who they were. You think they were looking for you?" Rocky asked.

"I wish the fuck some off brand bitches would call themselves rolling up in my projects looking for a problem. Best believe they would've found one. I already told my cousin and them what went down and its on-sight wherever we catch them broads. You know the Shower Cap Posse don't fuck around!" Claudette said heatedly.

The Shower Cap Posse was a group of hood boogers that Claudette's cousin hung out with. They were notorious for swarming

90

on women, and sometimes men, in packs and dishing out ass whippings.

"Damn I wish you would've called me as soon as you saw them," she slammed her fist into her palm.

"I wasn't thinking about it. Besides, looks like you had your hands full with dude in the car. Who was that anyhow?" Rocky asked.

"Oh, that was this dude I met last week named Holiday. He's trying to submit his application for a taste of this sweet pussy," Claudette boasted.

"You didn't fuck him yet?" Rocky couldn't hide her surprise.

"What do you think, I'm some kind of ho or something?" Claudette asked in an offended tone. "No, I didn't let him fuck me, but I did give him some head. He's been on my back ever since trying to get me to let him beat."

"What's stopping you? He looks like he's getting money."

"Oh, Holiday is a major player in the game and that's the main reason I haven't fucked him yet. Holiday is baller, running with one of the strongest crews in the city. He's used to bitches throwing their pussies at him like Frisbees, so me playing hard to get is something new. With dudes like Holiday, the more you make them wait, the more they'll be willing to do for you to hit it. By the time I'm finished with this nigga he's gonna wanna wife me."

"Damn, you got it all mapped out," Rocky said.

"Hell fucking yeah. Bitch, I'm tired of being broke and living in these slum ass projects. I ain't too proud for a sponsor, and you need to get you one too. As a matter of fact, you should roll with me

91

tomorrow night. Holiday's boss is having a party for his wife and he wants me to be his date. I told him I'd go if I could bring a friend. That way I'll have an excuse to dip out on him if shit goes sour. I was gonna hit Nikki, but why don't you come out with me?"

"Claudette, my money is kinda funny so I ain't in the position to really go nowhere. My hair ain't even done," Rocky yanked at a loose strand of her mop.

"Girl, I can throw a pressing comb to that wig, gel them edges down, and have you combat ready in under an hour. As far as money, fucking with a baller comes with its perks. Holiday and them are gonna cover everything. All you gotta do is find something decent to wear and we in these streets, baby girl."

Rocky was hesitant. She was totally unprepared to go out, but what else did she have to do? Her social life had been on the bench for too long and needed to get some playing time. It would be nice to get out and be fawned over for a night, even if it was by some thug ass dudes that Claudette knew. "Okay, but his friend better be cute," she relented.

"That's my girl," Claudette beamed. "I'll have him make sure you don't get stuck with some Pookie-looking nigga."

"You better not," Rocky warned.

"Girl, quit worrying, I told you I got you. This party is going to be everything! I hear even them niggas from Big Dawg might be coming through too," Claudette told her.

Rocky made a confused face. "What the hell is a Big Dawg?"

NO SHADE: A Hood Rat Novel

CHAPTER 11

The air inside the spacious room was so heavy with smoke that it was a struggle to see your hand in front of your face. There was more chronic smoke in their air than oxygen, making it hard to breathe, but no one dared step out. They were too afraid they might miss the miracle when it finally manifested.

Two girls, Tracy and Kima, sat on a love seat near a glass coffee table. On the tabletop were several bottles of water, boxes of cigars, and an open plastic bag that had once held almost a pound of weed. It was down to half that thanks to the constant rotation of blunts being sparked or handed out by one of the girls. That was their position at the company, the official blunt rollers for the crew. The girls made more twisting up spliffs than some people made working regular jobs.

Gathered inside the studio were the usual suspects. Tone was sitting in the recliner, talking on the phone, and doing something on his iPad at the same time. Every so often, he would pause to say something to the producer before going back to his gadgets. He was all business all the time. Tone was the mortar that held the company together, but the man sitting to his right was the brick it was built on.

Don B. was sunk in his plush leather chair, with one jeweled wrist hanging over the side lazily. Pinched between his fingers was a smoldering blunt of Afghan Kush. Every so often, he would lift the blunt to his thick lips and take deep puffs. A black Yankee fitted was pulled down over his head, shadowing most of his face to his thick beard. Hanging from his neck was a bejeweled Rottweiler head.

93

K'WAN

From behind his mirrored sunglasses, he surveyed his subjects and the kingdom he had built.

The self-proclaimed Don of all Harlem was a kid who had fought his way from the bowels of the ghetto to the top of the food chain. The former crack dealer, turned music mogul, had used the money he'd made on the streets to build one of the most successful record labels in the last decade. But for as successful as Big Dawg and its founder were, they were equally notorious. Don B's name as well as his company had been mentioned in several homicide investigations over the years, including those of some of its own artists. The running joke about Big Dawg was, you had to die to go platinum. Still, even with the rumors surrounding the company, it didn't stop hungry young artists from seeking out Don B. Two such artists were in the studio that afternoon.

Working the huge control panel of lights and knobs that dominated a good portion of the room was one of the newer members of the family, an Asian kid named Charlie Wong, who adopted the moniker of Keys. He was wearing a white t-shirt, black Atlanta Falcons fitted cap, and black skinny jeans. Over his ears, he wore large headphones, which funneled sound from the recording booth into his brain. As he bobbed his head to the melody of his latest track, the small Rottweiler pendant at the end of his gold chain clanked against the control panel. Chink's skin might've been yellow, but he had more soul than most black folks did. Keys was a musical genius and who could play several different instruments. His ear for music was unmatched and when he created tracks it like he was anointing it with the Holy Spirit. In under a year, Keys had produced eight songs, which all hit the Billboard charts. He was one of two of the record company's most prized assets and top earners. Inside the recording booth, was the other one.

She was hailed as the second coming of Mary J. Blige, possessing a soulful sound and around the way girl appeal. The media couldn't get enough of her and her hard luck story, and everyone knew she would be the next big name in music, but before that, she had simply been Vera Petty, a former gospel singer from a small town in Texas. She showed up in New York on a bus with little more than the clothes on her back, the Bible her grandmother had given her, and stars in her eyes. That all changed when Don B. had taken her under his wing and re-made Vera in his image. He retired her conservative look, put her on the cutting edge of fashion, and brought in some of the best stylists and make-up people in the business to give her a new, racier look. The day she signed her contract the shell that had been Vera Petty was burned away and from the ashes rose Venus, the first lady of Big Dawg.

Even before her transformation, Venus had been a beautiful girl and the fellas found it hard not to admire her, especially considering what she wore inside the recording booth. The tattered black leggings hugged her legs and hips tightly, leaving very little to the imagination. It was hot as the devil inside so she had come out of her shirt and was wearing nothing but a sport's bra and a towel around her neck, which she used to wipe the sweat from her coco colored face. A red bandana was tied around her head, ensuring she didn't ruin the expensive weave Don B. had started her wearing. Venus caressed the microphone stand as if it was a familiar lover, and she needed him to hear her words. She had a voice so beautiful that it was easy for even the hardest cats to get choked up when they heard it. By the time, she had gotten to the end of her song; there was hardly a dry eye in the room.

"That was beautiful," Kima told Venus when she stepped out of the booth. She was dabbing the corners of her eyes, trying to keep her mascara from running.

"Thank you," Venus said with an easy smile.

"That wasn't beautiful, that was Big Dawg," Don B. corrected her. He was beaming like a proud father. Venus was truly blessed, but more importantly, she was the property of Big Dawg and the one Don B. saw as his next cash cow.

"I don't know, I think it still sounds like it could use some fine tuning," Keys said.

Venus frowned. "Fine tuning? I've been singing this damn song over and over for hours; it ain't gonna get no more perfect than that."

"If Keys says it needs fine tuning then it needs fine tuning," Don B. said.

"I've sang the song like a hundred times already," Venus protested.

"And you'll sing it one hundred and one if that's what it takes," Don B. told her.

Venus sucked her teeth and the whole room went silent.

Don B's face became hard. "Something you need to say, Venus?"

"No, I'm cool Don," Venus tried to shrug it off.

"Nah, you sucking them thirty-thousand dollar teeth I gave you like you ain't feeling what I'm saying. Have I ever told you anything that wasn't to your benefit?"

Venus gave him a look as she thought of some of the less than intelligent things Don B. had convinced her to do.

"Of course I haven't," Don B. answered for her. "Everything I tell you or anyone else is for the betterment of your careers or this company. Yeah, I know I work y'all niggas like slaves, but how else do you expect to be number one? I hold all you muthafuckas to a certain standard because I understand what it takes to make it. Big Dawg is at the top of the food chain because we work harder than anyone else. Now, if you wanna sign to a record label that doesn't mind if you slack because they put out shitty music anyway, then you know where the door is. But, if you wanna be remembered as one of the greatest of all time, I suggest you get your ass back in that booth."

Venus mumbled something under her breath before storming back inside the recording booth, slamming the door behind her hard enough to rattle the glass partition.

"That's what the fuck I thought," Don B. said.

"Don, why you go so hard on that girl? I think the song sounded good," Tone said. He had taken a break from his networking to add his two cents on Venus's behalf.

"Oh, it was perfect, but I ain't gonna tell her that. If you don't keep these bitches hungry they start to get complacent and you know we can't have that," Don B. explained.

"Must y'all throw the B-word around so freely in the presence of ladies?" Tracy asked. Her brown eyes were red and hanging low from all the weed, she had smoked. She was a short, dark-skinned chick with thick hips and a slick mouth.

"You ain't no lady, you're a fucking employee, and I don't recall censoring what comes out of my mouth as being part of your job description. Now stop bumping your gums and roll me another blunt before I send your ass back to the unemployment line!" Don B. snapped. "Kima," he addressed the other girl, "you got a problem with me using the word bitch too?"

Kima raised her hazel eyes from the blunt she was about to light. "Nope, my baby daddy calls me a bitch all the time and I ain't getting a crumb from him, so it don't bother me none when you say it so long as you cutting a check." Kima didn't particularly care for her arrogant employer, but as long as he kept her bills paid and money in her bank account, she would turn a blind eye and a deaf ear to his bullshit.

"See, that's what I'm talking about. Kima is a team player," Don B. said. "Tracy, you need to take some pointers from your girl and loosen the fuck up."

"Whatever nigga," Tracy said and went back to her blunt rolling.

Their banter was broken up by the buzzing of the intercom.

"I hope that's the food we ordered. I'm hungry as hell," Don B. said.

"Me too," Venus said from inside the booth. They hadn't realized the two-way mic was on.

NO SHADE: A Hood Rat Novel

"You'll eat after you lay this song," Don B. told her.

"I'll check and see who it is," a grumbling voice said from a dark corner near the door shortly before a man with a shaggy beard and long cornrows emerged. G had been so quiet they'd almost forgotten he was in the room. G did everything quietly. Even when he spoke, it was rare that he ever raised his voice. G was the newest addition to Don B's security detail. He'd joined them during a chance encounter in Florida where he had been instrumental in saving Don B's life. Devil, who was the head of security, had been against recruiting the stranger.

They didn't know much about G except what he'd told them, and Devil was distrustful of men with secrets. Still, Don B. felt like he owed him a debt and agreed to let G eat from the Big Dawg bowl. When G looked at the security monitor, he frowned when he saw the two young men standing in the lobby. He didn't particularly care for either them, but they were a part of the dysfunctional ass family he'd joined, so he buzzed them in. A few seconds later, Dolla and Wise came ambling into the studio.

"Greetings fellow scum bags and degenerates," Dolla gave dap to all the men in the room. When he got to G, the quiet man looked at Dolla's hand as if it was something vile. "Word, it's like that? Well fuck you too."

G took a step towards Dolla, but a look from Don B. backed him off. "Bitch ass nigga," he mumbled.

"Dolla, why you always fucking with G?" Don B. asked in frustration. Dolla was always trying to antagonize G, and it would only be a matter of time before he lost his cool.

"Nah, big bro. I be trying to show the nigga love and he always acting like he ain't feeling me," Dolla explained.

"That's because I'm not," G said plainly. "You're a troublemaker and sneaky as a fucking viper in the weeds. I got no tolerance for little candy ass niggas like you and if I had it my way, I'd leave you stinking in a ditch somewhere."

"Good thing you ain't the one calling the shots and my big bro is," Dolla said spitefully.

"So, where are you two dick heads coming from?" Don B. asked, changing the subject.

"Just bending a few corners," Wise answered.

"As usual," Tone shook his head. "You know, if you two niggas spent as much time helping out around here as you do fucking off in the streets, you might actually amount to something."

"Now that's a terrible thing to say," Dolla faked offense. "What y'all see as us hanging around, getting drunk, and fucking random bitches, is actually us being your eyes and ears in the streets."

"And what news do my eyes and ears bring me that will make up for you disrupting my studio session?" Don B. asked. He was tired, hungry, and in no mood for Dolla's bullshit.

"Saw a man lose his hand a few days ago," Wise interjected. Unlike Dollar, he smelled the anger on the horizon and wanted no parts of it.

"Do tell," Don B. urged.

Wise opened his mouth, but it was Dolla who recounted the tale. "Yo, B, shit was crazy. One of them old niggas from the projects landed on the wrong side of Shai Clark, and got dealt with," he went on to tell Don B. the story of how Carl had lost his hand, embellishing certain parts here and there. "Word up, the kid had like a hundred blades on him and used every last one on Carl. It was ugly, B."

"Damn, he cut him up that bad and nobody called the police?" Tracy asked.

Dolla looked at her as if she was the dumbest person on earth. "Who in their right mind is gonna call the police on one of Shai Clark's boys, especially the Turk?"

"The Turk? What the fuck is a Turk?" Don B. asked, as he was unfamiliar with the name.

"The Butcher's Boy," G spoke up. "They call him the Turk on account of his father being Turkish. His daddy, Ahmad Kaplan, was a legend in his day. As the story goes, the Butcher was the one you went to if you wanted somebody to go missing and never be found. They say he'd hack up bodies in the back of his butcher shop on Saturday and sell the meat half price to the church ladies on Sunday mornings. Poppa Clark used him on a bunch of contract jobs back in the eighties and nineties."

Just then, Tone's phone rang. He looked at the number on the screen and smirked. "Speak the devil's name and he shall appear," he excused himself to take the call.

"Sounds like a cold piece of work," Don B. was still stuck on the story of the Butcher. "We could use a man like that on our side."

"Last I'd heard, Ahmad Kaplan was retired," G said.

"That's a shame, but maybe his kid has inherited some of his skills," Don B. suggested. "Do you know him well enough to get close to him?" he asked Dolla.

"Yeah, I know him," Dolla lied, which got him a dirty look from Wise. "Well, he ain't my right hand man or nothing, but me and Wise can get at him if you want."

"Do that," Don B. told him.

"Well, it looks like you guys spoke Shai up," Tone said as he was ending his call.

"That was Shai on the line?" Don B. asked in surprise.

"Nah, it was his mouthpiece, Swann," Tone told him. "Shai is throwing a birthday party for his wife tomorrow night and apparently Don B. is one of her favorite artists. Swann says Shai would greatly appreciate it if you would agree to perform at the event."

Don B. frowned. "Fuck do I look like, some clown who can be hired for birthday parties and bat mitzvahs on a whim? I'm a rock star. Call that nigga back and tell twenty-four hours isn't enough notice, and that he should find himself another circus act to entertain his bitch."

"You sure you wanna play it like that, Don?" G asked. "It's not often that the boss of bosses calls on you for a personal favor."

"Well he ain't the boss of me. I don't give a fuck who he is, nobody orders the Don around," Don B. said.

"Maybe you should stop looking at it as being given an order and start looking at it as an opportunity," G suggested.

"How you figure that, G?" Don B. asked, curious to hear G's take. His insight into the criminal mind had often proved helpful to Don B.

"Well, if Shai Clark is throwing a party for his main lady, you know the guest list is gonna consist of a lot of heavy hitters…people that less than savory cats like us wouldn't normally be able to get next to. There's no telling what kind of networking opportunities for Big Dawg may come of this."

"Or problems," Tone countered. "Shai knows as many gangsters as he does businessmen and we ain't the most well liked muthafuckas in the streets."

"A very valid point, Tone, but I seriously doubt if Shai's gonna mix those two crowds, especially at a family function. But of course, this is just my humble opinion. The Don of Dons calls the shots," he mock bowed.

"You know what, you're right," Don B. agreed with G. "Tone, hit Swann back and tell him I'll do it."

Once that was settled, they went back to focusing on Venus's recording session. G returned to his shadowed corner, smiling inwardly. What he had said was true about it being a great networking opportunity for Big Dawg. Shai loved to show off, especially when it came to Honey, so there would definitely be some power players in attendance, all looking to earn the favor of the young king of New York. It was a golden opportunity for Big Dawg, but G had his own agenda.

K'WAN

CHAPTER 12

"You know that nigga has got an agenda, don't you?" Was the first thing out of Shooter's mouth when he re-entered Marcus's office. Wayne had cut out, but Shooter lingered around until after Trap and Moochie had gone.

"When does he not," Marcus said, pouring himself another drink.

"But I'll bet that didn't stop you from agreeing to whatever he came in here and asked you for," Shooter said. He didn't need Marcus to confirm or deny, the look on his face said it all. "Damn Marcus, how long you gonna keep playing the fool for this dude?"

"I ain't playing the fool for nobody, Shooter. You don't even know what Trap wanted and you're jumping to conclusions," Marcus pointed out.

"I don't need to know what he wanted; I know what he's about. Trap is a gangster and you're a businessman. Mixing those two worlds is a recipe for disaster," Shooter warned.

"I'm good enough in my comfort zone to know better than to step out of it," Marcus assured him. "Trap didn't come to me for anything illegal, he just needs a solid," he lied

Shooter snorted. "The last time Trap needed a solid an innocent man ended up shot and you found yourself indebted to me for fifty-large, or has the weed completely wiped your memory clean?"

Back when Marcus and Trap were still running tough, Trap had asked Marcus to take a ride with him to see some Haitian kids he was doing business with. It was supposed to be a simple pick up of

104

some guns Trap had bought, but in the blink of an eye, it turned into something else. The parcel of guns was short by one, a small .38. Trap didn't even give the dudes a chance to explain before he accused them of trying to cheat him, to the displeasure of the Haitians. They had impeccable reputations and felt like Trap's accusation was disrespectful. Marcus tried to be the voice of reason, but the situation spiraled out of control quicker than he could get a handle on it. Trap, being the hot head that he was, shot one of the Haitians and everything went downhill from there.

As it turned out, the gun dealer that Trap had shot was connected to some very serious people who didn't take kindly to one of theirs being put in the I.C.U. and were out for blood. Marcus ended up the victim of a kidnapping, and there was no doubt in anyone's mind that they intended to kill him. Fortunately, for Marcus, Shooter had a relationship with their leader and was able to negotiate for Marcus's life, but not without compensation. That was the turning point for Marcus and he decided to focus solely on his legitimate holdings and leave the streets for those who still had the stomachs for it.

"It's not gonna be like that this time, Shooter," Marcus said, sounding surer than he actually was.

"Or so you hope, but shit happens, especially when dealing with a man like Trap. Marcus, I'm from the streets so I understand how the code works. Your sense of loyalty to your former comrade is why you can't bring yourself to turn Trap away when he needs you, but you ain't a soldier no more and the rules no longer apply. The only person in this world you have an obligation to is that gal you

105

plan on marrying in a few days. You're a grown man, and I can't force you to do anything, but what I can tell you is to be careful and to be smart. If it comes down to a choice between you and Trap, don't be no hero. You feed that nigga to the dogs, you hear me?"

"Yeah, I hear you," Marcus said.

"A'ight, I'm about to cut out. Got a hot date in a couple of hours and I wanna make sure I'm powder fresh for this young tender," Shooter patted his processed hair.

Marcus shook his head. "The consummate pussy hound."

"You better believe it. I've paid my debt to the marriage Gods and what's left of this life of mine will be spent, rested, dressed, and knee deep in bitches half my age." Shooter gave him a wink and left.

Long after Shooter had gone, his words still rang in Marcus's head. Dealing with Trap was like handling a viper. Sometimes they bit you not out of malice, but because it was in their nature.

Marcus grabbed the bottle of Scotch and deposited himself on the chaise lounge. After pouring himself a stiff drink, he fished a half-smoked blunt from his pocket and fired it up. Between Trap's bullshit and the wedding, Marcus felt like he had the weight of the world on his shoulders. He had so many different things on his mind that he felt like his head would explode if he didn't get everything sorted out.

*

Marcus felt like he had only closed his eyes for a few seconds, but by the time he opened them again the sun was starting to set outside of his office window. He reached for his drink and found it and the bottle missing. It was then that Marcus noticed that he wasn't alone. Tammy was sitting at the edge of the chaise, watching him sleep.

"Tammy, what are you doing in here?" Marcus asked surprised.

"Sorry to startle you. I knocked but you didn't answer," she explained.

"Did you need something?"

"No, I was just checking on you. I overheard Shooter and Wayne talking about that guy, Trap, and I wanted to make sure you were okay."

"I'm fine," Marcus said, sitting up.

"Drowning yourself in scotch tends to do that to you," Tammy handed him a bottle of water.

"Appreciate it," Marcus cracked the seal and downed the water. He immediately started to feel more alert.

"From the dent you put in that bottle of scotch I'd say you've had a pretty rough day."

Marcus sighed. "Tammy, you don't even know the half."

"You wanna talk about it?" she asked.

"Not really," Marcus said flatly.

"Sorry, I didn't mean to pry. I was just concerned," Tammy said in an apologetic tone.

"My fault, Tammy. I didn't mean to sound like that. I'm just a little stressed," Marcus told her.

"Well I think I know just the thing to help out with that," Tammy placed her hand on Marcus's lap.

"Cut it out, Tammy," Marcus moved her hand and stood up.

"What's the matter, baby? I'm just trying to make you feel better." Tammy got up and closed the distance between them. Seductively, she ran her hands down Marcus's chest and abs and began trying to undo his belt.

"Knock it off, Tammy," he took a step back.

"Marcus, you don't have to worry about anyone catching us. I locked the door behind me." She hiked her skirt, revealing she wasn't wearing any panties. "C'mon baby, just put the head in."

"Tammy, am I speaking another language or are you just not getting it? Ain't nothing popping."

"So, it's like that?" Tammy asked, clearly offended by his rejection.

"It ain't like nothing and that's what I keep trying to tell you. What is with you lately?"

"I don't know, maybe it's the fact that I'm not used to having a man make love to me then cast me to the side like I'm some jump off!" she shouted.

"First of all, lower your voice in my office. Second, we only fucked once Tammy and we both agreed that it was a mistake that should've never happened."

"No, you said it was a mistake, not me," she reminded him.

"Whatever, Tammy. Either way nothing is going to happen between us. You know where my heart is."

"Funny, because you weren't too worried about your heart when you had your dick in my mouth!" she snapped.

"Listen, Tammy," Marcus began, trying to keep his anger from bubbling over, "I slipped and I accept responsibility for that, but I'm about to get married. I don't want to take old baggage into my new life."

"So now all I am is baggage? Damn, you sure know what to say to make a girl feel special."

"Stop twisting my words, Tammy."

"Why not, when you're twisting my heart? I know it was just a fuck to you, but it meant more to me Marcus. I don't just give my body away like that. I know you love Billy and I respect that, which is why I'd never try to take you from her. If I have to play number two, I'm willing to do that if it means you'll still be in my life. All I'm asking is that you don't throw me away like trash," she pleaded.

"Stop talking like that, Tammy. You know I hate when you start talking that second fiddle shit because we both know you're better than that. You're a beautiful girl who is about her business and any man would be lucky to have you."

"So how come you don't want me?" she asked, with tear filled eyes.

"Tammy, don't make this any harder than it has to be. You know I can't do this."

"Well, neither can I," Tammy composed herself and left Marcus's office.

Marcus was left standing there, feeling like shit on a stick because he knew Tammy was a monster that he had created. He'd known Tammy had a crush on him, but he'd faked ignorance to it. She was an employee and he was her boss. Sure, Marcus had freaked off with some of the strippers, but Tammy was looking for more than a one-night-stand. They'd managed to keep it professional until one night all the rules went out the window.

Billy and Marcus were having problems in their relationship, and the fact that he had been spending most of his time at the club didn't help. He was dumping more money into it than he was getting out and he was trying as best he could to keep the place from folding. This presented a problem for Billy. She had even gone as far as accusing him of sleeping with the dancers he worked with, but at the time, he wasn't. He tried to get Billy to understand what was going on with him and the club, but she couldn't put her jealousy aside long enough to see that he was trying to grind them out of the hole. It eventually caused a rift between them, and that opened the door for what was to come.

One night Billy and Marcus had gotten into a big argument over something trivial, and rather than go back and forth with her, he left and went to spend the night at Shooters. It was their off night but Tammy and some of the other managers were there doing inventory. After the other managers had left, Tammy stayed behind with Marcus. She felt like he needed a friend. Marcus couldn't speak for her intentions, but he had no plans on sleeping with Tammy that night. It was something that just ended up happening. That night he had some of the most mind-blowing sex of his life. Tammy did things to Marcus, and let Marcus do things to her, that Billy would never go for. It was definitely memorable.

Tammy was fun, but Billy was his heart and the guilt of being unfaithful was killing him, so he cut his adventures with Tammy short. Tammy took it better than he had expected. Of course, she was hurt, but she understood. For a while, things seemed back to normal. Tammy flirted, but didn't try to cross that line. All was well until she found out that Marcus was getting married. She became moody and at times borderline insubordinate. Up until then Tammy been an invaluable employee, but lately, Marcus had begun to wonder if keeping her around was going to come back and bite him on the ass.

CHAPTER 13

By the time Billy made it back to Marcus's condo, she was tired, hungry, and irritated. The reunion between Yoshi and Reese had been a complete disaster. Billy hadn't expected it to be all hugs and kisses between the girls considering their unresolved issues, but she hadn't expected things to go nuclear. At one point, she thought they were going to come to blows, and had it not been for Ms. Pat and her pistol, they likely would've. She hated to see her friends at each other's throats, especially over a piece of dick.

Not long before she'd left New York, Yoshi had been seeing a guy named Gary, who she met on a video shoot. Gary wasn't a hustler or a killer like most of the men Yoshi had dealt with. He was a square with a decent job. Gary was hardly Yoshi's type, but he was good to her...at least in the beginning. Yoshi never told her friends about her relationship was Gary because she wasn't sure where it was going, but she was starting to develop strong feelings for Gary. Just about the time that Yoshi had decided to commit to Gary, she noticed a change in his behavior. She had been around the block enough times to know the signs of a cheating man, so she let Gary go. Her suspicions would be confirmed later on when Gary's dirt started coming to the light. She was able to deal with the fact that Gary was fucking three other girls that she knew of, but what broke her heart was finding out that one of them was Reese.

To Reese's credit, she didn't know about Yoshi and Gary in the beginning, and as soon as she found out what Gary was up to, she broke it off with him. Where Reese messed up was by not telling

Yoshi about it. Since Gary and Yoshi weren't seeing each other anymore, Reese figured she'd just let that fire burn itself out, and Yoshi would never be the wiser, but the streets started talking. As the saying goes, what's done in the dark always comes to the light and when the light shone on what Reese had done, it hurt Yoshi deeply.

Reese had tried to reach out to Yoshi on more than one occasion to explain, but the damage was already done. This isn't to say that had Reese told Yoshi in the beginning she wouldn't have been hurt, but they could've gotten past it, but because Yoshi heard it through the grapevine and not from Reese it looked suspicious, like she was being sneaky.

Not long after, Yoshi up and moved to California without warning. Billy didn't even know Yoshi was moving until a week before she left. Between Jah being murdered, her being raped, and a slew of other misfortunate events, New York had become a grim reminder of all the bad things that had happened to her in life. Billy couldn't say that she blamed her friend for wanting a fresh start; she just wished it had been under different circumstances.

As if the situation with Gary didn't make things bad enough, there was the issue with who would be Billy's Maid of Honor. In truth, she hadn't even thought about it. She had so much on her mind with planning the wedding that she hadn't given, as much thought as she should of, into the roles everyone would play.

Yoshi was one of her oldest and dearest friends, but it had been Reese who had stuck by Billy through the ups and downs over the last few years. They both deserved the honor, but it could only go to one of them. No matter which one of them she picked, the other would be offended, so she was damned if she did and damned if she didn't. Her wedding day would be upon her before she knew it and she had a tough decision to make.

When Billy put her key in the door, all she could think about was a hot bath and a cold glass of wine. The house was dark, but she could smell weed smoke in the air, which meant Marcus was home. She looked for him in his usual spot, the den, but found it empty. When she checked the bedroom she didn't find him there either. It wasn't until she was passing the kitchen that she spotted him…his silhouette actually. Marcus was sitting in the dark at the dining room table. The only reason she even noticed him was because she could see the burning ember at the end of his blunt.

"Why are you sitting here in the dark like a vampire?" Billy flipped the light switch. The fact that he was sitting there in a dingy looking tank top with a half empty bottle of Jack Daniels on the table was disturbing, but it was the pistol on the table next to it that frightened her. "Baby, what's wrong? Are you okay?" she cautiously approached the table.

"Yeah, I'm good. Just got a lot going on and trying to clear my head," Marcus told her. His voice sounded tired.

"You're trying to clear your head with a bottle of whiskey and a pistol? You do realize how fucked up that sounds, right?" Billy looked from the gun to her fiancé.

Marcus laughed. "What'd you think I was planning on offing myself? Ma, I love my life too much to go out like a sucka," he pulled her onto his lap. "When I die it's gonna be when I'm old, gray, and between your legs," he kissed her tenderly on the lips.

"Talk that shit Mr. Man," Billy straddled his lap so that she was facing him and plucked the blunt from his fingers. She draped her arms around his neck and gave him a shotgun, blowing the potent smoke into his face. "Sounds like we've both had shitty days. You wanna go first or should I?"

"I'll let you take the lead on this one," Marcus deferred.

"Well, it all started when we picked Yoshi up from the airport..." Billy went on to tell Marcus the story of her dreadful day.

"Damn, y'all ain't been back together for twenty-four hours and Reese and Yoshi are already beefing, over some dick at that." Marcus shook his head. "I guess some things never change."

"And what's that supposed to mean?" Billy asked in a defensive tone.

"Listen, you know I got love for Yoshi and Reese on the strength that they're your people, but let's look at this realistically. The world is a small place and both of those chicks play fast and loose with their pussies. Chalk it up as them getting caught slipping and move on."

Billy got off his lap and folded her arms. "Marcus, that's a fucked up thing to say."

"Billy, you know we tell truths between us so I'm giving you my truth," Marcus said seriously.

"Well the truth is that Gary was a piece of shit for playing my girls against each other!" Billy fumed.

"See, what you're looking for is a scapegoat in all this, but you can't put it all on the dude. All parties involved played a part in this turning out all fucked up. Gary is a scumbag for what he did, but to keep it one hundred, he's an outsider with no loyalties to either of them so what makes you think it was his place to inform them that they were sharing dick?"

"Because that's what a stand up nigga would've done," Billy declared.

Marcus chuckled. "Yeah, maybe in one of those K'wan novels you're always reading, but this is the real world. He was just being a dog ass nigga riding the wave. He lit the match, but the girls started the fire."

Billy looked at Marcus as if he had lost his mind. "Wait...let me see if I'm following you. This dude could've potentially ruined a friendship that goes back twenty years and it's their fault? Reese didn't even know Yoshi was seeing Gary too."

"Yes, but when she found out she should've said something. Reese made it worse by hiding it and Yoshi is not helping the situation by holding a grudge," Marcus said.

"She's hurt, it's to be expected."

"I'm not saying she isn't allowed to be in her feelings, anyone would be, but is she really willing to throw away all the history you guys share over someone who wasn't either one of their men to begin with? Jokers like Gary come a dime-a-dozen, but twenty-something years of friendship is slightly harder to come by. They both need to put on their big girl panties and get past it. I can't promise you it'll be easy, but you guys have gotten through a lot worse together."

Marcus's delivery was a bit harsh, but it didn't make it any less true. The girls had been through hell and back, but had always pulled through by leaning on each other for strength. This time would be no different, only Billy would have to be strong enough for all of them.

"Oh wow, I was so caught up in my problems that I almost forgot you had something on your mind too," Billy said.

"No worries," Marcus stood up and took Billy in his arms. "Seeing that beautiful face of yours always seems to make my problems go away."

"Get off me, smelling like a wino," Billy pushed at him playfully.

"Stop acting like me smelling like a backroom bar doesn't turn you on," Marcus pulled her closer. "Remember back when I used to creep by to check on you in the mornings when I would leave the club?"

"Yeah, I remember. You always smelled like liquor, weed, and cheap ass body spray."

"One of the many drawbacks of working at a strip club," Marcus laughed. "You hated that smell so much that you wouldn't let me get near you until I showered. On mornings when I was lucky you would come in and wash my back among other things," he pressed himself against her so she could feel him hardening.

"Well hello, stranger," Billy tugged at his dick through his pants. Their schedules had both been so hectic that their sex life had suffered slightly because of it. "You wanna move this little party to the bedroom?"

"Shit, we ain't even gotta go that far," Marcus lifted Billy and sat her on the table. He planted soft kisses on Billy's neck while undoing the drawstring of her sweatpants. He slipped his hands inside her panties and his fingers came out wet. He locked eyes with Billy and licked his fingers, slowly and deliberately. "Damn, you taste so good baby."

"That's just an appetizer," she slipped her sweatpants and panties down, scooting back on the table and spreading her legs. "You ready for the main course?"

Marcus knelt between Billy's legs and took in her scent. It was a sweetness of her essence, mixed with a slight hint of musk from being out all day, but not a stench. He kissed her on one thigh then the other, repeating the process while making his way onward. He could feel her squirm when the stubble from his face brushed her inner thigh. Marcus kissed her lower lips as tenderly as he would her mouth, sucking and inhaling so that he could taste her.

Billy gripped the back of Marcus's head and tried to force him deeper, but he resisted, keeping enough distance between his face and her vagina where they weren't touching, but she could feel the heat radiating from his face. When his tongue flicked out and graced her pussy lips, a jolt of electricity shot through her causing Billy to involuntarily arch her back.

When Marcus had decided he had teased Billy enough he grabbed her by the thighs and pulled her closer to him. At that angle, he could give her love nest his full attention. Marcus clamped his mouth over her entire vagina and closed it slowly, dragging his tongue down her slit as he went. Billy tried to wiggle out of his grasp, but he held firm. Using just the tip of his tongue, he invaded her space.

Billy's body went rigid when his tongue daggered her. Marcus flicked it this way and that way, making sure to greet each of her walls. Billy propped herself on her elbows and looked down at the top of Marcus's wavy fade. His head bobbed up and down and then in circular motions, causing the muscles in her stomach to constrict. One hundred and one different reasons as to why she loved him popped into her head, with his skills at oral stimulation making its way closer to the forefront. Billy's heart beat in her chest and spots danced in her eyes as he brought her to a climax. She felt herself cumming, over and over as if he had opened up a faucet that she couldn't turn off. Just when Billy thought she would die if he didn't stop…it happened.

"Damn," Marcus jumped back, but not quickly enough to keep from getting a spray of fluid in the face.

"Oh my goodness," Billy covered her mouth in embarrassment. "I…I…"

"Tried to drown me," Marcus wiped his face with his tank top.

"Great, make me feel more ashamed than I already am," Billy swung her legs around and got off the table.

"I'm only teasing," Marcus grabbed her arm. "Ain't no shame in your future husband getting you off. And now that I've gotten you off, how about a little show of appreciation," he looked down at his dick, which seemed to have magically appeared through his zipper.

Billy looked down at his throbbing muscle and licked her lips seductively. "Marcus," she purred in his ear, squeezing his dick in her hand. "I would love nothing more than to suck you until you moan my name, but you stink," she abruptly let his dick go and brushed past him.

Marcus was dumbfounded. "Hold on, so you just gonna leave me like this?" he held his dick.

"You've been in the streets all day and your balls smell like salami. See about me after you've showered."

"Billy that's some coldblooded shit. I made you squirt for the first time and this is how you repay me?"

Billy stopped short and looked back at him. "And who says it was my first time?" she winked and disappeared into the bathroom.

"Billy, don't make me fuck you up!" he called after her, but she couldn't hear him over the sound of the spray in the shower.

NO SHADE: A Hood Rat Novel

CHAPTER 14

Sitting in a hotel room, raiding the mini bar, and flipping through channels is not how Yoshi envisioned her return to New York when she boarded the plane at LAX, but there she found herself.

The plan had been for her to stay at Billy's crib while she was in town. They were going to eat ice cream, smoke weed, and reminisce like they used to do when they were younger, but that plan went out the window when she and Reese had their falling out. There was no way she could be under the same roof with her, let alone the same room, and trust herself not to try and kill her friend.

Before she agreed to attend Billy's wedding she had told herself that she was going to let the past be the past and forgive Reese, and she meant it, but seeing her face after all these years re-opened old wounds that she thought were healed. When she looked at Reese, instead of seeing one of her closest friends who had been there for her through some truly dark times, she saw the bitch who had slept with the man she had opened her heart too.

Yoshi was more hurt than angry over the whole thing. After losing Jah, she had given up on finding love, but over time opened herself up to the idea of a little happiness. In Gary, she saw someone who wasn't like the other men she'd dated. He worked a legal job and didn't live in the hood. She thought she had finally found someone different, but as it turned out, he was just like the rest.

The more Yoshi thought about it the crazier it made her. When she looked up at the mirror on the wall of the room, above the writing desk, she didn't recognize the person staring back at her.

121

K'WAN

Through the abuse, the rape, and the murder of her soul mate she had always pulled it together and stood tall. She was not some weak basket case who went all to pieces when she got her feelings hurt. She was a warrior…a survivor. Somewhere along the line, she had lost that part of herself and needed to find it again. Billy's wedding was still the focal point of her trip back home, but that night it would be all about Yoshi.

Yoshi pulled herself out of bed and went about the task of preparing herself. She dumped her suitcase on the bed and pieced together an outfit that reflected her mood. After a quick shower, she beat her face and did her hair. After dressing, she stood in front of the mirror that had earlier reflected who she had become and now saw what she used to be. Throwing on her sunglasses, she smiled wickedly. "You wanted her, you got her. The bitch is back."

*

No matter how much New York had changed some things would remain the same, or so Yoshi hoped. She took a taxi from mid-town to 147th and Broadway. Back in the day, there had been an after-hours spot up that way that Yoshi sometimes frequented when she was feeling especially adventurous.

When Yoshi reached the block, she was disappointed to find the rundown storefront she was looking for had been replaced by a small floral shop. It saddened her because she had been looking forward to revisiting some of her old stomping grounds. Seeing a familiar face or two was just what she needed to pull out of her slump, but she

122

wouldn't find it there. She was about to tell the taxi driver to take her to a different spot when something struck her as odd. The security gate, which obscured the view inside, was secured across the main window, but not the doorway. Upon closer inspection, she thought she saw shadows moving behind the smoky glass door. What was a florists doing open at 2 a.m.?

"I'll get out here," Yoshi paid the fare and slipped from the back of the taxi. The temperature had dropped making her wish she'd put on stockings under the short black skirt she was wearing. A little chill was the price she would have to pay for wanting to be cute. The sharp heels on her thigh-high boots clicked across the concrete as she approached the entrance to the floral shop. She had almost reached the small entrance when seemingly out of nowhere; a burly Puerto Rican man appeared in her path.

"You lost, Chula?" he asked her.

"Nah, I know just where I'm at," Yoshi tried to step around him, but he moved with her.

"I don't think you do. Everybody out here at this time of night is either looking to get high or selling pussy," he reached out and touched Yoshi's arm seductively. "Which category do you fall into, mami?"

Yoshi looked from his hand to his smirking face. When she spoke, there was ice in her tone. "I fall into the category of a bitch who'll have you murdered if I tell Killer Boo how you tried to disrespect my pedigree. Go fetch your boss and tell him Yoshibelle is here," she commanded. Yoshi watched him, holding her breath, while he measured her words. After a few seconds, he nodded and disappeared inside the florist. She had just taken a hell of a gamble by bluffing him. She wasn't sure if the after-hours spot was still in that building, or had moved when they replaced the storefront with the flower shop. Even if it was, there was no guarantee that it was still run by the same person. A few minutes later when the Puerto Rican came back with a black dude, she knew her gamble had paid off.

At six foot four and weighing at least two-hundred and fifty pounds, Killer Boo was a very imposing figure. He had chopped off his signature cornrows and now wore his head bald. His beard and goatee were peppered with gray, showing sings that age and hard living were finally starting to catch up with him. His dark eyes landed on Yoshi and drank her.

"Is this the ho bitch you said was looking for me?" Killer Boo quoted what the Puerto Rican had told him when he came inside.

"Yeah, this is the bitch," the Puerto Rican said smugly.

Killer Boo nodded before open hand slapping the Puerto Rican. The blow was so vicious that it took the Puerto Rican off his feet and deposited him on the ground several yards away. Killer Boo picked him up by the front of his shirt and shook him violently. "The next time you call yourself disrespecting a woman, make sure she doesn't have a big brother who'll break your fucking neck first," he snarled before letting the Puerto Rican go. When Killer Boo turned back to Yoshi, the anger had drained from his face. "Give me some love, baby girl," he spread his massive arms.

"Hey Killer," Yoshi hugged him. He had gotten so big that she almost couldn't get her arms around him.

NO SHADE: A Hood Rat Novel

"Stop that Killer shit. That's for niggas in the street. You're family, Yoshibelle," Boo told her. "Now come inside and let's get a drink. I haven't seen you in years and I want to hear all about what's going on in your life these days."

*

Killer Boo led Yoshi through the flower shop and down some stairs in the back, which opened up to a large room. To say she was surprised at what he had done to her old hang out would've been an understatement. Yoshi remembered the after-hours spot as being a hole in the wall spot with a bar and a few flimsy card tables and folding chairs, and a small dance floor where she and her friends would dance until all times of the morning, but Boo had made some upgrades.

The card tables were gone, replaced with black lacquer wooden ones and the sticky wooden floors were now carpeted. The bar still dominated one whole side of the room, but the dented metal one she remembered had been replaced with one made of smoked glass and fully stocked with everything from premium liquor to rotgut. One either end of the bar, there were large cages, where girls dressed in bikinis danced. The once rundown neighborhood hangout now looked better than some of the clubs in Midtown. If what he'd done with it was any indication of what Boo had been up to since he was released from prison, it was safe to say he was definitely on the come up.

K'WAN

Yoshi knew Boo from the neighborhood, but they didn't establish a relationship until she started dating his baby brother Jah. She would sometimes go up with Jah when he visited Boo at Green Haven Correctional Facility, which was like a second home to the eldest Dutton brother. Boo was one of the few people who could call her Yoshiebelle and it didn't get under her skin. She's once asked him why he refused to call her Yoshi and he told her it was because that was the name she went by when she was still dancing in the clubs, and he wasn't comfortable with those kinds of images of his little brother's future wife. They had gotten so close that Yoshi would sometimes go and visit him without Jah and spend hours talking about life.

When she had to make the trip to tell Boo about Jah's passing it was one of the hardest things she ever had to do. Boo was a stone cold killer and a very composed man, but that day he went completely to pieces. He took it so hard that they had to cut the visit short to take Boo to the infirmary because they thought he was having a psychotic break, and in truth, he was. Paul, the middle brother, had raised Jah, but Boo was like a surrogate father to him. Losing Jah was like losing a kid and he had never fully recovered. Yoshi kept in contact with him through letters until he was released from prison a few years prior. She had heard through the grapevine that he had taken over the old after-hours spot.

Boo perched himself on one of the bar stools and slid the other one out for Yoshi. He was gangster as hell, but still a gentleman. Mrs. Dutton had raised them well. Without having to ask, the bartender deposited a bottle of Hennessy on the bar.

126

"I see you still off that brown water," Yoshi nodded at the bottle.

"You know a leopard don't change its spots," Boo popped the cork and chugged from the bottle. "You still drink Absolute?"

"Nah, it's Ciroc these days," Yoshi informed him.

Boo had the bartender bring her a bottle of Pineapple Ciroc and poured her a glass. "To the Dutton boys," he raised his bottle. "May they have a pound of Granddaddy and a bad bitch waiting on me when I see them on the other side."

"To the Duttons," Yoshi touched her glass to his bottle before downing her drink. "So, I gotta ask; how on earth did you manage to get ahold of this place? Old man Suarez has run this since the beginning of time and I was a little surprised to hear that he had passed the torch."

"Oh, he didn't pass it, I took it and his hand along with it," Boo laughed. "When I was on the streets me and my crew made a lot of these old niggas rich, but not one of them dropped so much as a dime on my account the whole time I was away. So when I came home I made my rounds and collected what I felt niggas owed me."

Yoshi shook her head. "You still on that goon shit, huh?"

Boo shrugged. "Sometimes it's a necessary evil. Lately, I just been chilling though. I got a team of wild ass young dudes out here putting it in for me. We were wild in our day, but these kids are on another level with it. Human life don't mean shit to 'em if it's about a dollar. This one young cat I got under me, who goes by the name of Fate, is the wildest of the bunch. I think I took such a liking to him because he reminds me of Jah."

"Shit, ain't nobody on it like Jah was," Yoshi said.

"You might be right about that. I used to sit in my cell in total shock hearing about some of the shit my brother was out here doing. Jah was the last of a dying breed."

"Indeed he was," Yoshi agreed. She suddenly became silent like her mind was drifting.

"You think about him a lot?" Boo picked up on her vibe.

Yoshi smirked. "All the time. There's not a day that goes by when I don't think of Jah and what could've been. He was my heart."

"I miss my little brother too. Not to say that I don't miss Paul, I had love for both of them, but my relationship with Jah was different. I raised that little dude from a pup. Even after I got locked up, I stayed in his ear trying to keep him straight. I guess I didn't do a very good job of that," he said sadly. Boo had always blamed himself for Jah getting killed. Had he been there for his family instead of in prison, then maybe, things would've played out different.

"You can't beat yourself up about what happened to Jah, Boo. He always had a touch of the wild in him and I don't think there was anything me, you, or anybody else could've done about it. Sometimes I felt like Jah loved the streets more than he loved me," Yoshi joked in an attempt to lighten the mood.

"Nah, you had his heart, Yoshibelle. There was no denying that. You know, when Jah first started seeing you I tried to get him to cut you loose," Boo confessed.

"Oh really?" Yoshi was surprised. She's always thought Boo liked her.

"Just hear me out before you get in your feelings," Boo urged her. "You have to understand that Jah was my baby brother and it was my job to protect him from harm. He was young and impressionable and you were...seasoned, let's just say."

"But you didn't even know me back then, Boo," Yoshi pointed out.

Boo chuckled. "You think because I was in prison I didn't still have power and reach? There's not a woman who came in and out of my brothers' lives that I didn't get a full run down on. I tried to warn Paul's simple ass about Rhonda, but he was always a fool for his heart. No disrespect to the dead of course."

"So you thought I was on it like that?" Yoshi asked in an offended tone.

"I didn't know anything outside of what I was hearing and I'm sure I don't have to tell you what the streets were saying. Jah was a gangster, but he was still a kid and inexperienced at love. Getting his heart broken so young could've fucked him up more than he already was, and I couldn't have that."

"So, what changed your mind about me?" Yoshi asked.

"Meeting you and judging your heart for myself," Boo admitted. "When Jah brought you up on that first visit I was prepared to let you know I wasn't feeling the relationship, but once I sat down and talked to you, I realized I was wrong. The way you looked at my brother and the bells in your voice whenever you said his name was all the proof that I needed to know you were the genuine article. You and my brother had discovered something that most of us never will, true love. I had no right to try and block that blessing."

"I don't know whether to be flattered or offended," Yoshi said.

Boo shrugged. "Take it however you need to, I'm just keeping it tall with you, ma. Yoshibelle, the one good thing about doing all that time in prison was that it taught me to appreciate the things I once neglected, like love and family. While I sat in prison worrying about shit that really wasn't important, I lost everyone I loved. I couldn't even hug my family when they laid my little brother to rest because I was shackled at the waist. In short, what my bid taught me was; when God puts blessings in our lives like love and family we should cherish them because some people will never know the joys of either one, or worse, won't realize what they had until it's too late."

A butterscotch colored young man wearing a black sweatshirt and black White Sox cap materialized beside them. Yoshi hadn't even heard him approach. After a respectful, "Excuse me," he leaned in and whispered something in Boo's ear. Yoshi couldn't hear what he was saying, but from the change in Boo's facial expression, it wasn't good.

"Yoshi, I hate to cut out on you, but gotta go handle something that's probably gonna take most of the night," Boo explained. "While you're here make yourself at home. My people already know you're fam, so everything is on the house. Take my number," he slipped her a business card. "If you ever need anything, and I mean anything, you call your big brother. Let's go, Fate," Boo told the young man in the White Sox cap before disappearing in the crowd.

Yoshi sat there for a while, nursing her drink thinking about her conversation with Boo. Though he was speaking about his own life experiences, Yoshi felt like the words were meant for her. She could think of a half dozen people she had shared a laugh with one day only to find out they had died or befell some other tragedy the next day, like her friend Rhonda. When she was killed, it proved the point that nobody was promised tomorrow. Life was too short to be petty, which was what she was doing by holding a grudge against Reese for making a mistake. They had been through far too much to go out like that, and when next she saw her, she intended to put it to bed for good.

Yoshi hadn't even realized she was crying until she felt a tear splash the back of her hand. She took a napkin from the holder on the bar and dabbed her eyes, careful not to smear her make-up.

"Fuck him," someone said from just behind Yoshi. She turned around and saw a brown-skinned dude, wearing excessive jewelry standing behind her.

"Excuse you?" Yoshi didn't understand what he meant.

"I said fuck him," he repeated, inviting himself to the stool beside Yoshi. "Any nigga who would break the heart of someone as gorgeous as you is a fool. So again, fuck him."

"And what makes you think I had my heart broken?" Yoshi asked.

"Your mascara," he took his finger and gently wiped a streak of black from the corner of Yoshi's eye.

Yoshi laughed. "You're pretty observant aren't you?"

"Not to sound like a stalker, but I've been watching you since you walked in. I was going to come over and offer to buy you a drink, but I saw you with your dude so I fell back."

"Well, Boo isn't my dude, he's my brother. And I wasn't crying over a broken heart," Yoshi told him in a matter-of-fact tone.

He raised his hands in surrender. "I didn't mean no disrespect. I guess that's what I get for assuming. Well since dude ain't your boyfriend, how about that drink?"

Yoshi raised her bottle of Ciroc. "As you can see, I've already got that covered. Besides, I don't accept gifts from strangers."

"Damn, where are my manners? They call me Trap," he extended his hand.

Yoshi stared at his hand as if she was contemplating whether to shake it. "Yoshi," she relented.

"See, now we're not strangers anymore," Trap smiled. "As you already pointed out, you got the drink part covered so I guess all I can offer you is a little company."

"Company, huh?" Yoshi raised her eyebrow.

"Sweetheart, don't take this the wrong way but if I wanted to fuck you then I'd have come out and said it. I ain't so beat for no pussy to where I play games to get it. My bread is too long and my patience is too short. I just saw an attractive woman who looked like she could use somebody to talk at the moment. If I overstepped, let me know and I'm out of your hair."

The young man who called himself Trap was a piece of work. He was cocky, and borderline arrogant, but there was a charisma about him that intrigued her. Maybe it was because she had been dealing with the men on the west coast for the last few years, or maybe it was because he was right and she could use someone to talk to…but she wasn't ready for him to leave just yet.

"Fuck it," Yoshi turned the bottle of Ciroc up then slid it across the bar to Trap. "Stick around for a while."

CHAPTER 15

Billy got up early the next day to get a jump on the things she needed to do. She was surprised to see that Marcus was already up and out. Because he worked nights, Marcus usually didn't stir until at least 1 p.m. unless he had something going on, which she suspected he did. It was clear to her that something was going on with her man, but he didn't seem to want to talk about it and she didn't press him. Billy had learned long ago that trying to force Marcus to talk about his problems only made him more reluctant to open up. She would eventually get to the bottom of what was going on with Marcus, but she had her own issues to deal with first.

The first order of business was checking with the wedding venue to make sure that everything was as it should be. They had rented a mansion for their ceremony and were to exchange vows in the garden, standing in the shade of a copper tree. The innkeeper who maintained the property plugged Billy in with a company that would provide her with the tables and chairs they would need without charging an arm and a leg. Billy had pretty much everything covered, except the food.

The first catering company Billy had hired was a bit pricey, but they came highly recommended. To their credit, their food was up to standard, but their certifications weren't. Just days before the wedding, the health inspectors closed them down and left Billy scrambling to find someone to feed the hundred or so guests she was expecting. Every one she reached out to was either charging way too much because it was such short notice or the food was less than tasty. Thankfully, Kat had a friend of a friend who owned a restaurant that was willing to take on the job without killing their budget. They had an appointment for that morning to roll through and do a tasting at the restaurant, before Billy made her decision.

Billy invited all the women in her wedding party to attend the tasting with her. It would be an opportunity to kill two birds with one stone. She'd be able to see if the food was up to par while trying to bridge the gap between her two friends. The rift between Yoshi and Reese had been bothering her, and not just because she needed them in her wedding party, but also because she hated when her friends were at odds. She knew neither of the girls would willingly sit down to hash it out, so she neglected to tell both of them about the other's invitation on the outing.

Reese was an easy sell to come out and meet with Billy that morning, but she couldn't seem to get ahold of Yoshi. She had been calling and texting her all morning but with no reply. Billy was concerned, but not particularly worried. Yoshi had been navigating the streets of New York longer than any of them and knew how to take care of herself. She figured her lack of response was due to her still being in her feelings, so she left the time and location on Yoshi's voicemail and just hoped she showed up.

*

Billy picked Reese up on her way to the restaurant. She had offered to drive, but there was no way in hell Billy was going to ride in that hot-box again. The whole ride Billy kept checking her phone to see if Yoshi had called back, or at the very least responded one of the half dozen texts she sent her, but still nothing.

The restaurant was located in East Flatbush, which was a melting pot for different Caribbean ethnic groups. The location was small, somewhat rundown, and had an outside seating area where guests could enjoy their meals on nice days. It wasn't much to look at in the way of décor, but you could smell the food as soon as you hit the block. Several troublesome looking men lingered in front of the spot, staring at Billy and Reese like they were steak dinners. One of them said something vulgar in a thick accent as they passed. Reese, being Reese, was about to make a slick reply, but Billy pulled her along. The restaurant was Billy's last hope and she didn't need Reese causing a scene and ruining things because she couldn't control her mouth.

When they got inside, they found Kat already waiting for them. She was sitting at a quiet table in the corner, drinking wine, and whispering into the ear of an older man with dreadlocks. From the way, he was smiling, only God knew what she was saying. When she spotted Billy and Reese walk in, she waved them over to the table. As they approached the table, the man stood up and smoothed his clothes over in an attempt to look presentable, but he couldn't hide the slight bulge in his pants.

"Hello ladies, glad you're relatively on time for once," Kat stood and leaned in to kiss them both on their cheeks. She was already tall, but the heels she wore made her seem to tower over the two girls.

"I'm sure you found a way to keep yourself occupied while you waited," Reese snickered, which got her a sharp elbow from Billy.

Ignoring Reese, Kat made the introductions. "Langston, this is the bride-to-be, Billy. Billy, this is Langston the owner of The Yard."

"Nice to meet you, Langston, and thank you for accommodating us on such short notice." Billy shook his hand.

"Anything for a friend and a friend of Kat's is a friend of mine," Langston said in a proper accent. "Kat has filled me in already on the trouble you had with the last caterer and let me assure you that you won't have those problems with us. To spite our modest opinion we pride ourselves on our quality of both service and food."

"I hope so, because I'm kind of short on time," Billy said honestly.

"We'll take good care of you, sister," Langston assured her. "Now if you'll follow me outside we have a private table set up for you and several dishes for you to sample which are being prepared as we speak."

"Good because I'm starving. I just hope everything isn't jerked or has curry in it, because I got bad guts," Reese said, to Billy and Kat's embarrassment.

Langston laughed. "No worries, m'love. We specialize in traditional Caribbean food, but I think you'll find our Special Events menu quite diverse and to your liking."

*

137

Langston wasn't lying when he said The Yard's Special Events menu was diverse. In fact, it was so diverse that some of the foods listed Billy had never even heard of. To showcase his wares, Langston had his staff prepare samplers for three courses consisting of five dishes per course. For the appetizers, they sampled everything from salads to soups to cold bars and finger foods. Reese's greedy ass gorged herself on the lobster puffs, which were made from scratch with fresh lobsters they would import daily. The first four samplers from the dinner course consisted of the basics, chicken, fish, or pork. The fifth sampler of the dinner course was chef's choice, and probably the most impressive in Billy's opinion. It was herb-roasted quail, served over a bed of wild rice with green beans.

It was Billy's first time having quail and she loved it so much she ordered a whole one to take home with her. Their assortment of sweets was even more out of this world, bursting with different flavors, shapes, and textures. Before they'd even made it halfway through the desert course, Billy had already decided that she wanted Langston's people to cater her wedding.

"Oh my God, I can't believe how great the food is here!" Billy said while taking another bite of the slice of chocolate ganache cake. It was the flavor she had selected for their wedding cake.

"As I said it would be," Kat boasted. "The Yard may be located in the hood, but they're a first class eatery. You know nothing but the best crosses these lips."

"Yeah right," Reese snickered.

Kat rolled her eyes. "Reese, I know you ain't trying it with all the mileage on your tonsils. I might suck a little dick here and there, but it's always on my terms and never without its rewards. Unlike yourself, it takes slightly more than a couple of drinks and a night at Joe's Crab Shack to get these jaws working. While you're over there low-key throwing shade at me you need to see about that dried frosting around your mouth. I'd hate for people to think you were up to your old tricks."

"Fuck you, Kat," Reese covered her mouth with her hand in embarrassment and put down the plate of coconut cake she was eating. "Where's your bathroom?" she asked Langston.

"C'mon, love. I'll show you where the washroom is. I've got to get the paperwork for your friend anyway." Langston took Reese by the hand and led her inside.

"Kat, you know you didn't have to go in on her like that," Billy said once Reese was out her earshot.

"Fuck that, Billy. Your little friend has a slick mouth, which is why I jump in her ass every time she opens it. With bitches like that, the moment you let them get away with talking crazy to you they'll think they can do it whenever they feel like it. I don't play no games with these hos."

"You sure don't," Billy said, taking out her phone. She tried Yoshi again, but got her voicemail. "Damn."

"What's the matter, mama?" Kat asked.

"I've been trying to get Yoshi on the line all day and can't seem to reach her. I'm starting to get worried," Billy said.

"I wouldn't be. Yoshi is tougher than most chicks; history has already showed us that. You might actually be lucky she's not answering the phone. You know there's still bad blood between her and Reese. I'm surprised you even got Reese to come knowing that you invited Yoshi too."

"Reese doesn't know," Billy admitted. "I figured if I could just get both of them together we could dead all this foolishness."

Kat shook her head. "You were playing with fire trying to ambush them like this, Willamina. Both of those chicks are bullheaded, and you know Yoshi's got a nasty temper."

"I know, Kat, but I can't see any other way to handle this. My wedding day is almost on us and my bridal party is divided over some dumb shit. Before the day is over I'm going to get these two petty bitches together and put an end to this once and for all."

"Well, you may not have to wait as long as you thought," Kat motioned towards something just beyond Billy.

When Billy turned around, she had to blink twice to make sure her eyes weren't playing tricks on her. A powder blue Porsche truck had just pulled to the curb next to the Yard. A beefy woman with dreadlocks got out from the driver's side and walked around to open the rear passenger door. Billy couldn't help but to feel like she had seen her somewhere before, but wasn't sure where. She couldn't see who was inside the ride, but she could see who was getting out. Yoshi exchanged some last words with whomever she had been riding with, before slipping a pair of dark sunglasses over her eyes and making her way towards The Yard. From the way she was dressed, and walking, Billy suspected she had been out all night.

What exactly she had been doing while she was out, remained the lingering question.

"Well look what the cat dragged in. Last time I saw you, I think you were trying to get yourself arrested," Kat said referring to when she and Yoshi were both dancers at Brick City. One of the patrons had gotten out of line and Yoshi taught him a painful lesson in respect.

"That was a younger, wilder me, but I'm all grown up now. Can't you tell," Yoshi did a little twirl and stumbled, but quickly recovered.

"Bitch, are you drunk before 11 am?" Billy asked in disbelief.

"No, Willamina. I'm liberated," Yoshi threw her hands up before plopping down in the seat across the table, nearly knocking over a glass of water.

"Liberated my ass, you're loaded!" Billy leaned in and sniffed her. "Jesus, what did you do, bathe in vodka?"

"That ain't nothing but a little Ciroc," Yoshi waved her off. She looked around at the picked over sample plates. "Damn, you couldn't wait for a bitch to get here before you started the tasting?"

"Yoshi, I've been calling your ass all morning and haven't heard from you. I didn't even think you would show up," Billy told her.

"My phone was dead, but I did get your voicemail. I'm mad as hell that I missed it because the munchies are on my back!" Yoshi said, looking around to see if there was something, she could salvage. Her eyes landed on the chocolate ganache Billy was eating and she liberated it from her.

"That nigga in the fancy car you were with must not have been about too much of shit if he dropped you off without making sure you had breakfast," Billy capped.

Yoshi paused from devouring Billy's cake. "Oh, he fed me alright. Make no mistake about that. I'm just starving now because we smoked like two blunts of Afghan on the ride over here."

"And who exactly was that again?" Billy asked.

Before she could answer, Reese had returned from the bathroom. When she saw Yoshi sitting there, her eyes tightened. She looked at Billy for an explanation, but found only an apologetic look on her face. Obviously, the fix was in. Her gaze went back to Yoshi, who was staring back at her from behind dark sunglasses. The tension was apparent between them, so much so that you could feel it in the air. Neither of the girls wanted to break the ice, but one of them would have to. In a strange twist, it was Reese who decided to be the bigger person.

"Sup," Reese broke the silence.

"Chilling, how are you?" Yoshi replied.

Reese shrugged. "Been better...been worse. I could complain, but who gives enough of a shit to listen?"

"I'd listen," Yoshi said. It wasn't quite the cool ass response she'd prepared in her mind, but it's what came out when she opened her mouth.

Reese was surprised to hear the admission, but didn't show it. Instead, she folded her arms and twisted her lips. "That's funny, because you haven't been trying to hear anything I've had to say since you got back to New York."

"Well I've been drinking and thinking," Yoshi told her.

"Obviously," Reese shot back.

Yoshi's eyes narrowed as if she was having trouble focusing. "Look bitch, I'm trying to have a moment with you, so stop cutting me off," she pointed at Reese drunkenly. "When I found out you'd been keeping your involvement with Gary a secret, I was really hurt. Part of that hurt came from the fact that you kept it from me, and I thought we were bigger than that, but the salt on the wound came from the fact that it was you he chose you over me."

Reese was confused. "What are you talking about? You two were broken up when this happened."

"We were, but it's what happened after that made this situation even uglier, and me look like a chicken head. After I found out, I was beyond pissed and needed to get some things off my chest, so I went to Gary's house to confront him. I was so mad that I wanted nothing more than to spit in his face when he opened the door, but as soon as I laid eyes on him I couldn't find the hateful words, I had been practicing the whole way over there. Even after how he had done me, I still had feelings for him. I didn't plan on fucking Gary, but before I knew it, I was ass naked and we were going at it. When it was over I told Gary he had to make a choice, me or you, and Gary chose you."

This came as quite a shock to everyone, especially Reese. After she cut Gary off he tried to reach out to her a few times, but Reese wasn't trying to hear it. She had washed her hands of Gary.

"Wait, so you've been holding a grudge all this time because a nigga who dogged you wouldn't allow you to put yourself in a

143

position for him to shit on you again?" Kat shook her head. "You young bitches got the game twisted."

"It wasn't because he didn't choose me; it was because he chose her over me. You have to understand something, since we were young, I was always the one who got the guy with the looks, the money, or the car, and Reese got the tag along. No disrespect to you Reese, but you know I'm not lying. When the shoe ended up on the other foot, I couldn't take it."

"I sure hope this isn't your way of trying to make me feel better about all this," Reese said.

"No, it's my way of saying I accept my part of the blame in all this. I know you were only trying to protect my feelings, Reese, and I lashed out to cover my own shame. I went out like a straight bird over some dick and it almost ruined a friendship that meant more to me than anything. I miss you, Reese, and I miss our friendship," Yoshi said emotionally.

"I miss you too, Yoshibelle," Reese threw her arms around her. Yoshi had always been the toughest and most emotionally removed of their group, so to see her bare her soul like that was a rare thing.

"See, y'all gonna make me fuck up my make-up with this Lifetime Channel shit," Kat dabbed the corners of her moist eyes with a napkin.

"Group hug," Billy pulled them all together. Seeing her friends back together was one of the best wedding gifts she could have asked for.

"Billy, I owe you an apology too," Yoshi said.

"For what?" Billy asked.

"For being such a bitch about this whole Maid of Honor thing. This is your day and instead of being petty, I should be thankful that you thought enough of me to be included," Yoshi said sincerely.

"About that —" Billy began, but was cut off when Yoshi let out a drunken burp loud enough to draw the attention of anyone close enough to hear it.

"What was that, some kind of hood rat mating call?" Kat frowned, fanning as the stench of old liquor and whatever Yoshi had been eating wafted across the table.

"Are you okay?" Billy asked, noticing the color had drained from Yoshi's face.

"No, I think I'm gonna be sick," Yoshi leapt up from the table, headed for the bathroom, but her drunken legs wouldn't move fast enough. She made it as far at as the restaurant entrance before vomiting on the restaurant floor, and Langston's shoes. He had been on his way out with Billy's contract.

Langston looked from his ruined shoes to the drunken girl in front of him, to Billy who was clearly embarrassed by what her friend had just done.

"Sorry," was all Billy could think to say.

"I'll be sure to include the cost of my shoes in your final bill."

CHAPTER 16

Marcus's day wasn't going much better than Billy's. He'd started it earlier than he would've liked, but he didn't have a choice. The driver who was delivering the liquor had called him to let him know he was outside the club, but there was no one there to let him in, which came as a surprise. Tammy was supposed to be there to receive the delivery, but apparently, she hadn't shown up for work. He tried calling her phone, but she didn't answer so he had to take care of it.

He was pissed, but more concerned than anything. No matter what was going on, he was normally able to depend on Tammy to handle business when it came to the club. For her to pull a no-show without even so much as a call was unusual. She was probably still in her feelings from the argument they'd had the evening before. When he had a free minute, he would send somebody by her house to check on her. Once he was sure she was okay, he was going to fire her. No matter how great a manager she was, once she started letting her emotions fuck with his money, she made herself expendable.

After taking care of the delivery, Marcus called one of the night managers to come in and cover for Tammy while he ran some errands. Billy had to go into Brooklyn to see about securing another caterer for the wedding so he promised her that he would follow up with the people providing the furniture, which proved to be a headache. He had an eleven o'clock appointment, but the owner of the rental place didn't show up until almost noon. To make matters worse, they had messed up with the colors. Billy requested white

146

furniture, but they brought in green. Instead of owning their mistake, they tried to make it seem like Billy and Marcus had been the ones who made the mistake. It was resolved when Marcus threatened to have some of the homies roll through and break the owner's legs. He hated to jump out of character like that, but violence was the only language some people understood. The owner assured Marcus that they would have the mistake corrected and deliver the proper furniture the day before the wedding. If he didn't make good on his promise, Marcus was going to make good on his.

From there, he had to shoot up to Midtown Manhattan to meet his groomsmen to pick up their tuxedos, and oversee a last minute fitting. One of Marcus's groomsmen, Dre, had gotten locked up on a child support warrant, which left Marcus scrambling to find an alternate at the last minute. He had never been a man of many friends so it wasn't easy task, but Wayne had a solution. This is how cousin Mud became a part of the wedding party.

Mud was Wayne's cousin who ran around with them back in the days. He was slightly older than they were in age, but years behind mentally. Mud had been in and out of prison for as long as any of them could remember so he found himself forever trapped in the era in which he was a scrapping young man whose name still meant something in the streets. Mud was a cool cat until he got a drink in him. He would yap on for hours about how things were back in his day, or his exploits in prison, with each re-telling of the story more outlandish than the last. When Mud was drunk, he could be unpredictable and sometimes violet so Marcus was on the fence about using him as an alternate in his wedding, but Wayne assured him he'd keep his cousin in check. Marcus hoped so because the last thing he needed was Mud causing a scene on the biggest day of his life.

As soon as Marcus arrived and saw the look on Shooter's face he knew there was a problem and he wouldn't have to wait too long to find out what it was. He could hear Mud's boisterous voice coming from inside one of the fitting rooms, right before the tailor came scrambling out. Her face was flushed red and she was yammering something in Chinese that didn't sound pleasant at all.

"Is everything okay, Mrs. Lee?" Marcus asked.

"No, everything not okay! I no measure if dirty man keeping trying poke my eye with nasty worm!" Mrs. Lee snapped.

"This ain't no worm, baby. It's a full grown snake," Mud came stumbling out of the fitting room wearing his tuxedo jacket and boxers, showing off his erection.

"Have some shame and cover yourself," Marcus turned his head away.

"My fault, cousin. Mrs. Lee's magic hands just made me a little excited. I think we made a love connection in there. She was feeling this pimpin'," Mud laughed. "Ain't that right, Lee?"

Mrs. Lee opened and closed her scissors threateningly. "You connect with these if you wave nasty worm in face again."

"I love it when they play hard to get," Mud blew a kiss at her.

From the glassy look in his eyes and the stench of vodka coming off him, Marcus knew he had been drinking. "Damn, Mud, it ain't even two o'clock, and you're drunk?"

"Wasn't nothing but a sip," Mud shrugged it off.

NO SHADE: A Hood Rat Novel

"Smells more like a gulp," Shooter capped.

"Mud we're already behind schedule and this is the last possible day to get you fitted and make sure your tuxedo is ready by the wedding. So I'm going to need you to put that alcoholic shit on pause for a minute so we can get this done," Marcus told him.

"I ain't no alcoholic. Alcoholics go to meetings," Mud said defensively.

"Whatever makes you feel better, just get your ass back in the fitting room so Mrs. Lee can finish."

"You got it, Marcus. I'll behave," Mud held his three fingers up making the Boy Scout sign. "Come on, Lee. Let's get back to it, baby," he staggered back into the fitting room.

"Thanks for putting up with him, Mrs. Lee. I'll make sure I leave a nice tip for you," Marcus promised.

"Okay, I do it because you good guy Marcus, but anymore funny business from old drunk and your groomsmen show up naked because I no do fitting," she told him before following Mud into the fitting room and pulling the curtain behind him.

"What the fuck Wayne? You said you had this under control!" Marcus snapped.

"Man, he was already saucy when I picked him up," Wayne explained.

"Word to everything I love, if Mud pulls this wino shit at my wedding he's gonna come up missing and you're gonna help me dig the fucking hole," Marcus bumped past Wayne and sat in the chair next to Shooter.

"Well damn, who pissed in your Cheerios this morning?" Shooter asked, picking up on Marcus's foul mood.

"I've had a rough ass morning. Tammy was supposed to receive the liquor delivery but she never showed up, so I had to get up at the crack of dawn and take care of it," Marcus fumed.

Shooter shook his head. "That girl has really been getting beside herself lately. Any idea what might've brought on this change of attitude?" his voice dripped sarcasm.

"Don't start with me, Shooter. I'm not in the mood. I'm going off damn near no sleep and I still have to make sure everything is ready for tonight. You guys gonna swing through?"

"Nah, I'm gonna take a pass on this one. I don't dig the rap scene, and I dig the rappers you're having there tonight even less. Standing too close to that particular pack of dawgs you're liable to come away with rabies," Shooter said.

"Shit, speak for yourself because I'm all up in that thang! You know how many bitches are gonna come out to see Big Dawg perform? It's gonna be wall to wall pussy!" Wayne said excitedly.

"You're welcome to it, but if you happen to find yourself drinking with Don B., you better double check your glass to make sure there ain't nothing extra floating around in it," Shooter joked. "On another note, you boys figure out when you're doing the bachelor party?"

"Marcus claims he don't want one," Wayne said disappointedly.

Shooter gave Marcus a funny look. "What you mean you don't want a bachelor party? That's every man's rite of passage before crossing over into the great beyond, which is matrimony. Shit, that's the best part of getting married."

"I'm around big butt bitches shaking their asses for dollars every night, man. I ain't moved by that shit," Marcus told him. "If y'all wanna hook up for some drinks or something, I'm with that, but I don't wanna do nothing too over the top."

Wayne shook his head. "Sometimes I wonder if you're really my best friend or just a dude wearing his skin."

A loud shriek coming from the fitting room drew everyone's attention. Marcus bolted over, followed by Wayne and Shooter. Marcus threw back the curtain to find Mrs. Lee covering her mouth in embarrassment. Behind him, he heard a soft chuckle from Shooter. Mud was standing in front of the mirror, looking down at himself in disbelief. A small puddle pooled under his right foot, soaking his sock. Mrs. Lee had finally managed to taper the black slacks to fit Mud, right before he pissed in them.

Mud looked around and without an ounce of shame said, "I told her I had to use the bathroom and she didn't move fast enough to let me out. You know I got a weak bladder."

Marcus collapsed back in the chair and placed his head in his hands. "We should've just eloped."

CHAPTER 17

"Bills and dick, that's all some niggas are good for." Honey was schooling her sister Trish as they perused the racks of yet another store in the mall. They had been in and out of at least seven different establishments in the last couple of hours, with no sign that they would be leaving anytime soon.

It was the day of her birthday party and she still hadn't found the perfect outfit yet. Besides that, mall outings were the only time she and her sister could bond without anyone hovering over them. Since they were both married with children now, they didn't get to spend as much time together as they once had, largely in part of their choice in husbands taking their lives down two different paths. Trish had married a banker and Honey had taken her vows with a King Pin.

"I know, Melissa," Tish called her by her government name, "but you don't expect that kind of hurt to come from someone you love."

"And why not?" Honey asked, while fingering the fabric of a dress she was trying to decide if she wanted. "It's the ones who you love that'll hurt you the most, even when they don't mean to, especially men. We can fuck them, feed them, and spend countless hours in the gym to keep them enticed, but they'll still find a way to fuck up, no matter how good of a dude they are."

"But not Milton, he isn't like that," Trish said.

"Milton is a man, Trish. They're all like that. No matter how much you give a nigga they're always gonna want more. I call it a genetic defect of the species."

While they were shopping, Trish had revealed to her younger sister her suspicions about her husband being unfaithful. A friend of hers from work had come to her saying she'd seen her husband in the company of another woman. When she'd confronted him about it, he'd told her it was a client. She wanted to believe him, but wasn't sure she could.

"So you think Milton is dirty?" Trish asked.

"No, I'm not saying he is, but I'm not saying he isn't either. Before you take this broad's word as the gospel you have to examine the motives behind her telling you."

"The girl who told me is married, so I don't think she has designs on Milton," Tish said.

"Just because she doesn't want him doesn't mean she wants you to have him either. Milton is fine as hell and he takes good care of you. Maybe her husband is a fucking creep who treats her like shit and she wants you to wallow in misery along with her. Being married is one thing, being happily married is something else altogether, and sometimes you can shine too bright for a bitch's liking."

"You're right, but I'm still gonna keep my eye on him," Tish said.

"You'd be a fucking fool if you didn't. Let me tell you something, big sis. No matter how good the men in our lives are, they're still men and sometimes their nature makes them weak."

153

"I'll bet you don't have those kinds of problems out of Shai," Trish said.

"And who says I don't? I know we seem like the perfect couple on the outside, but don't think our relationship isn't without its problems. To be honest, I've probably got it worse than most."

"I find that hard to believe, Melissa. Shai adores you."

"Indeed he does," Honey agreed, "but that doesn't mean he's incapable of cutting up. My husband is the boss of a major organization and worth millions to boot. These shameless hos throw themselves at him all the time, and I can't babysit him twenty-four-seven to make sure he doesn't get out of pocket. I have to trust him to do the right thing."

"Has he always done the right thing?" Trish asked.

Honey thought on her answer for a few seconds. "I wish I could say he has. Me and Shai have had some situations in the past while he was still sowing his oats. Even after giving him two beautiful kids there was still little shit here and there. There were times when I didn't think we would make it from one year to the next, but by the grace of God and plenty of vodka, we're still holding on," she laughed.

"Milton cheating on me, I could understand because I'm such a plane Jane," she tugged at the formless brown dress she was wearing, "but Shai would have to be a fool to step out on you. I mean look at you, little sis," Trish pointed at Honey's reflection in one of the store's mirrors.

Honey was probably the only person in the entire mall walking around in stiletto heels, tight leather pants, and her face fully beat like she was about to go to the club in the middle of the afternoon. Some people would've looked at it as Honey was doing the most, but that's just how she was. Long before her good fortune, she was a girl who had always craved the finer things in life.

Honey adjusted her blonde weave in the mirror, and wiped a smudge of lipstick from her bottom lip. "Yeah, I am a bad bitch ain't I? Sadly, it's the beautiful people who are always getting tried. Ain't that right, young'n?" she addressed the young man who had been shadowing them through the mall.

"Huh?" Turk asked. He had been more focused on his phone than the women's conversation.

"Haven't you been paying attention to anything I've said?" Honey asked.

"It's my job to guard you, not ear hustle Mrs. Clark," Turk said respectfully.

"That's fine. You can play the strong silent type if you like. You're better eye-candy than a conversationalist anyhow. This little dude is fine, ain't he Trish?"

"Stop picking on that boy, Melissa," Trish scolded her.

"I'm not picking on him; I'm just stating the obvious. He's a fine piece of man meat. With those pretty ass eyes and that good hair, I'll bet these little bitches go crazy over you," Honey reached out to touch Turk's hair, but he took a step back. "No need to be scared, Turk. I don't bite...much."

"It's not you that I'm afraid of, Mrs. Clark," Turk said. He had been around the Clark family long enough to know that Honey liked to play twisted little games. He had also been around long enough to know that it never went well for those dumb enough to entertain her.

"You're pretty and smart...those are good qualities, especially in somebody so young. You're going to make a fine lieutenant one of these days, maybe even a Capo."

"I should only hope so, Mrs. Clark. I've been working very hard to earn your husband's approval," Turk said.

"Apparently not hard enough, or you would be in the field with the others instead of playing my shadow. What exactly did you do to get on Shai's shit list anyhow?"

"I'd rather not say, Mrs. Clark," Turk replied.

The truth of the matter was Turk had landed guard duty as punishment for what he had done to Carl. When Shai found out what he'd done, he went ballistic. Shai was against leaving messes in the street, especially ones that could lead back to him, which was what cutting off Carl's hand in front of two dozen witnesses had done. The only thing that had saved Turk from a far more severe punishment was that he was acting on Swann's orders. Still, an example had to be made, so he had pulled Turk off the streets and assigned him menial tasks, like guard duty, until further notice.

"Well, if you're not going to talk to me you can at least make yourself useful," Honey shoved her shopping bags into his arms. "Take these to the truck and bring it around to the front of the mall. I'll be ready to go when I pay for my stuff in here."

"Right away, Mrs. Clark," Turk took the bags and left the store. He breathed a sigh of relief once he was away from Honey. She was never cruel to Turk like she was to some of the other soldiers who drew her detail, but she made him uncomfortable. She was always doing things like touching him suggestively, or stopping in his path so he would walk into her. Turk didn't think she'd ever let him hit it, nor was he foolish enough to ever try his hand with the boss's wife, but just the idea was enough to put him in a bad situation. Nickels had once told him a story about how Shai had a man beaten to within an inch of his life for making a slick remark to Honey in the streets and Turk wanted no parts of that action.

Turk had enough problems with the royal family as it was and didn't need any more black marks added to his service record. Since he had officially become a soldier in the Clark family he had been going out of his way to impress the higher-ups, but it always seemed to backfire on him. He was either doing too much or not doing enough. His best efforts never seemed to be good enough to please the young king. Turk had himself to blame really. He was constantly trying to step out of the shadows of a man he hardly knew, and live up to a name that wasn't his.

Turk came up on the rough side of town, raised by an aunt when his mother became too far gone on drugs and booze to contribute anything positive to his life. Growing up a clearly bi-racial child in an all-Black neighborhood had its ups and downs. The girls loved his sandy skin and pretty hair, but those qualities made him an outcast amongst the boys. Having inherited his mother and father's genes equally made it difficult to tell exactly what his ethnicity was, but he looked closer to Arab than Turkish or African American. Some of the kids had taken to taunting him with remarks about Sand Niggers and going back to Iraq. His foreign appearance made him a target

157

and he was always fighting because of it. It was his willingness to knuckle up that stopped the taunts, and he even managed to make a few friends, but he was never really accepted.

Turk's aunt felt as if he was starting to spend too much time in the streets so she arranged a summer job for him the year before he turned fourteen. It was grunt work at a butcher shop ran by an old Turkish man named Ahmad Kaplan. Kaplan was horrible person who drank way too much and had a gambling problem, but his skill for cutting meat was second to none. Ahmad saw what he did as more than butchering animals; it was art. Every swing of the blade was a stroke on the canvas. This was the approach taught his young apprentice Turk.

Working for the butcher wasn't all bad. Turk always had extra meat to take home to his family, and he developed relationships with all the local gangsters who frequented Kaplan's shop. Whenever some of the really important men from the neighborhood would come in, Kaplan would let Turk work the register while he went into the back to take care of their special orders. Turk loved when the gangsters came because they always gave him healthy tips, and treated him like he was family. It always puzzled Turk how such a seemingly harmless old man knew so many killers and thieves, and why they treated a half-breed orphan like he was one of their own, but one late night, he would find out.

Kaplan had just finished taking care of a special order and had to run out for a while. In an attempt to score points with the old man, Turk decided to clean his work area. It was while emptying one of the slop bins that he discovered a human finger. He never mentioned his discovery to Kaplan, but there was something about the way the old man looked at him after that day that made Turk think he secretly knew. One thing was for certain, Turk would never take meat from the shop home to his family again.

That fall, Turk's aunt unexpectedly decided to send him away to boarding school in upstate New York. When he asked her where she got the money for the tuition to the prestigious school, she fed him a story about him having been awarded some kind of scholarship for underprivileged kids that was provided by the state. It was obviously a lie, but she was adamant about getting him out of the city so he went. It was at the school where he would meet his crime partner Baby Doc, and later on Nickels Clark. The three friends would go on to create all sorts of criminal mischief, which is how he ended up indentured to Shai Clark, who had to clean up one of their messes. It would be two years before he'd seen Ahmad Kaplan again, and it would be under tragic circumstances.

Turk found himself back in the city to attend the funeral of his estranged mother. They'd found her dead from an apparent overdose. Turk tried to mourn his mother, but he didn't know her well enough to be saddened by her passing. He was surprised to see how many people had turned out for the funeral, including Ahmad Kaplan. He seemed more broken up than most over the death of Turk's mother, which Turk found odd considering to his knowledge they'd never met. It wasn't until one of Turk's uncles had gotten drunk at the repast and spilled the beans about Turk's paternity that everything started to make sense.

The next evening, Turk went to the butcher shop to confront the old man about his uncle's drunken accusations. He'd expected Ahmad to deny them, but he didn't. He was actually very candid with Turk about things that until then had been kept from Turk, but were common knowledge in underworld circles, including his paternity. That night, over a bottle of vodka and two loaves of Pide, which was Turkish bread, Ahmad Kaplan bared his soul.

He told Turk of his immigration from Istanbul to the states, and of his heinous deeds, which earned him the title of The Butcher, and how alcohol and a gambling habit had destroyed his once notorious reputation. He also told him how he'd fallen in love with the black prostitute who would give birth to his one and only son. Also about his marriage to the daughter of a powerful mafia chieftain who had forced him to turn his back on the boy, under the threat of having the child killed to hide the shame his infidelities had brought to their family name. After their talk, Turk wasn't sure if he felt better or worse, but at least some of the blanks that had been his life and history were now filled in. That was the last time Turk would ever set foot in the Butcher's shop and the last time he had laid eyes on his biological father and namesake.

*

Turk had just finished loading the bags into the back of the truck when his cell phone rang. "What it do, Holiday?" he answered. Turk listened for a while and frowned. "Nope, I ain't gonna do it. Last time I let you set me up on a blind date the broad had a mustache.

160

Get Nickels or Baby Doc to tag along on your little outing." After a few more minutes of Holiday's pleading and the promise of speaking to Shai about getting him off guard duty, Turk finally relented. "A'ight, but if this bitch is a booger you're on your own," he told him and ended the call.

Turk hated blind dates, especially when Holiday set them up. For a man in his position you'd have thought he would've been a bit more selective in his choice of women, but Holiday's dick did not discriminate. He loved hood rats like fat kids loved cake, and nine times out of ten, whomever he was setting Turk up with would be just as ratchet as the rest. Still, if helping Holiday out could get him back on the streets and away from Honey, he would grin and bear it. Besides, attending Honey's party might be a quicker way to get back into Shai's good graces. He still didn't trust Holiday to set him up with someone who wasn't busted, but it would only be for a few hours. He would smile, buy a few drinks, and cut out. What was the worst that could happen?

PART III

A CLASH OF KINGS...AND A QUEEN

K'WAN

CHAPTER 18

Honey hadn't added much input when it came to planning her birthday party, except stressing the fact that she wanted it to be off the chain. Turning thirty was a big deal, and she wanted to say goodbye to her twenties in high style. She trusted Shai to make sure it would be nice, but what she wouldn't expect was an extravaganza of that magnitude.

The Clark entourage was three cars deep. The lead car carried Holiday and Angelo, who always ran point when they attended public events. They were the first to enter and the last to exit. The middle car was an armored Hummer, which carried Shai, Honey, Swann, and his lady for the evening, some light skinned T.H.O.T who talked too much and listened too little. Honey wasn't happy about Swann rolling out with a woman other than Giselle, his daughter's mother, but she held her tongue. Swann and Giselle had an on and off again relationship that Honey was never comfortable with and when Swann brought other chicks out she felt like she was being disloyal to Giselle. She had history with Giselle and the others were just space-fillers in Swann's life.

Trailing the first two cars was a black Lincoln Navigator. Riding in it were Swann's goon squad, several armed and dangerous men ready to pop off at the first signs of trouble. They were foot soldiers whose sole purpose was to protect Shai at all costs.

They were able to spot Shooters several blocks before they actually arrived. Two searchlights of pink and gold, Honey's favorite colors, were erected in front of the club, crisscrossing and letting people for miles around know that was the spot to be. A projector was set up on the curb, playing a photo montage of some of Honey's finest moments.

"Damn, you went all out babe," Honey said to Shai as she looked out the heavily tinted window of the Hummer.

"Nothing but the best for my lady," Shai told her while adjusting his tie.

"I still wish we had come out in one of the other cars. These windows are so thick and so dark, nobody can see us," Honey said.

"That's the general idea; you can't shoot at what you can't see. You know there are people in the world who would rather see me dead than happy and ain't no sense in making their jobs easier," Shai told her.

"Don't you worry, Shai. Nothing is gonna happen to your lady on my watch," their driver, Andrew volunteered.

"That's Mr. Clark to you, lil' nigga," Swann corrected him. "And you ain't getting paid to do security, you're getting paid to drive, so do that, and shut the fuck up!" He hadn't meant to be so short with the young man, but Andrew had a knack for getting under Swann's skin. The only reason he'd given Andrew a job is because he was fucking his older sister.

"Let the little nigga live, Swann," Shai told him. Andrew irked him sometimes too, but he knew how it was to be young and want to fit in. "And you," he turned to Honey, "are gonna get more than enough attention with that outfit."

"I paid enough for it," Honey tugged at the front of the dress to make sure her breasts weren't popping out.

K'WAN

"You mean I paid for it," Shai said jokingly. "Now let's go greet your adoring public."

The front of the club was so jam packed that you'd have thought they were having a sold-out concert inside instead of a birthday party. A few would get lucky and make it in, but most would be turned away. It had been Swann's idea to leak the information about the party and performance to the popular site Baller Alert, who specialized in being in the know when something big, was going down. When you wanted to know where the fabulous were partying, you visited their site. In exchange for access to the party, they'd get the word out on all their social media networks and people would come in droves. The plan was to have as many people as possible show up and then hand pick who would be allowed entry. This would ensure that Honey's party was the talk of the town, and judging by the crowd, they'd be talking about the party all week.

The goons were the first ones out of the vehicle. Lead by Holiday, Turk, and Baby Doc they fanned out along the sidewalk and formed a human walkway between the Hummer door and the entrance of the club. Shooters had top-notch security, but Shai didn't trust the wellbeing of his wife to anyone but his own people.

Andrew scurried around curbside and opened the door for the royal couple. Shai slid out looking like every bit the power player that he was dressed in a perfectly tailored black suit and blood-red silk tie. He squinted against the flash of at least a dozen cameras as media and spectators alike tried to get pictures of him. Shai was quite the celebrity around town. Unlike his father and brother, who shunned the spotlight, Shai welcomed it. He was the king wore two crowns, one of the corporate world and one of the underworld. Once he felt like the paparazzi had gotten a good enough look at him, he extended his hand to his queen.

Honey was breathtakingly beautiful in her black Zac Posen silk gown. The dressed stretched past her ankles, giving you only glimpses of her metallic Pierre Hardy sandals as she walked. Her blonde hair was laid to the Gods, freshly curled not even forty minutes before they'd arrived. The main attraction was the diamond-filled tiara, which crowned her head.

As Shai led Honey across the red carpet towards the front of the club, they found themselves the center of attention. Honey couldn't help but stop for a second to take in the crowd of on-lookers. There was a lot of love in that crowd, but there were also some sour faces. Honey couldn't say that she blamed them. They all wanted to walk a mile in her shoes, but she doubted many of them were built to navigate the road she'd taken to get where she was.

She thought about the gutters she had to crawl through, and the degradation she was forced to suffer before life finally showed her some love, and reasoned she would do it all over again if the roads led to the love of her life, Shai Clark. As a child, Honey's mother had always told her that there were no such thing as fairytales, but she couldn't tell because Honey had surely been rescued by a king. "All hail the queen bitches," Honey said through clenched teeth as she smiled for the different cameras as Shai lead her to the club entrance. "All hail the muthafucking queen."

*

Turk hung back and watched as the king and queen were escorted inside by soldiers deemed more deserving than him and his lot. He knew those assigned to guard Shai and Honey would reap all the benefits for half the work while grunts like him would go unmentioned on the big night. It stung a bit, but he sucked it up. So long as he was back in the action, he was willing to accept a lesser role.

"Look alive ladies," Angelo ambled up to the young men. He was dressed in a gray suit, as usual, and soft black shoes. Following closely behind him was Holiday. "This joint is gonna be packed tonight and I need everybody on their toes. I'd prefer if you didn't drink at all, but if you insist on taking a sip, know your limits. The last thing I need is for one of you little shit birds to get so twisted that you can't rise to the occasion if it goes down."

"We on it, Angie," Baby Doc said a bit too enthusiastically for Angelo's tastes.

Angelo didn't like Baby Doc being out with them on a night where anything could happen. He was still young and inexperienced and that would make him a liability if things got hectic. Had it been up to Angelo, Baby Doc wouldn't have been there, but Shai felt like it was time for him to cut his teeth.

"Don't worry about it, Angie. He's gonna be okay," Holiday said as if reading his mind.

"The last time you told me he was going to be okay he almost got his head blown off," Angelo said, reminding Holiday of he and Baby Doc's run in with Animal. Baby Doc had almost become a casualty because he came between Animal and his prey, which was

166

Holiday. Thankfully, Baby Doc came away with his life but he'd lost partial hearing in one of his ears when Animal fired a gun next to it.

After giving a few last minute instructions, Angelo and the goon squad made their way towards the club entrance.

"Holiday...Holiday!" someone was calling from the crowd of people waiting to get in. Angelo looked over and saw a young girl jumping up and down, trying to be seen over the security guard who was blocking her from entering the club.

"You know that bitch?" Angelo asked Holiday.

"Oh yeah, that's one of my little jump-offs. Tell them niggas to let her through," Holiday said, rubbing his hands together.

"You know you're on the clock, right?" Angelo reminded him.

"I know man, but shorty ain't gonna come between me and handling business," Holiday told him.

"She'd better not," Angelo told him before giving security the signal to let the girl through before going inside.

Claudette was all smiles when security parted the rope. She made it a point to cut her eyes at some of the other girls who weren't fortunate enough to make the cut. "Hey boo," Claudette threw her arms around Holiday to add salt to the females she knew were watching. She tried to kiss him on the lips, but he turned his face away.

"Sup, lil' mama?" Holiday greeted her in a cool drawl. "You're looking good," he admired the two sizes too small skirt she had wiggled into. He hoped to God that she wasn't wearing any panties underneath.

"You know I couldn't be on your arm looking all crazy, knowing it's a big night for you," Claudette said.

"Who's your friend?" Holiday asked, looking over at Rocky. She was standing a few feet behind Claudette, looking nervous.

"Oh, this is my girl Rocky," Claudette pulled her over.

"A pleasure to meet you," Holiday shook her hand, while openly admiring her. She was a little on the homely side, but cute in her own way.

"So where's ya man who's supposed to be keeping my girl company tonight?" Claudette asked, looking over the posse of vultures that had gathered behind Holiday to see who he was talking to. They looked hard and in some cases unwashed. From the look on Rocky's face, she wasn't feeling them either.

Holiday scanned the crowd and spotted Turk near the velvet rope talking to one of the bouncers. "There he is right there. Yo, T!" he called out.

Rocky had to do a double take when she saw the man approaching them. Dressed in a white shirt, black blazer, and jeans, she almost didn't recognize the mystery man she had been fantasizing about since the night they'd collided in the projects. "So, we meet again," she said, trying to hide the nervousness in her voice.

"So it would seem," Turk smiled.

"Wait, y'all know each other?" Claudette asked, looking from Turk to Rocky.

"It's a long story," Rocky said.

"Very," Turk added.

"Well you two can tell us all about it when we get inside. Now let's go turn up," Holiday said and led the group inside.

K'WAN

CHAPTER 19

Marcus stood on second floor balcony of Shooters, which overlooked the main floor. In one hand, he held a smoldering L of some primo bud, and in the other a glass of champagne. It was a little early to be celebrating, as it was only midnight, but he couldn't help but to give himself a well-deserved pat on the back. When everyone said that he couldn't he showed them that he could by planning and executing what would go onto be hailed as the party of the year.

The amount of people who turned out that night was more than Shooters had ever seen. Everybody wanted to get into that party and when people found out it wasn't open to the general public, they threatened to riot. Even with the added security Marcus had brought in for the night, they still didn't have enough manpower to keep the crowd at bay if they decided to buck. For a minute, Marcus thought they were going to tear his club apart, but then the king spoke appeared.

Shai moved with an air of power about him that you could almost physically feel. With a wave of his hand, the unruly crowd grew still and quiet. It was the most amazing thing Marcus had ever seen. Though it was to be a private event, Shai agreed to allow Shooters to let in a certain amount of guests. One half of the club would be sectioned off for his private party while the other patrons would be allowed to occupy the other half, provided they paid three times the cover charge. His security team didn't like it because they felt like Shai was taking an unnecessary risk. Marcus, however, understood the method to his madness. By this simple act, Shai had accomplished two things; he earned the respect of the people by proving that he was a compassionate king, and made himself a nice piece of change. From the triple fee Shooters collected at the door, Shai would be given proper tribute. Breaking bread didn't bother Marcus because even with Shai taking a cut, he still stood to make more money that night than Shooters would normally clear in a week.

Inside, Marcus had everything set out for the Clarks. A red carpet went from the entrance and led a winding path to what would be the Clark's personal section. Bottles were on chill and some of their sexiest servers had been assigned to take care of their every whim for the night. Marcus had even gone the extra mile and rented two thrones for Shai and Honey to sit upon for the night. Marcus had done his homework on the royal couple and knew just what to do to properly stroke the egos of the royal couple.

The highlight of the night was probably when Big Dawg took the stage. From the moment Don B. opened his mouth, the crowd was his to control. The crowd mouthed every word to every song he performed. Marcus had never been a big fan of Don B's music, or him as a person, but he had to admit that there was a magnetic quality about the man. He'd been skeptical about honoring Honey's request to have the gangster rapper at his spot, not only because of the crowd he would attract, but also because of his history with Reese, and the circumstances surrounding the paternity of her daughter. Billy had gone through the roof about Marcus allowing

Don B. to perform, but this wasn't about personal feelings, it was about a dollar.

Honey seemed to be enjoying the show more than anyone. She was as excited as high school kid to see the rapper perform and didn't bother to hide it. At the end of Don B's set, the crowd erupted into a deafening roar. It took the combined efforts of half their security staff as well as the Big Dawg bodyguards to keep people from mauling them as they made their way to their reserved section. No matter what Marcus might've thought about Don B. personally, there was no denying his star power.

The whole time Marcus had been working the party, Tammy was blowing his cell up. She had called and texted him so many times that Marcus eventually shut his phone off. He wasn't interested in anything Tammy had to say after the stunt she pulled. Marcus had sent Bear around to her house to check on her, and found Tammy very much alive. She had given him some lame excuse about having left a message on the club's answering service, but it was bullshit. Any other time she needed the day off, she would call him or one of the other managers directly. Once Bear confirmed the girl wasn't dead or in danger, Marcus fired her via a formal email. It was a coldblooded way to go about it, but it ensured he had a paper trail in case she tried to sue the club. Tammy was done testing his authority and his patience.

Marcus watched from his perch as one of Shai's men, Swann, escorted Honey over to the table, and introduced Honey to Don B. Her smile was so wide that you could see all thirty-two of her teeth. Marcus was uncomfortable with the way that Honey was gazing at the rapper and if Shai was a smart man, he would keep an eye on that situation.

Marcus was about to go downstairs to check on the bar when something, rather someone, caught his eye. He'd instructed the doorman to alert him as soon as Trap had arrived, but somehow the gangster had managed to slip in. His shadow, Moochie, loomed behind him ever vigilant for signs of danger. From the way he was aggressively bumping through the crowd, Marcus knew he'd been drinking already. Trap and alcohol always made a bad combination. The fact that Trap was in Marcus's club drunk was disturbing, but even more unnerving was the fact that he was headed straight for Don B. and his crew.

*

By the time Trap's Porsche truck pulled up in front of Shooters, there was a good-sized mob gathered out front. It took them an extra ten minutes just to be able to pull up to the valet.

Moochie was out first, tossing they keys to the valet before muscling a few people back so she could let Trap out of the passenger side. Trap damn near spilled out of the car, slightly buzzed off the fifth of Hennessy he had been punishing on the ride over. He was slightly tipsy, but as soon as he saw the paparazzi heading his way with their cameras, he straightened himself out. Though he wasn't a major act like Big Dawg, Trap had made a name for himself on the underground circuit and the streets loved his music. He

173

stopped to take pictures with a few fans before making his way to the entrance.

No sooner than they tried to cross the threshold, they were met by security. The beefy man looked at Trap and Moochie like they were rabble trying to sneak inside. "Private party tonight. Come back tomorrow."

"I know, but I'm a guest of Marcus. The name is Trap," he introduced himself.

The bouncer glanced down at his clipboard. "Yeah, I see your name. Still, there's a dress code so I can't let you in," he looked at Trap's black t-shirt and big chain.

Trap cocked his head to one side and looked up at the taller man. "You really wanna do this like this, my nigga?"

"I'm ready to do this any way you wanna do it, shorty," the bouncer capped.

Moochie took a step forward, ready to take the bouncer's chin off with one of her thick mitts, but Trap stopped her. He spotted Wayne standing near the coat check and waved to get his attention. When Wayne spotted him, he looked like he was contemplating leaving Trap and Moochie outside, but decided against it.

"They're good. These are Marcus's people," Wayne explained.

The bouncer knew Wayne from seeing him come in and out with Marcus so he took his word for it. "A'ight, but I still gotta pat y'all niggas down."

Trap spread his arms. "Knock yourself out."

NO SHADE: A Hood Rat Novel

The bouncer patted Trap down, rougher than he needed to, and once he was sure Trap wasn't carrying any weapons, he let him pass. "You too, homie," he told Moochie.

"Fuck outta here. I'm a female, so you better either get a broad to check me or take me at my word that I'm clean," Moochie snarled.

The bouncer had to take a good look at her to make sure she wasn't lying about her gender because he could've sworn she was a dude. He looked around for a female member of the security team, but there were none in earshot. His good mind told him to make her wait until someone could come over, but he didn't want any trouble with Marcus so he let her pass.

"Appreciate that, big homie," Trap told Wayne once they were inside.

"No problem. Just don't make me regret it," Wayne told him.

"I'd never smudge your name, big Wayne. Say, where's Marcus?"

"I don't know. He might be up in the office or something. I'll go check."

"You do that. In the meantime, me and Moochie gonna hit the bar and get something to drink."

"Try not to get in any trouble while I'm gone, Trap," Wayne said.

"Now what could I possibly get into between here and the bar. You run along and get the boss man. I'll mind my manners until you come back."

Wayne gave Trap one last warning look before disappearing into the crowd to find Marcus.

"Some niggas is just extra," Moochie said after Wayne left.

"Cut him some slack, sis. You know big Wayne is just being a mother hen. Say you got those?" Trap asked.

"Of course I do," Moochie peeked around to make sure nobody was watching before digging into her bra. From her bosom, she produced two .22s. "These niggas must be crazy to think we gonna roll anywhere unarmed," she said, slipping the small guns into her pockets.

"That's my girl," Trap pounded her fist. "Let's hit the bar. I'm suddenly feeling very parched."

Moochie led the way through the crowd to the bar, which was surrounded by a sea of thirsty partygoers. A few well-placed elbows and a murderous stare got the siblings to the bar in under three minutes. Trap ordered a bottle of champagne for himself and Red Bull on the rocks for Moochie. The placed their backs against the bar and surveyed the crowd.

"A lot of paper in the room tonight," Trap said, sizing up the different groups of ballers. They were rocking big jewels and spending big money. "Had this been a few years ago, we'd have had half these niggas in here naked and tied up."

"Yeah, we were some bad ass outlaws back then, but that was the past and we need to be focused on the future, which is staying legit," Moochie said.

"I know, sis. Just thinking out loud. That's all," Trap said sipping from his bottle. He noticed a crowd formed in the corner

176

around one of the tables and craned his neck to see who was sitting at it. Suddenly, a smile spread across his lips. "As I live and breathe," he tapped his sister and pointed to who he was staring at.

Moochie laughed, which was a rare occurrence. "You know I thought this was a classy joint, but it seems that they'll let in any dawg off the street."

"No sense in being rude. Let's go over and show the proper respect to the great and powerful Don," Trap dragged his bottle off the bar and walked off.

*

"Yo, sun, you straight murdered that shit. Hands down that had to be the performance of the century," Dollar gushed after Don B. had returned to their section.

"I did my thing, but it's the crowd that made it special. The Don is only as great as the people who support him. Don't ever forget that," Don B. told Dollar while cracking open a bottle of water. Between the blunts and cigarettes he seemed to be getting winded earlier and earlier during his sets.

"He ain't lying. I think I saw two bitches faint when you did your verse from 'Slap Ya Self.' Ya shit was so hard I'm sure nobody even remembered that True and them were on the original record," Wise added. He was trying to do his part to stroke Don B's ego, but all he ended up doing was crossing a very delicate line.

Bad Blood was the first act signed to Big Dawg. The group was comprised of young dudes Don B. knew from the hood that had the

177

talent and swagger to make something of themselves in the rap game. Unlike most, they were actually living the things they rapped about, and it would be their lifestyles that led to each of their deaths, including their front man True.

True, was Don B's protégé and best friend. He had been a stand up dude and a star in the making, but when his past and future collided, he paid the ultimate price. Don B. had buried many friends, but it was True's murder, which affected him the most. Though True lost his life due to something that had been brewing since long Don B. came to into his life, the mogul always felt like the blood was on his hands. Maybe if he had done more, or set a better example, True would've lived to see the success Don B. had always promised him. In death, he sold more records than he ever would in life, but Don B. would've gladly traded it all to have his friend back.

Don B. turned to Wise. "What the fuck do you know about it? You was still going $2.50 on a bag of smoke with ya mans when True and Bad Blood were on the charts. Don't talk about shit you don't know nothing about. As a matter of fact, why the fuck are you even talking to me right now?" he snapped.

"Chill, bro. He didn't mean anything by it. Wise was just trying to give you your props," Dollar tried to quell the situation which earned him his own dose of Don B's wrath.

"I've been praised by millions, what the fuck do props from either one of you simple-minded niggas mean to me? You wanna do something for me, go to the bar, and grab some more bottles. We getting light over here," Don B. told them.

NO SHADE: A *Hood Rat* Novel

"Why we gotta go get the bottles when that's what our waitresses are for?" Dolla asked.

Tone rested his hand on Dolla's shoulder and gave it a little squeeze. "Know when it's time to take a walk."

Dolla picked up on what Tone was throwing down. "Say no more. We gonna spin the floor right quick," he got up. "C'mon Wise."

Don B. tapped a cigarette on the table angrily, watching Dolla and Wise bumble through the crowd. "The things we do for family."

"I swear, sometimes I wonder what you see in them," Venus said tugging at the leather booty shorts their stylist had made her wear that night. They were uncomfortable as hell, but looked good on her and she had the attention of every man in the room when she took the stage. She was eye candy, and Don B. wanted to capitalize on that during their performance. Venus had sung her heart out during the cameo she had made during Don B's set. She had done shows before, but it was her first time taking the stage with the Don. She marveled at the polarizing effect he had on the crowd and dreamed of the day the fans held her in such high regards.

"I'm inclined to agree with the lady," Devil spoke up. He was Don B's personal bodyguard and the person he trusted the most other than Tone. "You should've left those two idiots in the shit-hole town down south where you found them."

"I called myself looking out for them by bringing them up," Don B. said.

"Well you didn't do them any great favors by bringing them up north. At the rate they're going it'll only be a matter of time before

179

they get into something you can't buy them out of or somebody kills them."

"You might be right about that one, Devil," Don B. agreed. "Times like this I wish G rolled with us because them two niggas always make themselves scarce when he's around. Why didn't he come again?"

"He said he wasn't feeling too good," Tone answered.

"Pussy," Devil snorted. "I remember back in '83 I fought in a ten round amateur bout with walking pneumonia and a hundred and four degree fever and these young niggas call out of work if they got tummy aches," he shook his head.

"Well this ain't '83 and niggas ain't made out of steel no more," Don B. joked. "But on some gangsta shit, I don't know how I feel about G leaving us on stuck on a night as big as this one. He's always been reliable until now."

"I told you about trusting new niggas," Devil reminded him. "You want me to fire the nigga?" he asked, meaning murder.

Don B. thought on it for a few seconds. "Nah, not just yet. Keep your eye on him though. I'll let you know when and if it's time to retire that nigga's number."

"Look alive. We've got company," Tone nodded beyond the rope, where Swann was escorting a beautiful woman over to their table.

"Well hello," Don B. peered over his sunglasses at the curvaceous girl with the blonde weave.

"Put your fangs away. That's Shai's lady which means she's off limits, unless you wanna get yourself whacked," Devil warned him.

"Take it easy, Devil. I was just admiring the merchandise," Don
B. said.

"Red Devil, what it do, blood?" Swann greeted him with a
complex handshake.

Devil shrugged his shoulders. "Same old, same old. I see you're
still up to your old tricks. Funny, because I heard you were relieved
of your duties."

Word on the streets was there had been some kind of falling out
between Shai and Swann over something no one was quite sure of.
Whatever it had been was serious enough to where Swann had fallen
off the grid for a while. People speculated that Shai had his best
friend executed for the offense, until about a year prior when Swann
reappeared like he never left. Nobody was stupid enough to ever ask
Shai or Swann what had happened, but Devil had his suspicions.

"Nah, I just took a little break to sort some personal things out.
I'm back where I belong now, busting my gun at enemies of my
family," Swann said proudly. "While we're on the subject of guns, I
heard you guys have got a new hitter working for you. I'm surprised
he's not here tonight to watch the Don's back."

"I got Don's back covered," Devil informed him.

"Of course you do, Devil. You've been looking out for Don B.
for years, which is why it was newsworthy when you brought in
somebody else to help out. I hear he's a cold piece of work and was
hoping to meet him tonight."

"He wasn't feeling well so he sat this one out," Tone told
Swann. "By chance, would you care to share with us how you're
more familiar with the Big Dawg employees than our own Human

181

Resources department?" He wondered if Swann asking about a man who they were just discussing was just a coincidence or a sign.

Swann smirked. "You of all people should know that the Clarks have eyes and ears everywhere. But let me not get sidetracked," he motioned for Honey to step forward. "Don B., this is the birthday girl, Honey. I promised her I'd introduce you before the night was over. She's a big fan of your music, though I can't figure out why," he chuckled.

"Swann, you don't have to be an asshole all the time," Honey scolded him.

"It's cool, being a dick is in his nature," Don B. mustered a phony grin. "A pleasure to make your acquaintance," Don B. took Honey's hand and kissed the back of it.

"The pleasure is all mine," Honey blushed. "I wanted to come over and thank you personally for agreeing to perform at my party on such short notice. It was the best birthday gift ever!"

"It was an honor and a privilege to help ensure the queen of the city had a great birthday," Don B. gave her a mock bow.

"Damn, seems like every time we bump into each other you're bending over," someone spoke from behind Don B.

Devil and the other members of the security team immediately swooped in to form a barrier between Don B. There was a brief commotion, which brought over the club security to help get it sorted out. Don B. was furious. He shoved his way through the wall of bodies, anxious to see who would dare mock the Don in public. When he got to the front of the crowd and saw who it was, his jaw dropped. Of the millions of people, he could've run into at a random club in New York City, why did it have to be him?

CHAPTER 20

From the time Turk walked in the club, he knew the night was going to go to the left. The first sign was when he and Holiday showed up in the Clark's section of the club with the two girls and were barred entry. They were only allowing friends and family on that side and the girls were neither. They could've let Turk and Holiday slide with getting the girls in, but Honey made a big deal about it. Her exact words were, "Them bitches can't sit with me."

Being treated like a second-class citizen in front of his guests didn't sit well with Holiday. He had painted himself as the man next to the man for Claudette, and the treatment he received betrayed his true status on the food chain. Turk could tell from Claudette's body language that her perception of Holiday had changed, but Holiday didn't seem to notice. He smoothed things over by splurging on bottles and bribing one of the bouncers to let them have a rickety table in the back of the club. The view of the festivities sucked, but at least they weren't standing up anymore. About twenty minutes in, Holiday slid off with Claudette into one of the bathrooms leaving Turk to entertain Rocky.

Rocky didn't talk much. She mostly looked around curiously at everyone while trying to act like being in a room full of half-naked girls and killers didn't make her uncomfortable.

"You good?" Turk asked in an attempt to break the awkward silence that lingered between them.

"I'm okay; it's just a little loud in here!" She had to shout over the music for him to hear her.

184

"I guess it's to be expected, considering we're in a club," Turk said. He meant it as a joke, but Rocky didn't laugh.

More awkward silence.

"Is Turk your real name?" Rocky asked.

Turk shrugged. "It might as well be. It's the only thing anyone has ever called me since I was a kid. Rocky your real name?"

"No, it's shorty for Raquel. I never liked it, but it was my grandmother's name," Rocky told him. "So, you think they'll be gone much longer?" Rocky looked at her phone impatiently.

"I can't speak on another man's stamina. You're more than welcome to go in and check on them if you like."

"Thanks, but I'll pass," Rocky said with a roll of her eyes. She went back to checking the time on her phone.

"Listen, if you wanna get out of here we could —"

"Let me stop you right there," Rocky cut him off. "Just because my friend is fucking your boy in the bathroom doesn't mean you'll be bending me over any sinks, stalls, or small-packaging me in the backseat of a car. I don't get down like that."

"Shorty, you need to slow your roll. All I was gonna suggest is that we go outside in the back where the music isn't so loud," Turk informed her.

Rocky's face turned red from embarrassment. "Sorry, I just thought —"

"That because your friend is a ho I automatically assumed the same about you? That would be kind of closed minded on my part, but dumb ass thug niggas like me ain't supposed to be big on tact, are we?"

185

"I never called you a thug," Rocky shot back.

"But you thought it, didn't you? No need to lie, shorty. I saw it all in your face the first time we met and bringing you here amongst Holiday's ignorant ass and the rest of these niggas only reinforced it."

Rocky opened her mouth to counter, but she couldn't. She did think he was a thug, among other things, that she would never admit.

"See, I told you," Turk laughed. "Don't feel no type of way about it. I'm used to it. People have been making assumptions about who I am for as long as I can remember."

"Okay, I accept that. So why don't you tell me," Rocky crossed her arms, "who are you?"

The question caught Turk off guard. He didn't have a logical answer, because no one had had ever asked him the question. "I'm just the Turk, I guess."

"I'm just the Turk," Rocky mimicked him. "Speaking about yourself like that you sound more like something to be owned instead of a person."

"With as much time as I spend trying to advance at my job that's how it feels," Turk admitted. More often than not, he felt more like a tool of the Clark organization than a part of it. They took him out of the box to use whenever necessary then put him back in.

Rocky shook her head sadly. "That's a shame. Throwing yourself so deep into your work that you don't take a minute to enjoy life should be a crime, take it from someone who knows. You need to get out and have a little fun once in a while."

"Who says I don't?"

"You just did, Mr. Work-a-holic."

"You're one to talk, Ms. Uptight."

Rocky faked offense. "I am not uptight."

"The hell you aren't. The whole time we've been sitting here all you've done is scowl and look at your phone. It's not exactly the most fun I've had on a date."

"Is that what this is? A date? I thought we were just thrown together to keep each other company while our lustful friends fornicated in a public bathroom," Rocky joked.

"I guess you do have a sense of humor after all," Turk said.

"Stick around long enough and you'll find I'm full of surprises," Rocky said playfully.

"Is that an invitation, Ms. Raquel?"

"I guess that'll depend on you, Mr. Turk," she replied.

As it turned out, Rocky wasn't so bad after all. Once she loosened up, she proved to be quite interesting. Rocky was funny and surprisingly smarter than Turk gave her credit for when they'd first met. She was nothing like Claudette, which was why Turk found it so puzzling that they were hanging out together. Rocky confided in Turk that she hadn't known Claudette very long and that they weren't exactly besties, but she didn't have many friends in the housing projects she'd moved into.

Claudette must've felt them talking about her because she suddenly reappeared, with Holiday in tow. Holiday was smiling like the cat who had swallowed the canary, but Claudette looked irritated. Her hair was slightly askew and there was a wet spot on her skirt, as if she had recently tried to scrub out a stain.

187

"We were about to send a search and rescue team looking for y'all." Rocky gave Claudette a dirty look, letting her know she didn't approve of her ho-ish behavior.

"I wish you would've." Claudette sat down. She grabbed one of the bottles of water and rinsed her mouth, spitting into an empty glass. The expression on her face said she had a less than favorable time.

"Everything cool?" Turk asked Holiday.

"Yeah, I'm cool. I don't know what the fuck her problem is," Holiday told him.

"Nigga, don't even get me started," Claudette rolled her eyes.

There was obviously some tension between Claudette and Holiday that neither Turk nor Rocky wanted any parts of. They continued making small talk amongst each other, but their angry friends showing up had affected the vibe. Turk was saying something to Holiday when he spotted a commotion in the Big Dawg section. He was just going to watch in hopes of seeing a good ass whipping, or someone getting dragged out, but then he spotted Honey and Swann near the center of the disturbance.

"Excuse me for a second," Turk got up from the table. He patted Holiday on the shoulder before making hurried steps towards the disturbance.

It took Holiday a second to figure out what was going on but when he caught on, he was out of his chair and on Turk's heels.

*

"So what happened?" Rocky asked Claudette after the boys had gone.

"Girl, where do I even begin?" Claudette filled a glass with Hennessy. "I spent fifteen minutes sucking his little ass dick because it acted like it didn't want to get hard. Then when we finally get to the business, he lasted a shade over five minutes before shooting his load all over my damn skirt. If this shit leaves a stain I'm not going to be able to return it in the morning," she fumed.

"Wait, you fucked a nigga you barley know with no condom?" Rocky was appalled.

Claudette waved her off. "Holiday ain't got nothing. He don't look sick. Anyway, what happened with you and his pretty ass friend? Did he crack on you for some pussy too?"

"No, Turk was actually a perfect gentleman," Rocky told her.

Claudette rolled her eyes. "You are one lucky bitch. I wish I'd met Turk before that asshole Holiday. I'd let that nigga put a baby in me. Our kids would probably have some good ass hair."

Rocky pinched the bridge of her nose, listening to Claudette's ignorant ass was starting to give her a headache. "So what now?"

"Now, we drink up all these nigga's free liquor and move onto greener pastures," Claudette refilled her glass. The way she was tossing them back, she'd likely be drunk before long.

"Claudette that is so tacky," Rocky said.

"Fuck all that. From the looks of things they're going to have their hands full for a while anyhow, tending to Shai and his bitch," Claudette cast a dirty look over at Honey. "If it wasn't for her uppity ass we'd be sitting with some real ballers, instead of these two

189

fucking grunts. I swear, girl, I'm not leaving here without getting some rich dick and a few dollars for my troubles."

"I heard somebody call my name," Dolla appeared at their table as if out of thin air. As usual, Wise wasn't far behind.

"Out of the frying pan and into the damn fire," Rocky twisted her lips in disgust at the sight of Dolla.

"I see you still ain't managed to pull that stick out of your ass, huh, Rocky?" Dolla invited himself to a seat between them and turned his attention to Claudette. "What's up, ma? I'm surprised to see you two here, since it's a private party."

"I could say the same about the two of you," Claudette replied. "We were invited by some friends, but things didn't work out the way we planned. How did y'all manage to slither in here?"

"You wound me with your accusation," Dolla faked hurt. "I'll have you know we didn't have to slither in anywhere, we're with the star attraction," he nodded in the direction of the Big Dawg section.

"You know all this time I thought you were full of shit when you claimed to be a part of Big Dawg," Claudette moved in closer to Dolla. Normally, she wouldn't have given Dolla's thirsty ass the time of day, but that night she saw him as a means to an end.

"I told you I'm connected, ma," Dolla ran his hand up Claudette's skirt.

"What the fuck are you doing?" Rocky whispered to Claudette.

"Trying to make the best out of a bad night. Now shut your ass up and play along."

CHAPTER 21

"Is this how you greet your all your friends, Don? Or is this special treatment for little old me?" Trap looked down the line of angry faces flanking Don B.

"What you doing here, Trap?" Don B. asked in a less than friendly tone. He and Trap had history that stretched back to when Trap was an unknown rapper trying to come up. Like the rest, Trap wanted to get down with Big Dawg, but a misunderstanding between he and the Don blew the deal and landed Trap on a bus back to Florida. He had been holding a grudge ever since.

"Who says I wanted anything?" Trap asked. "As it happens, I've got business here tonight."

"Bullshit, Shooters is shut down for the private party. No outsiders allowed tonight," Don B. said.

"Oh, but I ain't no outsider. I happen to be a personal friend of the owner," Trap informed him.

Tone laughed. "Funny because I've known Marcus for a while now and I can't see you and him having much in common."

"Me and Marcus got more in common than you might think, but it ain't for me to put another man's business in the streets."

"We were kind of in the middle of something when you rolled up," Don B. told him, letting Trap know that his presence wasn't welcomed.

Trap's face saddened. "I'm not detecting a lot of love coming from you, Don. I know things ain't been right between us since you shitted on me and left me broke and stranded in New York, but I ain't holding no grudges so I don't see why you are. As a matter of fact, I'd have thought you'd be happy to see me, especially after me doing you that solid back in Miami. Do your new friends know about Miami, Don B?"

Don B. had tried to forget about Miami, but he couldn't. To that day, he still had nightmares about the things he had endured during their trip to the sunshine state. He and the Big Dawg crew had gone down to Miami on business, but of course, Don B. had to mix in a bit of pleasure. He had met a dancer named Reign and found himself smitten. Reign was beautiful, cunning, and about her money, a perfect match for the Don. He had visions of making her his queen, but Reign had visions of making him her fool.

Unbeknownst to Don B. at the time, Reign was using him in a plot she had to avenge her sister Unique, who had been murdered. The young girl was a casualty in the war the man known as Animal had been waging in streets across the country. Don B. didn't have anything to do with Unique's death, but his connection to Animal, and being a New Yorker, put him in Reign's crosshairs. During their last encounter, Don B. came expecting a bout of mind-blowing sex, but instead received a dose of his own medicine. Reign drugged him, tied him up, and put him through hours of sexual torture. The worst part about it was that she videotaped the whole incident.

By the time Reign was done violating Don B., he was ready to die, but the world wasn't quite ready to let him go. Just before his final moment, he was rescued by Trap and Moochie. Reign died that day, taking the secret of Don B's humiliation with her. Don B. never told a soul the truth about what happened to him, not even his closest

192

confidants. The only proof was the tape, which unfortunately was in Trap's possession. He had been saving it as his trump card to use against the Don whenever the mood struck him.

"I'm feeling a bit uncomfortable with ya goons hovering over me, Don B. Why don't you tell them to give us a little space?" Trap phrased it as a suggestion, but it felt like an order.

All eyes turned to Don B. for direction as to how to proceed. Had he given the word, Devil and the team would've happily beaten Trap to death, but sadly, this was not to be.

"Stand down," Don B. said in a defeated tone.

"Don, you sure?" Devil asked. He was itching to crack Trap's forehead to the white meat.

"Are you hard of hearing? I said stand the fuck down!" Don B. snapped.

Devil didn't like it, but he did as he was told and gave the signal for everybody to fall back.

"That's more like it," Trap smiled. He took the seat Don B. had seconds before vacated and put his feet up on the table. "This is a nice set up you got going on over here, Don," he picked up a bottle of Hennessy and chugged from it. "You don't mind, do you?" he asked as an afterthought.

"Knock yourself out," Don B. said through clenched teeth. It took everything out of him to not have Devil knock the smug grin off Trap's face.

"Mighty kind of you, Don...mighty kind," Trap said sarcastically. He looked around and his eyes landed on Honey and Venus. "Hello ladies. What are y'all names?"

"Spoken for," Swann pushed Honey behind him protectively.

"Baby is this yo' nigga?" Trap asked, ignoring Swann.

"Maybe you didn't hear me when I said she was spoken for," Swann said.

"Oh, I heard you, but I was talking to her," Trap shot back. "What's the matter; you don't know how to talk?"

"We speak a different language around these parts," Turk stepped through the crowd. His thumbs were hooked in his belt, showing off the handle of the meat cleaver sticking out of his pants. After what he'd pulled with Carl, Swan didn't trust him to carry a pistol that night, but he'd be damned if he went into a den of wolves without some type of weapon. "Maybe you're familiar with it?"

Trap leaned forward. "Are we gonna have a problem?"

Turk looked him directly in the eyes. "If you continue to disrespect my O.G.'s lady, absolutely."

Trap laughed. "Moochie, you see the balls on this little nigga?"

"Yeah, I see 'em," Moochie said from behind Turk. She held both the .22s at her sides. Turk had been so focused on Trap that he never saw her ease up on him, and neither did Holiday who was supposed to be watching his back.

Trap folded his hands on his lap. "So, am I speaking your language now?"

*

"I told you niggas I didn't want no shit in my club!" Marcus came pushing his way through the crowd. He had Wayne, Bear, and a half dozen bouncers at his back. "Fuck is going on here?"

"Ain't nothing," Trap raised his hands in surrender. "Just a little friendly banter amongst gangsters. You know how that goes, Marcus."

"You know this joker, Marcus?" Swann asked. His dislike for Trap and disappointment in Marcus was written all over his face.

Marcus looked at Trap who was watching him quizzically. "Unfortunately, I do. I apologize if he's been an inconvenience to you guys tonight, Swann."

"Is that O.G. Swann?" Trap asked, recognizing the name. "Man, y'all should've told me this was a Clark party and I'd have been a little more mindful. We ain't never met, but me and your boss know some of the same people," he told Swann.

"I seriously doubt that, but whatever," Swann dismissed him. "Marcus, we appreciate the hospitality you've shown us, but I think it's time we call it a night."

"Swann, y'all don't have to leave so soon, it's still early. They haven't even brought Honey's cake out yet. Let me have the girls bring y'all some more bottles while I personally check on the cake," Marcus offered. He knew if the Clarks left the money would follow.

"Nah, I think we've had our fill for the night," Swann looked Trap up and down. "I'm sure our paths will cross again soon."

"Of this you can be sure," Trap saluted him with the bottle of Hennessy he'd taken off Don B's table.

Swann strutted back through the crowd, ushering Honey in front of him, with his young goons watching his back. Turk spared a glance over his shoulder and found Trap watching him and smiling.

"Trap, I need to speak with you about something important," Marcus said, trying his best to hide his irritation.

Trap considered lingering around for a while longer just to make Don B. uncomfortable, but didn't want to test the limits of Marcus's hospitality. "Well," he got up, "it's been real fellas, but as I said earlier, I've got business here tonight." He took his time walking though Don B's entourage recklessly eyeballing each man he passed.

"Don't let the door hit you in the ass on the way out," Devil called after him, which caused Trap to stop short.

"I don't think I'll have to worry about that. Getting hit in my ass by anything ain't my forte. Damn shame I can't say that about everybody here," he cut his eyes at Don B. "Oh and Don, I think I'll be calling in that favor you owe me real soon," he snickered and left with Marcus.

"What's that nigga talking about?" Tone asked Don B. after Trap had gone.

"Nothing," Don B. lied. "He ain't talking about nothing."

*

"Why is it that you always do the exact opposite of what I ask you to do?" Marcus asked Trap.

NO SHADE: A Hood Rat Novel

"You asked me not to cause trouble in your joint and I didn't. All I was doing was rapping to the pretty lady in the dress and niggas got all in their feelings," Trap downplayed it.

"Rapping to that particular pretty lady could've gotten you murdered. That was Shai Clark's wife," Marcus informed him.

"Is that right? She looked kinda familiar. Did she used to dance?"

"I don't know and I don't care, neither should you. Now let's get down to business so I can get your troublesome ass outta here. You got the bread?" Marcus asked.

"What, you think I can fit a hundred grand in my pants pockets?" Trap asked sarcastically. "The money is in the trunk. I was gonna give it to you at the end of the night."

"No sense in waiting. We can walk over and get it now," Marcus said. He was ready to get it over with and Trap out of his hair.

"Okay, Mr. Pushy. Me and Moochie were about ready to call it a night anyhow. I got a date after I finish with you," Trap told him.

Marcus shook his head. "I pity the poor girl who's dumb enough to let your dog ass get in her pants."

"Nigga, I've had about enough of your insults for one night," Trap said seriously. "For your information, it ain't even like that with me and shorty. I kinda like her."

This surprised Marcus. "Trap you've always been the love 'em and leave 'em type."

"Yeah, I know, and that's because most of the chicks I come across ain't worth keeping around. This one is a little different. I don't know her that well yet, but she seems to have a head on her shoulders. I met her at this after-hours spot in Harlem," Trap said.

"Trap, I'm sure I ain't gotta tell you to be careful with bitches you meet in hole-in-the-wall clubs, especially in Harlem. She was probably in there selling pussy."

Trap laughed. "I thought the same thing at first, but after I got to talking to her I didn't get that vibe from her. She was just in there having a few drinks and blowing off some steam, same as I was. She lives in Cali and is only in New York for a few days."

"A Cali chick? Shit, they're probably more scandalous than the broads in New York. Don't go falling all head over heels for the broad until you see what she's really about," Marcus told him.

"Why not? You fell in love with Billy and you hardly knew her," Trap pointed out.

"It ain't the same thing. I didn't meet Billy in an after-hours spot," Marcus replied.

And what's that supposed to mean?" Trap asked defensively.

"It isn't supposed to mean anything. All I'm trying to say it…you know what? Forget it. Let's just go get this paper."

"Let me find out you throwing low-key shade, Marcus." Trap eyed-balled him. "What you're supposed to be the only one who can find somebody?"

It wasn't until that moment that Marcus realized that Trap might actually be serious and he'd offended him. "My fault, Trap. You know I ain't no hater. I'm just trying to make sure you don't go into anything blind. You're a pain in the fucking ass, but you're still my nigga and I'd never see harm come to you at the hands of a man or woman. Just take your time with it, that's all."

"You know I don't rush into nothing unless it's a gun fight," Trap said in a much lighter tone. "But seriously, thanks for being concerned," he gave Marcus dap.

"So, what's Ms. California's name?" Marcus asked. Trap was about to answer when a commotion broke out across the room. "If it ain't one thing it's another," Marcus said in frustration. "Hold that thought," he told Trap before making his way towards the disturbance.

CHAPTER 22

"That was some real dumb shit you did back there," Swann told Turk as they were walking back to their section.

"I saw niggas forming and I was just coming to cover your back," Turk explained.

"Man, I wanted to laugh like shit when Turk's crazy ass wanted to test that blade against them guns," Holiday snickered.

"I don't see what the fuck is so funny. You were supposed to be holding him down and you let that bitch get the drop. You know better than to not have your partner's flank covered," Swann scolded him. "Turk, I understand what you were trying to do, but you could've caused that situation back there to get ugly. I thought I told your hotheaded ass not to carry a weapon tonight? You're too irresponsible to carry when we're with Shai."

"You said don't bring a gun and I didn't. I brought my hatchet," Turk said sarcastically.

"Don't be a smart ass, you know what I mean. Now fork it over," Swann held his hand out. Reluctantly, Turk handed over his cleaver. Swann examined the fine razor edge. "I know you're not dumb enough to be still carrying the same blade you used to amputate Carl's hand?"

Turk just shrugged.

Swann shook his head. "For someone so smart you sure are dumb, Turk. Holiday, get rid of this then go find Andrew, and tell him to bring the car around back. It's time for us to go," he handed the cleaver to Holiday.

"Okay, let me go deal with these broads and I'll get right on it," Holiday said.

"Fuck them bitches. We need to get Shai and Honey out of here before something else happens."

"So I'm just supposed to leave them to get home on their own? That's rude," Holiday said sarcastically.

"Nigga, since when did you give a fuck about being courteous? For all I care those bitches can walk home. You're on the clock so you belong to me until I say otherwise. Now you can do what the fuck I told you to, or I can let Shai tell you himself right after I inform him how you and this mutt almost started a shoot-out!"

"I'll take care of it," Turk spoke up to try and defuse the situation. "Holiday, get the car. I'll drop some cab money on these broads and meet y'all outside," Turk said and walked off.

"You didn't have to talk to me like that in front of Turk," Holiday said once the youngster was gone.

"What, I hurt your little feelings? Suck it up and deal with it," Swann told him.

"Swann, I'm supposed to be a lieutenant and when you talk down on me in front of the soldiers, it doesn't do much to boost my position. All I'm saying is that it wouldn't kill you to show me a little respect," Holiday said.

Swann laughed. "Nigga, you want respect then you should try earning it by not letting pussy and partying cloud your judgment. That's what got your ass shot...twice. Now go find Andrew so we can bounce."

*

201

Turk was glad to be away from Swann. He was on some bullshit and Turk was no fan of his mood swings. Sometimes Swann could be the coolest dude in the world and others he could be a dick. It's as if ever since he had come back from wherever the hell he'd disappeared to, he'd been moving different. It sometimes seemed like he was working harder to gain Shai's approval than Turk, which he found odd since Swann was the Clark underboss. There was definitely something off about their relationship lately.

Turk was a bit put off when he reached the table where they'd left Rocky and Claudette to find two dudes sitting in the seats he and Holiday had vacated. Upon closer inspection, he realized that he recognized them. They were the same two knuckleheads from the projects.

Rocky spotted Turk first and the expression on her face betrayed her shock and shame. "Oh, hey. Didn't expect you back so soon."

"Apparently not," Turk looked at the two men sitting with them.

"Listen this isn't what it looks like…" Rocky tried to explain.

"You don't owe me any explanation. I ain't got no papers on you. We were just keeping each other company while our friends were…occupied. That is what you said, isn't it?"

"My bad, fam. I didn't know these belonged to you," Dolla spoke up. His words were slurred and his eyes were glassy. Probably due to the fact that they had drank almost all the liquor Holiday had tricked on.

"Nah, they don't belong to me. We good, homie. I was just coming over to tell the ladies that we were leaving and offer them cab money to get home, but I guess you guys can take care of it from here."

"Don't dip off so soon. Stay and have a drink with us. I needed to holla at you about something anyhow," Dolla told him.

"My G, we don't know each other so I can't see what we would have to discuss. I've said my piece and I'm gone," Turk turned to leave, but Dolla grabbed him by the wrist.

"That's kind of rude of you to give a man your back before he's done talking." Dolla could've let it go, but he felt like Turk was slighting him in front of the girls.

Turk looked at Dolla's hand as if it was something foul. "As I've already said, we don't have anything to talk about," he yanked himself free of Dolla's grip, which seemed to only make Dolla angrier.

"What the fuck is your problem? Here I am trying to make a business proposition on behalf of my big homie and you acting all funny-style about it," Dolla said much louder than he needed to.

"Let it go, D," Wise said. He felt the tension mounting.

"Shut the fuck up and stop acting like a pussy, Wise!" Dolla snapped. "See, that's the problem with some niggas. They get thrown a few scraps and they don't know how to accept a full meal when it's offered to them."

Dolla was pushing Turk, and as bad as he wanted to break his jaw, he kept himself in check. He had caused enough drama for the night and didn't want another incident. "You got it, big man. You guys enjoy the rest of your evening, and our liquor." Turk turned to walk away.

"Whatever nigga," Dolla turned his attention back to the table and the drinks. "I don't know why you think so highly of that dude, Wise. He ain't about shit, fake ass Chi Ali looking muthafucka. All them Clark niggas think they better than everybody else because they got money and a few guns, but ain't none of them about shit. Fuck the Turk and fuck Shai Clark!"

Everyone at the table became deathly quiet, except Dolla, who continued his drunk ramblings. Rocky didn't want to look up from the drink she had been staring at since the argument started, but she couldn't help herself. She raised her eyes in time to see Turk coming back to the table.

"Turk don't!" she shouted, but was too late.

*

One minute Dolla was talking shit and the next he had a mouthful of tablecloth when Turk slammed his face into the table. Before Dolla could collect his wits, Turk kicked his chair out from under him, depositing the loudmouth on the floor. Wise bravely tried to come to his brother's defense, but he wasn't a very skilled fighter. Unfortunately for him, Turk was. He hit the young man with a vicious combination of blows to the head that sent him reeling.

About this time, Dolla was staggering back to his feet. Seeing Turk beating the hell out of his brother sent him into a rage. He knew he was no match for Turk with the hands, so he pulled a gun.

He had Turk dead to rights, but him being drunk off his ass he forgot to take off the safety, which provided Turk with the precious split second he needed to close the distance between them. A powerful chop across Dolla's wrist sent the gun skidding across the floor and into the crowd, making it a fair fight…if that's what you could call it.

To his credit, Dolla was a better fighter than Wise, but Turk still outmatched him. Turk lit Dolla's face and head up with a flurry of blows. Angrily, Dolla tried to rush Turk and use his superior weight over him, but Turk reversed it and Dolla ended on lying on his back on the table. With murder in his eyes, Turk broke one of the bottles and wielded it like a dagger. Dolla knew his end was at hand. Turk would've surely killed Dolla had Marcus and his security team not subdued him. By then, a crowd of spectators had formed, including Tone and Devil. They had come over in the hopes that they would find Trap on the receiving end of an ass whipping, but were surprised to see it was one of their own getting mashed out.

"Get the fuck off me! Do you know who I'm with?" Turk struggled against the bouncers to no avail.

"I don't know who you came with, but I know who you're leaving with. Take this muthafucka outside and hold him until the police come," Marcus ordered his men.

"But it wasn't his fault," Rocky tried to explain.

"You with him?" Marcus asked.

"Well…yeah…kinda, but –"

"Then your ass is gone too," Marcus cut her off. "As a matter of fact, evict all these muthafuckas from my spot."

The bouncers were pulling Dolla to his feet, preparing to toss him and Wise out with the girls, when Tone interjected. "Those two are with us," he pointed at Dolla and Wise.

Marcus didn't look happy. "These two idiots are part of your camp?"

"Sadly, yes. I apologize on their behalf and we'll take care of any damages," Tone said, thinking how he had to clean up yet another mess because of Dolla and Wise. Keeping them around was starting to get expensive.

Marcus wanted to toss them out on their asses, after giving them a good beating, but didn't want to ruin any chances he might've had to make some more money with the record company down the line. "A'ight, let them go," he told his security people. "But they still gotta go, Tone. They pulled guns in my club and I can't have that."

"Fair enough," Tone agreed. "Let's go," he told Dolla and Wise.

"That nigga is lucky, because I was just about to get in his ass," Dolla boasted on wobbly legs.

"Shut yo' ass up," Devil shoved him forward.

Not wanting to miss her opportunity to come up, Claudette fell in step behind Wise and the others. She made it a few feet and realized that Rocky hadn't moved. She motioned for her to follow, but Rocky stood there, obviously conflicted. Claudette didn't have time to wait around for Rocky to figure out her moral dilemma so she abandoned her friend and got in where she fit in.

*

"What the fuck is wrong with you two niggas, B?" Don B. started right in on Dolla and Wise when they got back to the Big Dawg section.

"That wasn't on me, man. Dude started it and I was just finishing it," Dolla drunkenly threw some mock punches at the air.

"More like you were about to get finished," Devil pressed his thumb against the knot that had formed over Dolla's eye, causing him to flinch. "Y'all let that pretty little nigga wash the both of y'all up. I'm ashamed to have you flying these Big Dawg colors."

"Hold up, you mean to tell me one dude laced both y'all boots?" Don B. asked in disbelief. "Who the fuck did you pick a fight with, Black Dynamite?"

"They call him the Turk," Claudette blurted out. She wasn't sure why she'd spoken, other than the fact that she was determined to be noticed.

Don B. slid his sunglasses down and peered over them at Claudette. "I'm sorry, who the fuck are you and why are you speaking?"

"Oh, I'm sorry…" she stammered. "I'm Claudette. Dolla invited me to come over and hang out with y'all."

"Well if you wanna keep hanging out I suggest you keep your mouth closed unless one of us gives you something to put in it, smell me?" Don B. checked her. "Getting back to you two fuck-nuts," he turned back to Dolla and Wise. "You two were supposed to be recruiting the Turk, not volunteering to be punching bags for him. What the fuck is up with that?"

Wise deferred the question to Dolla with an accusatory look.

"Yo, on everything, I came at the nigga correct, Don. I tried to tell him how much sweeter his life could be if he was running with Big Dawg, but the nigga wasn't trying to hear me because he was in his feelings because his bitch chose me," Dolla lied, dragging Claudette into it.

Don B. looked her up and down from behind his shades. She wasn't much to look at, but she had a nice body. "So, you're the piece of pussy who started this fiasco?"

"Don't put that on me," Claudette snaked her neck. "Ain't nobody got no papers on me so I can't be held accountable for niggas who don't know how to act. I'm just trying to have a good time, if you know what I mean?"

"Yeah, I know exactly what you mean," Don B. smirked. He could smell the essence of ho all over the young broad.

"All that shit is irrelevant right now," Tone spoke up. "Marcus was cool about not pressing charges on these two for the gun in the club, but he says they gotta go."

"Nobody tells Big Dawg when it's time to go. We leave when we're good and ready. Luckily, for that square ass nigga, the Don is ready," Don B. said. "Round up a few bitches for the after-party and escort two of them to my chariot to keep me occupied on the ride back."

"Got you, Don," Dolla said confidently. "Let's go, baby. You're with us," he told Claudette. He reached out to take her hand, but to his surprise, she pulled away and moved closer to Don B. "Fuck is you doing?" he asked.

208

"It's like I said, daddy, ain't nobody got no papers on this," Claudette said coldly. She turned to Don B. "You got room in that chariot for one more?"

CHAPTER 23

It didn't take Shai very long to get bored with the scene at Shooters. It wasn't that their service wasn't excellent or they didn't have top choice girls, it's just that strip clubs weren't his thing. The only reason he'd even agreed to hold the party there was because Honey wanted it.

"I still don't see why we had to leave so early," Honey was complaining. She wasn't pleased with having to end her birthday celebration early.

Shai didn't care for strip clubs, but his wife loved them, probably because she had spent most of her teen and young adult years dancing in them. Shai had retired her from the pole years ago, but she still found her way back whenever time allowed. She said she liked to blow money in the strip club because she knew how hard the girls had it and it was her way of giving back, but Shai sometimes wondered if it was deeper than that. In her day, Honey had been a star, and sometimes he felt like she had trouble adjusting to life as a housewife.

"Shit is getting crazy in there, sis, and it ain't a good idea to wait around for it to get crazier," Swann explained. He was walking closely behind Honey and Shai, trying to help his date stay on her feet. The girl had consumed way too much alcohol way too soon.

"You're just overreacting because of what happened with that guy at Don B's table," Honey told him.

"It ain't about him, Honey; it's about not waiting around for the other shoe to drop," Swann said. No sooner than the words left his mouth, they heard a gunshot coming from a few blocks away. Instinctively, Angelo, Baby Doc, and the goons closed ranks around Shai and Honey.

"Where the fuck is this nigga with the car?" Shai asked, looking up and down the alley. They'd sent Holiday to tell Andrew to bring the car around nearly twenty-minutes prior but there was no sign of the car or Holiday. Just then, the latter came out of the back door they'd just exited.

"What are you doing back inside when I sent you to get the car?" Swann asked.

"I did go and look for Andrew, but couldn't find him. The Hummer is still out front, but I don't know where Andrew is. I was coming back inside to tell you, but y'all had already cut out the back," Holiday explained.

"Then why didn't you bring the car personally?" Swann asked angrily. His gut had been doing flip-flops since his confrontation with Trap and he had a bad feeling.

"Because I don't have the fucking key!" Holiday shot back.

"Can you guys please stop yelling? It's making my head hurt," Swann's date slurred.

"Shut yo' drunk ass up," Swann snapped. He propped her against the wall.

"Don't even worry about it. I've got a spare key, so we can walk. I'm tired of standing in this damn alley like a cat burglar," Shai said.

"Not to question you big homie, but do you think that's a good idea?" Baby Doc asked. "The front of this place is packed with random people with random motives. Walking out into all that, even for a few seconds…" his words trailed off. "You got soldiers; let us do our job which is to protect the king."

"Spoken just like your dad," Angelo chuckled.

Shai was inclined to agree. Sometimes it was hard for him to see Baby Doc as more than a nerdy ass kid who was always in the house reading, and sometimes he forgot that the blood of gangsters ran through his veins, same as he did. Times like that, he was reminded. Shai tossed Baby Doc the spare Hummer keys. "Don't crash my shit."

"I got you, big homie," Baby Doc said gleefully and ran off down the alley.

"Ironic that for as hard as his dad worked to keep him outta this shit, he's a natural fit for it," Angelo thought out loud.

"Some people are just born to break the law," Shai said, thinking how his father had also tried to keep him away from the criminal side of his business. Poppa Clark never wanted this for his youngest son, but fate handed him the reins.

After a few minutes, they saw the headlights of the Hummer at the opposite end of the alley. Baby Doc, being short, was almost invisible behind the wheel of the big truck. He struggled a bit controlling it, but managed to reach them without crashing. "Told you I had this," Baby Doc jumped down from the driver's side, smiling proudly.

"Ladies first," Angelo held the back door open while Shai helped Honey inside before moving to the side so Swann's date could climb in. She was so drunk that her foot missed the step and she fell halfway in, with her skirt rising up for all to see her ass.

"Drunk ass bitch," Swann said in an irritated tone. He tried to help her up, but she jerked away.

"Get your damn hands off me. I can manage," the woman said belligerently. She tried to climb into the vehicle but slipped again, this time falling backward. Had Shai not caught her, she'd have fell flat on her ass.

"Easy, lil' mama," Shai said, helping the girl stand up straight.

"Shai, you're such a gentleman. Your asshole friend should take some pointers from you," she slurred. She threw her arms around Shai's neck, almost knocking them both off balance. Shai had just pried her arms loose from his neck to put a little distance between them when her head exploded, covering his suit with her brains.

"It's a hit!" Swann yelled, drawing his pistol.

Shai stood there in wide-eyed shock, looking down at the headless corpse at his feet. He wanted to turn away, but he couldn't. Baby Doc tackled him inside the open back door a split second before a second bullet struck the door, shattering the window.

"Stay down," Baby Doc covered Shai with his body.

Swann was down in a crouch, gun raised and ready, as he swept the darkness at the end of the alley for the shooter. Near the mouth of the alley, under the flickering light of a restaurant that had closed for the day, he spotted a hooded man. "I got him," Swann said, bolting down the alley, gun spitting fire at their enemy.

"Fuck y'all standing around for? Go with him!" Angelo barked at the goons, while jumping behind the wheel of the Hummer. Without waiting for the back door to close, Angelo peeled out.

"Swann," Shai said when he was finally able to find his voice. "We can't leave him."

"Swann can take care of himself. We gotta get you and Honey out of here," Angelo said, barreling down the alley. He didn't slow down until they were safely out of the alley and away from the club.

Honey was curled up in the corner, babbling incoherently as Baby Doc tried to comfort her to no avail. Shai sat there, still covered in blood looking straight ahead. He'd had some close calls before, but never that close. Men tried to kill Shai all the time, it came with the territory, but this time was different, his wife was with him. If the assassin made his play only a few seconds earlier, Shai's kids would've been orphans all because of the legacy he had inherited.

"This was a set up," Baby Doc said to no one in particular.

Angelo looked up at him through the rearview mirror. "What you back there going on about?"

"We were set up," Baby Doc said.

"Maybe, maybe not. Swann leaked the info to the blogs so everybody knew where we'd be tonight. This could've been just some random ass nigga trying to get his stripes," Angelo reasoned.

Baby Doc frowned at the suggestion. "A random nigga might've been able to guess we'd exit using the back door, but they'd have no way to know what time. We cut out early, remember?"

214

"So you suggesting one of ours was in on this?" Shai asked Baby Doc.

Baby Doc shrugged. "Big homie, I don't have enough clout in the organization to suggest anything, but what I know is that if you dangle enough money in front of a cat anything can happen. My dad sitting up in prison over some bullshit is proof of that."

"Baby Doc, go ahead somewhere with those conspiracy theories," Angelo scolded him.

"No, he may be onto something. Who was unaccounted for when we left?" Shai asked.

Angelo thought on it for a few seconds. "Only Andrew and Holiday's boy, Turk."

"Nah, Turk is solid. He wouldn't have been in on it," Baby Doc said in his defense.

"Wasn't it you who just said that if you dangle enough money in front of a cat anything could happen?" Shai reminded him.

Baby Doc was silent.

"Angie, once we make sure my wife is home safely, call a meeting. I want everybody who went conveniently missing standing in front of me by sun up, or laying at my feet by sun down."

CHAPTER 24

Marcus was beyond thrilled when the night started winding down at Shooters. It was one of those nights were Marcus hated being the boss because he was kept running to handle this or that the whole time. The club was still jumping, but the heavyweights had gone, and their troubles along with them. All told there had been a half dozen ass whippings issued by security, and a few quiet arrests made by off-duty cops Marcus kept on staff. Thankfully, the property damage had been kept to a minimum and nobody got killed…at least not yet.

While there was a break in the action Marcus decided to handle his business with Trap so he could be on his way. He found Trap and Moochie sitting at one of the tables in the corner. Trap was enjoying a drink while Moochie enjoyed the company of two of the dancers. She had ass cheeks in one hand and a fist full of singles in the other.

"Glad to see you guys are enjoying yourselves," Marcus said sarcastically.

"Yeah, you got a nice line up of bitches in here. They ain't Florida bitches, but they nice," Moochie said, never taking her eyes off the moon-sized ass shaking directly in front of her face.

"Trap, you about ready to handle business?" Marcus asked, wanting to get the transaction over with.

Trap spared a last glance at a stripper who had been trying to get his attention then back to Marcus. "Yeah, I got something I need to take care of and I'm already late," he got up. "Moochie, you ready to bounce, sis?"

216

NO SHADE: A Hood Rat Novel

"I'll catch up," Moochie told her brother before burying her face in the bosom of the girl straddling her lap.

Marcus gave a few last minute instructions to his staff before leaving Shooters with Trap. The crowd had thinned out considerably, but there were still a few people outside wanting to try their luck with getting in. Marcus told the doorman it was cool to open it up for the rest of the night. All the VIPs were gone, but the coins of the common folk spent just the same.

Trap had stashed the money in the trunk of the car, which the valet had taken to their private lot, which was two blocks away. When Marcus had taken over Shooters, it was his idea to rent the vacant lot and convert it. They charged half what the garage around the corner did and offered valet service, so he was undercutting the competition and reaping the benefits. They could've just had the valet bring the car around, but the less people who saw the exchange, the better. It was a short walk, and Marcus's car was also parked there, which made it convenient. After he got the money, he could jump in his whip and go home and let the managers close the club for the night.

Trap's truck had been parked near the back where the street light couldn't reach so they had the cover of darkness on their side.

"Marcus, thanks again for doing this for me. I know I put you in a bind, but I was desperate," Trap said sincerely. "These crackers wanna throw everything but the kitchen sink at me, bro."

"I know you're in a bad situation, Trap. It doesn't make me any less mad that you're putting this on me, but I understand your position. I'm gonna do this for you, Trap, but I need you to

217

understand what I'm putting on the line here. If you burn me, I stand to lose everything."

Trap gave Marcus a serious look. "Man dig these blues; I ain't shit, that's just a given, but I'm trying to be better. Marcus, I'm a career criminal holding onto a farfetched dream and that dream is the only thing keeping me from diving back into the streets headfirst. I ain't got much, but I worked for what little I got. I know what I stand to lose if I don't do the right thing, but I also know you stand to lose a whole lot more by helping me. I ain't got nobody, but you're about to have a wife and one day a family who are gonna need you, and I'd never intentionally come in the way of that. If it came down to it, I'd gladly eat this whole charge before I let it fuck up the life you're trying to build. I put that on my mama's soul."

When Trap spoke, there was the same conviction in his voice that was in Marcus's when he vowed to wash his hands of the streets. Trap was notorious for playing games and double dipping, but this time around, Marcus felt like he was sincere. He was tired and Marcus understood.

"We gonna stand out here talking all night or we gonna get that hundred grand out the trunk?" Marcus asked. It was his way of letting Trap know that he was with him.

Trap nodded, letting Marcus know he'd gotten the message. "I got it right here," he popped the trunk of his Porsche, and flipped up the panel that held the spare tire. On top of the doughnut was a black leather bowling ball bag. Trap pulled the bag out and handed it to Marcus. "It's all there, but you can count it if you want."

Marcus accepted the bag and tested the weight. "Nah, I'll count it when I get home. I'm ready to call it a night."

"Me too. I was supposed to meet shorty over an hour ago. I hope she ain't too pissed," Trap said, closing the trunk. When he and Marcus stepped from behind the truck, they noticed a woman standing there. It was the same woman who had escorted Trap to Marcus's office.

"Tammy?" Marcus almost didn't recognize her because she looked such a mess. She was wearing a pair of pajama pants, a bathrobe, and furry slippers that were so worn they looked like she had walked all the way from her house to Shooters in them. Her hair was askew and her eyes were red and swollen like she had been crying.

"I tried calling your phone, but you weren't answering," Tammy told him. "Can we talk?"

Marcus sighed. "Tammy, it's been a long night and I ain't got time for this shit. The email said it all, so there's nothing else for us to talk about."

"I've held you down during some dark times, and never asked for anything but some appreciation and I ain't even worth you firing me to my face. You got some fucking nerve, Marcus!" Tammy's eyes flashed hurt.

Marcus wasn't sure if it was the fact that he was hungry, tired, or just fed up that made him choose that moment to explode, but one thing was for certain; he was tired of Tammy's shit. "Okay, you want an explanation then I'll give you one! I told you that once that if that nut-ass shit you was on started to effect business that we was

219

parting ways, but from the way you continued to carry it, obviously you thought I was bullshitting and I had to show you different. Because of all that, here we stand…I'm short a manager and you're unemployed. What the fuck else do you want me to tell you?"

"I want you to tell me you care!" Tammy shouted, before producing a .9mm from her robe and pointing it at Marcus. "Marcus, Marcus, Marcus…you just can't see all the sacrifices I've made in the name of trying to get you to love me. Jesus, I'm studying for my doctorate do you think that managing a strip club is the best that I could've done for extra income? I've devoted my life to that slum ass club because it represents a piece of the man I love!"

"Listen," Trap spoke up, "it's obvious that the two of you got some problems to work through that don't have a damn thing to do with me, so why don't I leave you lovebirds to it," Trap took a step, but froze when Tammy turned the gun on him.

"The hell it doesn't," Tammy sneered. "Me and Marcus were good until you showed up. I saw the devil in you the moment you walked into Shooters, and now you're trying to corrupt my Marcus!"

"Tammy, just be easy," Marcus said softly. "How about you put that pistol down and we talk about this like rational people."

Tammy shook her head violently. "Nigga, I'm out here in my pajamas and slippers! Do I seem rational to you? I'm so sick of men like you who think women are toys to be taken out of the box and played with whenever they feel like it and put back when they're done!" Her hand trembled with rage.

"Tammy, you don't want to do this," Marcus said nervously. He thought about going for the gun, but she was too far for him to make it without getting shot.

"I don't want to, but I have to. I'm sorry, Marcus, but if I can't have you then neither can that bitch."

There was a popping sound and Marcus instinctively closed his eyes. While he waited for the end, he thought about Billy and how she would take his death. All she wanted was to be his wife and he her husband, but because he couldn't keep his dick in his pants, they'd never have the chance to exchange vows, all because he couldn't keep his dick in his pants.

After a few seconds, Marcus realized that he was still on his feet. He slowly opened his eyes, expecting to see Tammy still standing there with the .9mm pointed at him, but instead she was lying on the ground. Her eyes were open, but she saw nothing. Beneath her head, blood began to pool on the ground, from the slug that had entered it. Standing over her was Moochie, holding a smoking .22.

"Why is it that every time I leave you alone somebody tries to kill you, lil' bro?" Moochie asked, tucking the pistol.

"This one wasn't on me," Trap cut his eyes at Marcus.

"You killed her," Marcus said in disbelief. He was staring at Tammy's corpse but his brain was having trouble processing what he was seeing.

"Would you rather I let her shoot you?" Moochie asked sarcastically.

"We gotta clean this shit up," Trap bolted back to his truck. He retrieved the plastic cover used to keep dirty tires from soiling the trunk's upholstery. "You got cameras in this lot?" he asked, while spreading the plastic on the floor next to the body.

"Yeah, they stream to the security system in my office," Marcus said.

"Good, go get the tape then get back here so you can help us dispose of this body," Trap told him.

"Dispose of the body? Nigga we should call the police. This was a clear case of self-defense," Marcus said.

Trap stopped what he was doing and looked up at Marcus. "Are you drunk or just stupid? We're in a parking lot with a corpse, two unregistered guns, and a hundred grand in drug money. You think anybody is gonna believe that shit? Nigga, I ain't going to prison for you or nobody else, so you best get with the program before the program gets with you," he said coldly.

"I'll be back in a minute with the tape," Marcus reluctantly agreed, and headed back to the club. The whole time he was walking all he could think about was Shooter's warning about dealing with Trap. Money laundering was one thing, but being an accessory to a murder was a whole different animal. Whether Marcus wanted to be or not, he was all in now, he just hoped that he could make his way out.

NO SHADE: A Hood Rat Novel

CHAPTER 25

It was almost dawn by the time Turk was released from custody. The club didn't press charges, so after processing him to make sure he didn't have any outstanding warrants Turk was given a desk appearance ticket with a future court date and released. When he came out of the precinct, he was surprised to find Rocky sitting on the steps waiting for him.

Rocky had managed to find out from one of the officers who'd arrested Turk which precinct he'd be taken to and walked the eight blocks to it. She felt bad and partially at fault for what had happened to Turk. If Claudette hadn't invited Dolla and Wise to the table then none of it would've happened. Because Rocky wasn't immediate family the desk Sergeant wouldn't give her any information, other than the fact that he had been brought to that precinct. With little other choice, Rocky waited and hoped.

"Didn't expect to see you here," Turk said.

"I didn't expect to be here," Rocky replied. "I kinda felt bad about you getting arrested because of us."

"I didn't get arrested because of you; I got arrested because home boy had a big ass mouth. I don't know you very well, but I'm a bit surprised by your taste in men. You didn't strike me as the type to fall in with scumbags."

"I don't, that was all on Claudette. She's a bit…"

"Loose?" Turk finished her sentence for her. "Yes, I picked up on that. In any event, thank you for coming to check on me, as you can see, I'm good," he made his way down the steps.

"Wait a second," Rocky went after him. "I come down here and spend half the night waiting to make sure you're okay and you're just gonna blow me off?"

Turk stopped short. "I said thank you, didn't I?"

"Look, you don't have to be a dick to me because of how Claudette carries herself. I'm not like that," Rocky told him.

"Rocky, I don't know what you're like, because we were interrupted before I had a chance to find out. What I do know is that I just spent the last few hours in jail for getting in the middle of something that had nothing to do with me. Chivalry is for suckers," Turk told her.

"So you're a sucker because you did what you thought was right? That makes you a good dude in my book."

Turk chuckled. "Shorty, I'm anything but good, trust me on that one."

"Why do you always do that? Talk down about yourself?" Rocky asked.

Turk shrugged. "Habit I guess."

"Well it's a habit you should consider breaking. If you don't think highly of yourself how do you expect anyone else to?"

"What are you psychoanalyzing me now?" Turk asked defensively.

"No, I'm just making an observation. No need to get so pissy about it. Gosh, you pretty-boys can be so sensitive."

Turk laughed. "You got jokes."

"I gotta do something to make your sour ass smile."

"Mission accomplished, Ms. Raquel. Listen, I'm sorry for being such an asshole about all this. I should be grateful that you cared enough to check on me, especially because none of my so-called friends did," Turk said sincerely.

"Don't sweat it. Seems that neither of our friends lived up to that title tonight, so it's only right we look out for each other. Besides, I'm going to let you make it up to me on our next date."

Turk raised his eyebrow. "We didn't even make it through our first one and you're talking about a repeat?"

"Then I guess we'll just have to call it the Date Night Remix. Either way I'm not letting you worm your way out of it. After I walked all the way down here and sat on those hard ass steps for hours the least you can do is buy me dinner."

"It's a little early for dinner," Turk said looking at his watch. "How about we get some breakfast? I know a Halal diner on the east side that makes a pretty good omelet."

"Sounds good," Rocky slipped her arm around Turk's. "Lead the way."

Turk and Rocky walked arm-in-arm to the corner where they could flag a taxi. Coming in their direction was a homeless man pushing a cart full of flowers. "Flower for the lady?" the man asked, holding out a wilted looking rose.

"Man, don't nobody wanna buy no half-dead ass plant," Turk told him.

"Stop being so mean," Rocky pinched his arm playfully. "How much?"

"Ain't but a dollar," the homeless man told her.

Rocky looked at Turk.

"Okay, okay. Let me get five of them," Turk handed the man a twenty. "And I want my change too, nigga."

"Sho ya right, sho ya right," the man said happily. He collected six flowers from his cart and handed them to Rocky. "The extra one is for being so sweet."

"Thank you sir," Rocky smelled her flowers.

"My change," Turk reminded him.

"My fault," the homeless man dug in his pocket and came out with a zip lock bag full of loose change.

"You know what, never mind," Turk told him.

"Bless your heart," the man smiled showing off the hint of gold in his mouth before continuing on his way.

"See, there's hope for you after all," Rocky nestled closer to Turk. Their moment was interrupted when a black SUV pulled to a screeching halt beside them. Turk instinctively stepped between Rocky and whatever potential danger may have loomed in the vehicle. He didn't have a weapon and hoped to God that he wouldn't need one. His only hope was that if whoever it was happened to be on some bullshit they wouldn't be dumb enough to try and gun him down in the shadow of a police precinct. He held his breath as one of the windows rolled down. Behind it, he saw Holiday's scowling face.

"Nigga, you scared the shit out of me!" Turk barked.

"Get in the car," Holiday told him, completely ignoring Turk's outburst.

NO SHADE: A Hood Rat Novel

Turk could tell by Holiday's facial expression that something was wrong. "Everything good, Holiday?"

Holiday looked past Turk and noticed Rocky standing there. He shook his head in disapproval. "No, but it will be. Now ditch the bitch and let's go." He said the word bitch loud enough for Rocky to hear him.

Turk wanted to check Holiday, but realized it wasn't the time or place. Something serious was obviously going on and he didn't want to antagonize the situation. "A'ight, give me a second," he told Holiday and walked over to speak with Rocky. "Sorry, but I'm going to have to take a raincheck on breakfast."

"I understand. Duty calls. Put my number in your phone and call me later so I know you're good." She cast a dirty look at Holiday, who was staring daggers at them.

After the exchange of numbers, Turk dug in his pocket and pulled out some money. "Here, take this so you can jump in a cap," he held out five twenty-dollar bills.

"I told you, I'm not like Claudette," Rocky refused the money.

"Rocky, you said you walked here from the club so I know your pockets are a little light right now. Don't let your pride put blisters on them feet with you trying to walk back uptown," he shoved it into her open purse. "Don't look at it as me tricking to try and gain your affections, look at it as me being a good dude, as you say."

"Okay, but you have to let me pay you back," Rocky insisted.

"Oh, you will Ms. Raquel. Bank on that," Turk winked and slid into the back of the SUV. He held his thumb to his ear letting her know that he would call before the vehicle pulled off.

Rocky stood on the curb watching the taillights of the SUV before it disappeared into traffic, and reflecting on her night. Turk was a dangerous man, that much she could tell by the company he kept and the beating he'd put on Dolla and Wise, but he had a way about him that Rocky really dug. She wanted to get to know him better, and sincerely hoped that the night he got in the car with Holiday wouldn't be the last time she ever saw him.

*

Holiday didn't say too much on the ride uptown, but he didn't have to. His body language spoke volumes. Normally, he'd be cracking jokes, or at the very least cracking jokes about how he had fucked Claudette in the bathroom, but he was unusually quiet and seemed irritated. Turk tried to prod him to get an idea of what was going on, but all he would say is, "Shai needs to see you."

Turk wasn't sure what it was about, but if he had to guess, it'd be the fight at Shooters. Turk knew how Shai was when it came to his public image, and by getting into the brawl, it could've potentially damaged it. It had been a rough night for Turk and the last thing he needed was to get chewed out by his boss over something he'd honestly tried hard to avoid. It seemed like Shai was always in his feelings over small things when it came to Turk and to be honest, Turk was as sick of Shai as his boss was of him. He was tired of being a doormat and that would be the night he would give Shai a piece of his mind.

NO SHADE: A Hood Rat Novel

They pulled up in front of brownstone in Harlem and Holiday led the way upstairs to the third floor. Before Turk even reached the apartment, he could hear Shai behind the door going ballistic over something, likely him. When he walked into the apartment and saw Shai standing in the middle of the living room, yelling at his men, he knew it was bad, but he wouldn't realize how bad until he saw tears of rage welling up in the man's eyes.

"...My family," Shai was saying when Turk entered the room. "They violated in the worst possible way and all any of you can do is stand around and give me excuses about why I don't have the head of the shooter laying at my feet!"

"Turk is here," Holiday announced as if Shai couldn't see him standing there.

"And where the fuck were you when a nigga was trying to blow my head off in an alley?" Shai barked.

"Huh?" Turk asked, completely baffled by the question. He had no idea what was going on.

Shai stood directly in front of Turk and stared him down. "If you can huh you can hear. Don't play with me, boy. Tonight is not the night. Now where the fuck have you been for the last few hours?"

"I was in jail," Turk answered.

Shai looked to Holiday for confirmation. "It's true. I picked him up at the precinct. The police had him on a disorderly from the fight inside Shooters."

"Is anybody gonna tell me what's going?" Turk looked at the sea of morbid faces.

229

"Somebody tried to hit Shai outside Shooters," Swann finally told him.

Turk was stunned by the revelation. "Any idea who did it?"

"Right now, everybody is a suspect," Shai said in an accusatory tone. "There were only two people unaccounted for at the time of the assassination attempt, you and that fucking idiot Andrew."

"Well like I said, I was in jail, so you know it couldn't have been me," Turk said.

"I don't know shit!" Shai snapped. "For all I know, you getting conveniently locked up could've been a part of the plan so you'd have an alibi."

Turk took offense. "The Clarks have been good to me so why would I cross you?"

"The same reason any niggas goes off the rails, greed," Shai replied. "Maybe you're tired of being the low man on the totem pole and somebody put some big ideas in your head about stepping up."

"Shai, with all due respect, I know you're upset over what happened, but your anger and suspicions are misplaced. You need to calm down and think about this."

Shai grabbed Turk by the front of his shirt and pinned him against the wall. "Lil' nigga, who are you to tell me anything? I tell you, you don't tell me!"

Turk looked Shai squarely in the eye. "Shai, you are the king of kings with more wealth and power than most men could ever dream of. Me? I'm a street nigga who I ain't got much, but the one thing I do have which I place great value on is respect. I treat each and every man with respect and in return, all I ask is the same in return.

NO SHADE: A Hood Rat Novel

That being said; if you don't get your hands off me, I'm gonna have to ask you to step outside."

"C'mon, take it easy, Shai," Baby Doc placed a calming hand on Shai's shoulder. After a few tense seconds, Shai released Turk. "Turk is solid, he wouldn't cross us."

"You willing to bet your life on that, Baby Doc?" Shai asked seriously.

"Absolutely," Baby Doc said with confidence. Turk had come to Baby Doc's rescue on more than a few occasions when they were doing dirt in upstate New York, so he better than anyone could speak for his character.

"Glad to hear it, because now you'll share in the weight of what needs to be done and the consequences of what'll happen if it doesn't get done," Shai said seriously. He then turned to Turk. "For as long as I've known your troublesome ass you've always been out to prove how bad-ass you are, trying to outrun that big old shadow your daddy cast on you. Okay tough guy, you wanna prove you're a man who is fit to run in my circle then I have a task for you."

"Anything, Shai. Name it and it's done," Turk assured him.

"If you didn't do this then the only other suspect is Andrew. You track that fucker down and bring me his head. If you can't find him, bring me the heads of those closest to him," Shai ordered.

"Wait a second, Shai," Swann spoke up. "Now I can understand you wanting Andrew dead, but his family shouldn't be brought into this. They're civilians." Swann thought of Andrew's sister. She wasn't his main chick, but she was useful and losing her would hurt his side businesses.

"Well so is my wife, but that didn't stop the shooter from almost clipping her too," Shai shot back. "The rules go out the window on this one, Swann. It's personal."

"I understand, Shai. Well at least let me handle it so I can make sure it's done right," Swann offered.

"Nah, this one goes to the pups. It's time to see if they're ready to run with the wolves. Turk, if you really want to step out of your father's shadow and show me that you belong in this organization; you do this thing for me. You murder my enemies and your days as an outcast will be over. No more petty shit, you'll be a full Capo with your own street crew if you're successful. How does that sound?"

"It sounds like the stock in black dresses is about to go up." Turk rubbed his hands together in anticipation. All he ever wanted was to belong and now he would have the opportunity.

"That's what I like to see, a man who is enthusiastic about his work," Shai smirked. "Now you and Baby Doc get the fuck out of my sight. I don't wanna see either of you again unless you're dragging Andrew's body behind you."

*

On the other side of town:
Andrew awoke with a booming headache and a nagging urge for something he couldn't quite put his finger on. When he tried to sit up, his head bumped against something. That's when bits and pieces of what had happened to him starting coming back and he realized he was still in the trunk of a car with his wrists and ankles tied and

232

his mouth taped. He wasn't sure how long he had been in there, but judging by the fact his arms and legs had long ago gone numb and his bladder was full enough to burst, he reasoned it must've been a while.

Things were foggy, but the last thing he clearly remembered was standing outside the Hummer waiting for Shai and the others to come out of the club. A man with a beard had approached him and asked how to get to Ninth Avenue. When Andrew turned around to point him in the right direction, something sharp pricked his neck and the world started spinning. The next thing he knew, everything went black. He had tried to come back to consciousness several times, but each time he did his captor would stick him with something then it was back off to dream land. He wasn't sure what he had been drugged with, but it kept him sedated and his thoughts jumbled.

Outside the car trunk, he could hear what sounded like two people arguing. Their voices were muffled, so he couldn't tell what the argument was over. There was the unmistakable sound of a gunshot, followed by something slamming against the car. Andrew had no idea what was going on, but he knew he had to get the hell out of that trunk. He struggled but couldn't break the duct tape that secured his hands and ankles. In the middle of his struggling, the trunk came open and he was temporarily blinded by the overhead streetlight.

"Looks like that little heroin cocktail is starting to wear off again," a voice said. "I would give you another shot, but I don't wanna overdose you before you've had a chance to play your part.

233

K'WAN

You won't be in here too much longer, but in case you get lonely, I've brought you some company," the speaker said before dumping something heavy in the trunk beside Andrew.

When Andrew's vision finally cleared, he realized that what had been dumped in the trunk with him was a body. At first, Andrew didn't recognize him because his face was covered in blood, but then it dawned on him who it was and it only made his situation more confusing. The dead man who occupied the trunk with him was once his sister's steady boyfriend, Ron. Ron had come to Andrew a few weeks prior and started asking him a bunch of questions about his sister's fidelity. For some reason, Ron had gotten it in his head that Andrew's sister was cheating on him, and she was, but Andrew would never tell him that. He and Ron were cool, but Swann was putting money in his pockets. Ron had made it clear back then that if he found out his sister was cheating there would be severe consequences. If Andrew being in the trunk was a result of Ron making good on his threat, he could understand, but what baffled him was how the hell Ron ended up in the trunk too?

"From the look on your face I'd say you're plenty confused about all this, especially the part about you ended up in this here trunk," the man standing over the trunk patted the car. "I could let you continue to wonder what the hell is going on and how you play into it, but where's the fun in that?" He snatched the tape from Andrew's mouth.

"What's this all about?" Andrew croaked. Having his mouth taped for so long made it dry and his throat coarse.

NO SHADE: A Hood Rat Novel

"Redemption, what else?" the man said as if it should've been obvious. He leaned in and Andrew was finally able to get a good look at his captor's face. He was dark skinned with cornrows and eyes that had beheld things Andrew had only seen in his worst nightmares. On one side of his face, there were small burn marks, which started below his eye and trailed off into his shaggy beard. "You see, the bitch ass nigga lying next to you had been going all around town trying to find out who was laying pipe to his bitch. When I caught wind of it, I thought it my civic duty to give the poor love struck brother some direction. I'm sure I don't have to tell you how much it crushed him to learn that it was a nigga of Swann's stature that was knocking his broad off. He was mad as shit when he found out …mad enough to kill, but it took a bit of prodding to get him to finally buck," he poked the torso of the corpse with his index finger.

Andrew looked at the man as if he was insane because he had no idea what he was talking about.

"Oh, I forgot! Since you've been sleeping it off in the trunk, you missed out on all the fun. Your boys got themselves into a bit of a jam earlier. You should've seen the look on Shai's face when he thought the bullet that split ol' girl's wig was meant for him. That pompous little jackass thinks everything is about him. What's going to be even more priceless is what happens when he starts to put two and two together and fingers you as the shooter," he laughed maniacally.

The seriousness of Andrew's circumstances finally set in and a paralyzing chill ran through his body. "Wait a second, I didn't have anything to do with it!" he pleaded.

"True, but unfortunately you're the only logical suspect at this point. The only people who'll know the truth are the dead, the soon-to-be dead, and me. "

"This ain't right," Andrew broke down into tears as he thought about what lay ahead of him.

"No, it isn't right, but it's necessary. You should be proud though, Andrew. You're about to help me settle an old score," he laughed and brought the lid of the trunk down.

The last thing Andrew saw before he was one again engulfed by blackness was two rows of jagged gold teeth in the man's mouth.

PART IV

WEDDING BELLS & BULLET SHELLS

NO SHADE: A Hood Rat Novel

CHAPTER 26

After leaving Turk, Rocky took a taxi uptown and stopped at the corner store to get a sandwich. She was starving, but she was also tired. It had been an extremely long night, and she could barely keep her eyes open. Halfway through the sandwich Rocky ended up nodding off and woke up nearly choking on a soggy piece of hero bread. After her call with Turk, she showered, brushed her teeth, and tried to figure out what she was going to do that day. She didn't have to pick up her son until the next afternoon so she wanted to enjoy her last day of freedom.

As if fate was giving her a sign, she got a call from Turk. He was just hitting her up to let her know that he was good, but they ended up on the phone for nearly an hour, before agreeing to see each other again that night. Rocky was beyond relieved that her new friend had made it through the night unharmed. She might've been naïve, but she wasn't so foolish as not to know how dangerous the men were who Turk was dealing with. She didn't know Holiday outside of Claudette, but Shai Clark's name was ringing in the streets. He was bad news.

Now that Rocky had her plans for the evening mapped out, she needed to figure out what she was going to do for the day. She tried calling Claudette, but got no answer. She was probably off still doing only God knew what with Dolla and his cohorts. Rocky was disappointed in the way Claudette carried that whole situation. She'd always known Claudette was loose, but what she pulled at the club was downright thirsty. Seeing her for who she really was made

Rocky question her relationship with the girl. Claudette was cool, but Rocky didn't want her association with Claudette to give people the wrong idea about her. She was by no means an angel, but at least she had morals. After the night before, she couldn't say the same about Claudette.

Rocky had some change left over from the money Turk had given her so she decided to go out and score some weed. When she came out of the building, she found Boots talking to a portly, dark-skinned guy named Happy. Happy was an older dude from the neighborhood who had a thing for young girls. He would ply them with cash and liquor to lure them to his bedroom where they would satisfy his sick sexual fantasies. Rocky had heard through the grapevine that Happy had run through at least a dozen different females in the same projects, which explained why the same circle of women stayed in and out of the free clinic. As far as being lecherous went, Happy damn near had Dolla beat.

When Boots noticed Rocky behind her, she jumped as if she had just been caught doing something she had no business doing. If Rocky didn't know any better, she'd have sworn Boots' hand had just come out of Happy's pants.

"What you doing creeping up on people like that?" Boots asked.

"I wasn't creeping. You were obviously too preoccupied to notice me." Rocky spared a glance at Happy's open zipper.

"What's up new fish?" Happy greeted Rocky. It was chilly that morning but he was sweating like a pig.

"Not too much. What y'all up to?" Rocky asked.

"Enjoying a bit of refreshment," Happy hoisted the bottle of Cîroc that he had stashed under the bench. "Care for a taste?"

"No thanks. It's a little early to be drinking," Rocky said, looking at her watch. It wasn't even eleven-thirty.

"Baby girl, it's always Happy hour somewhere," Happy grinned, sipping from a large white foam cup.

"Hey Boots, I'm trying to smoke. Do you think you can call your friend from the other day?" Rocky asked.

"You ain't gotta spend ya money. I got what you need right here," Happy fished around in his pocket and came out with a fifty sack of weed. "We can get as high as you want."

"And what do you expect me to do in exchange for you lighting me up?" Rocky asked suspiciously. She knew there was always a catch with Happy.

"Nothing, just walk to the store and get some cigars to roll in," Happy said innocently.

"Okay, you wanna walk with me Boots?" Rocky asked.

Boots looked to Happy, who was watching her closely to see how she would answer. "Ah…I was in the middle of talking to Happy about something."

"I'll bet," Rocky rolled her eyes in disgust. "I'll be right back with the cigars," she started towards the avenue.

"Take your time!" Happy called after her.

*

239

Rocky went to the corner store and purchased two Dutch Master's and a bottle of water. She still had the cake-mouth from all the liquor she had consumed the night before and needed to hydrate. As she was walking back down the avenue, she noticed a taxi pull up to the curb near her building. Claudette climbed from the back of the cab looking a hot mess. Her hair was ruined and instead of the blouse she had left in, she was wearing a white t-shirt that looked three sizes too big.

"Looks like somebody had a rough night," Rocky walked up on Claudette. When she neared her, she noticed that there was a glassy look in her eyes and she appeared to be slightly disoriented. "Are you okay?"

"Yeah, I'm good," Claudette said. When she went to close the taxi door behind her, she winced in pain.

"So you gonna tell me about it, or leave me to guess why you look like you spent all night sleeping on the sidewalk?"

Claudette looked down at herself as if she was just noticing her disheveled appearance. "I ain't even got myself together yet and you're asking me a million and one questions. We partied, we drank, and we fucked…the end," she said sharply.

"Damn, why you acting like you got an attitude with me? If anything I should be cursing your ass out for leaving me while you went off with Dolla and his greasy ass crew," Rocky said.

"Trust me; you got the better end of that deal. You got any weed? I'm nauseous as shit and need to smoke to shake this hangover," Claudette said.

NO SHADE: A Hood Rat Novel

"I just came back from getting two Dutches. Happy and Boots are about to light me up," Rocky told her.

"That slimy muthafucka is back in the hood? I haven't seen him in a while. I heard he's been in and out of the nuthouse since Tionna got killed."

"Who's Tionna?" Rocky wasn't familiar with the name.

"A long and sad story. Let's go meet up with Happy before Boots gasses him to run off with her and the weed. You know that bitch is thirsty as hell. On the walk over you can tell me what happened after your sprung ass chased off after Turk," Claudette said playfully.

As they walked back to the building Rocky told Claudette the story of what had become of the Turk and how Holiday had swooped down on them, but Claudette was only half listening. She was too busy trying to piece together the last few hours of her own life. After they'd left the club, she rode in the limo with the Big Dawg crew back to one of Don B's cribs in Brooklyn where he was having a private after-party. When she got there it was on and popping. There was liquor, weed, and every other drug imaginable. Claudette was already drunk and high, but that didn't stop her from sipping from every bottle and hitting every blunt that came her way. She was trying to get her hooks in Don B., but got cock-blocked by a Puerto Rican chick with ass-shots, so that left her stuck with Dolla. He gave her something that he said was a Mollie and that's when things got fuzzy.

Claudette could remember Dolla kept trying to get her to fuck, and at first, she wasn't into him, but as the night wore on and the

241

higher she got, her resolve waivered. He couldn't have been much of a fuck because she passed out during their romp. As Claudette drifted in and out of consciousness, she could remember feeling multiple hands groping her and tugging at her clothes. She wasn't sure, if it was a dream or if it was really happening, but either way she was too gone to do much about it. There were flashes of different faces coming in and out of the room she had passed out in. One by one, the faces hovered over her, laughing and mocking Claudette. The last and cruelest of the faces she remembered seeing was Don B's. He said something to her, which Claudette couldn't understand right before she felt a sharp pain in her ass. After a while, Claudette became totally numb to what was going on and she blacked out. When she woke up, she was in the back of a taxi feeling like she just been body cavity searched and missing her underwear. If the unidentified substance dried in her hair and on her face was any indication of what had really happened to her, Claudette wasn't sure if she ever wanted to know the truth.

As they neared the benches, where Rocky had left Happy and Boots, they noticed some type of disturbance. Boots' baby daddy Bernie had popped up at some point and he was less than thrilled to find his lady with the larcenous Happy.

"So you fucking this nigga too?" they heard Bernie pressing Boots when they walked up.

"Bernie, we're just sitting here drinking. Why are you bugging?" Boots asked.

"Because you don't know how to keep your pussy to yourself!" Bernie shot back. "Do you know how fucking embarrassing it was for me to find out on live television that the kid I've been raising wasn't mine?"

"It was your idea to go on the show, so you can't blame me," Boots told him, as if it wasn't that big of a deal.

"She's got a point there," Happy interjected.

Bernie turned his rage on Happy. "You need to mind your business, homie. I'm about two seconds off your fat ass too. I told you to stay away from my baby moms."

"I ain't the one who you need to be telling to keep away," Happy told him.

Bernie looked from Happy to Boots. "What's this nigga trying to say, Boots? He trying to tell me you want him?" his voice was shaky with emotion.

"Bernie, you need to go ahead somewhere with that weirdo shit. I keep telling you I'm not fucking Happy or anybody else," Boots rolled her eyes.

"Well you gotta be fucking somebody because you ain't gave me no pussy in three weeks, and we both know you can't go more than a few days without getting dicked-down. Just keep it one hundred with me, Boots. If you're fucking this nigga then just tell me instead of having me feeling like I'm going crazy," Bernie pleaded.

Boots looked at Happy who just shrugged his shoulders. "Okay Bernie, since you wanna play it like this. Yeah, I'm fucking Happy! You satisfied now?"

Bernie looked like his heart had just been ripped out of his chest by the revelation. He had always suspected that his children's mother was creeping around on him, but he was never sure. To have it thrown in his face made it real. A lone tear ran down Bernie's cheek.

"Oh my fucking goodness. I can't believe you're out here crying. You're making yourself look real soft right now." Boots shook her head.

"Could we just talk about it, please?" Bernie asked, just above a whisper.

Boots seeing she had him in his feelings decided to twist the knife. "Bernie, ain't shit for us to talk about. It is what it is and it's gonna be what it's gonna be. I'll come get the kids in the morning and we'll all go stay with my mother."

"But Boots —"

"Are you deaf or retarded?" Boots cut him off. "You wanted the truth and now you have it, but your ass is still standing around like I'm speaking another language. I think you've embarrassed yourself enough for one day, Bernie. Just go home."

Bernie wanted to press the issue and demand that his lady talk to him, but he knew it would be pointless. Once Boots had made her mind up about something, it was almost impossible to change it. The thought of Boots and his kids not being in his life was too much to bear. Without them, he had nothing else to live for. With his head hung, and tears now flowing freely from his eyes, Bernie began slinking off to write his suicide note. That was when Happy dropped the straw that broke the camel's back.

"That nigga was way too tender for you anyway," Happy said to Boots loud enough for Bernie to hear. "You need a real man to raise them kids."

244

NO SHADE: A Hood Rat Novel

There is a little wall in the backs of our minds that separates the sane and insane. It's the thing that keeps us from engaging in irrational behavior, with the all-important pause, which allows us enough time to think before we react. When Happy threw his final insult, Bernie's wall came crashing down.

When Happy noticed Bernie coming back in their direction a broad smile spread across his lips, anticipating the chance to beat Bernie's ass. He had never particularly cared for Bernie, but he tolerated him for his own personal reasons. By keeping Bernie close, he could also stay close to Boots. Now that he didn't have Boots anymore, he was expendable. When he pounded Bernie out in front of his girl, it would only make him look like more of the man in Boots' eyes. He knew his last remark would push Bernie, but he had no idea how far until he saw the small gun in his hand.

By the time the first shot was fired, Happy had already pulled Boots in front of him to take the hit. The bullet struck her high in the chest. She looked up at Happy in disbelief at his cowardice, before her eyes glazed over and she slipped to the ground, leaving Happy exposed and at Bernie's mercy. Happy was a heavy man, but he moved as swift as the wind while Bernie was chasing him with that gun. Happy yelped as one of the bullets hit him in the ass and turned his sprint into a speedy limp. Bernie would've surely had him had Happy not flipped himself over the small black fence and made a break through the parking lot.

Bernie came back through the projects, eyes full of rage and hurt. The gun was now hanging at his side, but his finger lingered over the trigger. He looked at the terrified Rocky and Claudette with such hatred that for a minute they thought he was about to shoot them too. After a few tense seconds, his attention shifted to Boots.

"You see what you made me do?" Bernie barked at the non-responsive Boots. "All I wanted to do was love you and treat you like a woman should be treated, but that wasn't enough for you was it?" He began pacing back and forth. "It was supposed to be about me, you, and the kids, but instead you made it about you and every nigga with a few dollars and something to smoke!" He stopped his pacing and looked down at Boots. It was as if he was only just realizing what he had done. A wave of sobs racked Bernie's body. "It's all fucked up now...it's all fucked up!" He put the gun to his chin, and blew the top of his head off.

Rocky stood there in total shock. The way Bernie had fallen, his body landed next to Boots and aside from the blood, they looked like two sleeping lovers. Rocky tried to look away, but she couldn't. It just wasn't registering for her how a girl she was just speaking to five minutes earlier was now lying motionless at her feet. Rocky was so close that she thought she could smell the coppery tinge of their intermingling blood on the concrete. She had seen death in the newspapers and on the nightly news, but never up close and personal. It was a sight that would stick with her for the rest of her days.

NO SHADE: A Hood Rat Novel

CHAPTER 27

"Are you going to keep staring at that phone or make a call?" Baby Doc asked Turk. He was sitting in the passenger seat of the black Lexus Swann had reluctantly allowed them to borrow. He didn't want to loan the car out, but Shai had insisted. They had a lot of ground to cover and not a lot of time. Since Swann had indirectly made the mess, his car would be the sacrificial lamb to help the boys clean it up.

"Why you over there worried about what the fuck I'm doing, B.D?" Turk snapped.

"I was only fucking with you, nigga. Relax. Let me find out you over there stressing over that funny looking broad with the glasses," Baby Doc teased him.

"You know the Turk gets too much pussy to stress over a chick," Turk tried to downplay it. In truth, the fact he couldn't reach Rocky was bothering him. When he'd spoken to Rocky that morning they'd made plans to hang out later that night, but when he tried to call her back to confirm a time and pick up location, he got her voicemail. He'd tried her back three time since then and sent a text, but still no response. His ego was bruised because he felt like he and Rocky had made a connection and was genuinely interested in seeing where it would go, but obviously, the feeling wasn't as mutual as he'd thought.

"Homie, if she calls she calls. If she doesn't she doesn't. Right now, we need to focus on what we were sent to do, or a bitch not calling back will be the least of either of our concerns."

K'WAN

Turk and Baby Doc hadn't wasted any time hitting the streets in search of Andrew. They had put the word out to every criminal, low life, and drug misfit they knew that Shai was offering a reward for information about Andrew's whereabouts. Normally to earn favor with the Clarks people would've been falling over themselves to reveal Andrew's whereabouts, but much to all their surprise, no one had come forward with anything useful. It was as if Andrew had fallen off the face of the earth. The fact that they couldn't find him was good for Andrew, but bad for anyone he held dear. Shai had been clear in his instructions about how he wanted the situation handled, which is why Turk and Baby Doc found themselves staking out the building Andrew's sister lived in.

"So, do you think she'll know where he is?" Baby Doc asked.

"For her sake I hope so," Turk replied, running his thumb up and down the edge of the meat cleaver on his lap. He pressed his thumb against the tip of the blade causing a dab of blood to well up and drip down the blade's edge. As if he were performing a ritual, Turk gently smeared the blood along the side of the cleaver. He looked over at Baby Doc and there was an uneasy expression on his face. "Baby Doc, you don't have to roll with me on this one. I can handle it if you don't feel up to it."

"Nah, you know I'm down to ride with you," Baby Doc assured Turk, but there was something else behind his eyes. "It's just that...well, I'm down to murk this nigga Andrew because he's got it coming, but his sister ain't a part of this. I know Shai says we're supposed to put it on Andrew's people, but I'm thinking maybe we don't have to kill her. If she doesn't tell us where Andrew is, maybe we could just slap her around and put a good enough scare in her to get her to leave town. Nobody but us would know she's still alive."

"Yeah, we could go about it like that Baby Doc, but what do you think would happen if Shai ever found out? It'd look like we were in on it from the beginning and our lives wouldn't be worth shit…at least mine wouldn't. On the strength of your dad he might let you live, but I hold no illusions about what would happen to me. Make no mistake; I don't like this shit any more than you do, but it's gotta be done and I'd be rather be the one to do it and be rewarded than the one who fucks it up and has to take the weight for it."

Baby Doc didn't press it, but his face said he still wasn't comfortable with it and Turk couldn't blame him. Turk wasn't a killer like Swann, or even Holiday, but he was no virgin to taking a life. He was a survivor by any means necessary, even if it meant committing murder, but killing a woman was something different. He thought about how he felt when his mother had been taken from him and didn't look forward to inflicting that pain on someone else's child. His personal feelings didn't change the fact that she had to die and it would have to be by his hand. Turk understood that when he decided to devote his life to working for a man like Shai Clark there would come a time when he had to do something that totally went against what he believed, but he never realized it would come so soon.

"Is that her?" Baby Doc asked pointing across the street. There was an attractive brown-skinned woman, wearing an overcoat and carrying grocery bags in her hands headed towards the building they'd been staking out.

Turk squinted to get a good look at her face. He had met the woman once or twice with Swann so he would know her on sight. "Yeah, that's her."

"A'ight," Baby Doc cocked his gun. "Guess we better get to it," he reached for the door but Turk stopped him.

"Not so fast," Turk pointed across the street. A few seconds later, a young man of about thirteen joined her. His face and the woman's bore a very close resemblance, meaning they were related. He kissed her on the cheek before helping her into the building with her bags.

"She's got her kid with her. Maybe we should do this another time," Baby Doc suggested.

"No, we gotta do it now," Turk told him. "Now I can't make you do anything, Baby Doc, but I'm about to go upstairs and question this broad. Hopefully she can give me a line on Andrew and if not," he hoisted the cleaver. "She gets the horror show."

Baby Doc studied his friend's face. Though Turk was trying to be tough about it, he could tell he was conflicted. Baby Doc didn't like it, but he wouldn't abandon Turk. "Fuck it, I got your back, but we let the kid live, right?"

"Whatever helps you to sleep at night, Baby Doc," Turk got out of the car.

The two young men made hurried steps across the street, constantly scanning the street for signs of the police. In front of the building, there was a young man sitting on the steps, playing a hand held video game. He gave Baby Doc a curious look, but his eyes lingered on Turk. He seemed to take a special interest in the tattoo on his forearm.

"You the Baby Butcher?" the boy asked, much to Turk's surprise.

"Where'd you hear that name, kid?" Turk asked. The nickname was more a reminder of his sordid past than a compliment.

"None of your business if you ain't him," the smart mouthed boy capped back.

"Yeah, I'm the Baby Butcher."

The boy gave him a disbelieving look. "Prove it," he challenged.

"No problem," Turk grabbed the boy by the front of his shirt and yanked him off the stoop. As if by magic, his trusty cleaver appeared in his hand. He pressed the edge against the boy's neck just hard enough to let him know it was extremely sharp. "Now stop fucking around and tell where you heard that name before I show you how I got it!"

"Don't hurt me, man, I was only doing what he asked!" the boy blabbered.

"What who asked?" Turk shook the boy violently.

"A guy came around this morning and offered a hundred dollars to sit on the stoop and wait for somebody he called the Baby Butcher," the boy explained.

"And how the hell did you know it was me?" Turk asked.

"The tattoo," the boy pointed to the cleaver etched in the skin of Turk's forearm.

"And what were you supposed to do when I showed up?"

251

K'WAN

"Give you a message. The guy said to tell you that he can help you find what you're looking for," the boy told him.

Turk and Baby Doc exchanged glances. "You know where we can find the man who paid you to deliver the message?"

"Yeah, he said he would come around every day at about four to see if you received the message. He hangs out in there," the boy pointed across the street. About three doors down from where Turk had parked the Lexus there was a non-descript bar that was in such shambles you wouldn't even know it was open.

"Let's take a walk." Turk grabbed the boy by the back of his neck and ushered him forward.

The boy, with Turk's hand firmly braced around his neck, led the way into the bar. Baby Doc brought up the rear, with his pistol in his hand behind his back. The bar looked just as bad on the inside as it did the outside, and smelled twice as bad. It was as if instead of finding a bathroom the patrons simply pulled their dicks out and pissed wherever they felt. The spot was empty save for the bartender and two drunks at the bar. One of which was passed out on the bar, lying in a pool of his own drool. Sitting at the back of the bar at a single table, under one of the only functioning lights in the place, was a dark-skinned man who looked strangely familiar to Turk. From the way he was staring at Turk and Baby Doc, he knew without the boy having to say that he was the man who had given him the money and the message.

"Get your little ass home and stay off the stoop," Turk shoved the boy before starting towards the back of the bar.

NO SHADE: A Hood Rat Novel

The dark-skinned man's eyes stayed locked on Turk as he approached. He had both his hands laying palms down on the table, as if he was trying look non-threatening. There was a calm about him that said he was a man who knew he had the upper hand. Even when Baby Doc and Turk were standing menacingly over him, his facial expression didn't change.

"You know me from somewhere?" Turk glared down at him.

The man looked up at Turk with eyes so dark that they didn't even reflect the overhead light. "I didn't know that you had to know someone to offer them something they so desperately needed. From what I hear, you're a man in desperate need of something that only I can provide right about now, Turk, so you can spare me the mean mug."

"You think this shit is a game, homie?" Turk sneered.

"No, I think it's you about to cut your nose off to spite your face," the man said calmly.

Turk brought the cleaver down on the table, buried it in the wood between the man's hands. "I'll be cutting your fucking nose off if you don't stop bullshitting and tell me why you're looking for me and how you knew I'd be on this block!"

The man gave Turk an amused look. "Little boy, I been putting heads to bed since before you were big enough to cross the street by yourself. I ain't one who scares easily. I also ain't one to tolerate a whole lot of disrespect, especially from a nigga who didn't have the decency to threaten me with a gun," he looked down at the cleaver.

"He might not have a gun, but I got one." Baby Doc stepped up brandishing his pistol.

253

The man turned his attention to Baby Doc. "A hot head, just like your dad I see. I know the two of you are kind of uptight because time isn't on your side. Shai's given you a task and not a lot of time to do it. So instead of us going back and forth to see who's got the bigger dick, help me to help you by listening to my proposition."

After a few moments of silent debate, Turk gave Baby Doc the signal to stand down. "Okay," he turned back to the man at the table. "Okay, what's this about?"

Seeing that Turk obviously wasn't going to sit down the man decided to get to it. "I hear that Shai Clark is offering a reward for the whereabouts of a dude named Andrew."

"You heard correctly," Turk told him. "I'm assuming you've got a line on him."

"I wouldn't be sitting here if I didn't," the man told him.

"And how is it that you knew we'd be here?" Baby Doc asked.

"That was more about me knowing Shai's habits than yours. When you boys combed the streets and couldn't find Andrew the next logical move would've been for Shai to send you at his people. I figured if I hung around his sister's building long enough some of Shai's boys would pop up."

"But how did you know it would be me?" Turk wanted to know.

"Because the streets talk, and I'm always listening," the man said. "The underworld is buzzing about Swann's new protégé, the bastard seed of Ahmad Kaplan," he pulled the cleaver from the table and examined it. "They say you've got your father's skill, but haven't quite mastered his technique. Is this true?"

"Point me at that a snake muthafucka Andrew and you'll find out." Turk relieved him of the cleaver.

"Not so fast. I have a few conditions before I agree to show you my goodies," the man said slyly.

Turk motioned for him to continue.

"You boys come back here at midnight and I'll show you where Andrew has been held up, but when it comes time to get paid, Shai has to hand me the money personally," the man told them.

"Why does it matter who gives you the money as long as you get paid?" Baby Doc asked.

"Let's just say that I've been following his career since he took over the family business. The Clarks have always been my heroes and it'd be an honor to meet the reigning king of New York."

"No disrespect, but Shai don't sit with soldiers," Baby Doc told him.

The man looked at Baby Doc. "Get this straight, Junior, I ain't no soldier. I'm a muthafucking general. Those are my terms, take them, or leave them."

Turk looked at Baby Doc, whose face said he clearly wasn't comfortable with the arrangement. Truth be told, neither was Turk, but they were running out of options and time. "I'll speak to Shai and get back to you with an answer. How do I reach you?"

"By meeting me here at midnight," the man replied.

"Cool," Turk turned to leave, but stopped short. "It just occurred to me that I never got your name."

"Names only complicate things, but if you need to call me something…call me, G," the man cracked a hint of a smile and Turk could've sworn he saw a glint of gold in his mouth.

CHAPTER 28

Billy noticed that Marcus had started acting stranger than usual. Her first clue that something was off was when he came in from the birthday party at Shooters wearing a different outfit than the one he had left in. When she asked him about it, he gave her some lame ass excuse about having to help break a fight up and getting blood on his shirt. That would've been acceptable if he hadn't also changed his pants too. Even more peculiar, was that he stunk of what smelled like gasoline.

Billy left the issue of the outfit alone and asked him about the party, to which he gave a very dry, "Everything went cool." Marcus had been so hyped that leading up to the party it was all he could talk about and now he didn't want to discuss it. Something was definitely afoot.

She waited until Marcus went to get in the shower and headed straight for his cell phone. Marcus had a lock on his phone, but unbeknownst to him, Billy had cracked his code months ago. She trusted Marcus and never felt the need to snoop in his phone, but she needed some insight as to what was going on.

She started at the most obvious place, his text messages. She was surprised to find them completely erased. Even the conversation she and him had been having back and forth had been deleted. If Marcus wasn't up to anything then why delete all his messages? When she checked his calls nothing seemed out of the ordinary, but she did come across a Florida number that Marcus had saved in his phone as Bad News. Billy was curious about the number so she decided to call it from her cell phone. To her surprise, a woman picked up. "Sorry…wrong number," she said and ended the call.

Marcus had come out of the bathroom mere seconds after she had returned the phone to his pant's pocket. "What're you doing?" he asked, noticing her hovering near his discarded clothes.

"I was picking up after your messy behind," Billy picked up his pants as if she was in the process of putting them in the laundry hamper.

"I got it," Marcus snatched the pants away from her so hard that he almost broke one of Billy's nails.

"Damn, what the hell is your problem?" Billy asked with an attitude.

"I don't have a problem, so stop trying to create one," Marcus huffed. He began emptying his pockets, tossing his money, keys, and wallet on the nightstand but kept his phone in his hand.

"Look nigga; don't come in here trying to get on me because you had a bad night at work. You know I'm not the one," Billy told him.

Marcus sighed. "Baby, I'm sorry if I seem a bit snippy, but it was a rough night."

"I figured that because you came in later than usual. When I got up to use the bathroom at about 8:30 am you still weren't home." It was more than an observation than an accusation.

"That's because the party turned out to be more work than I expected. Between Shai's crew and them rapping niggas I was ready to pull my hair out."

NO SHADE: A Hood Rat Novel

"Well it was you who wanted to be the toast of the town by hosting this event," Billy reminded him.

"And I was. We made so much money that Bear and them were still helping count it when I left," Marcus half lied. It was true that they had made a huge profit, but he hadn't stuck around to count it. He left that task to the night managers and entrusted Bear to oversee it to make sure nothing came up short.

Billy found that odd. "You never leave before all the money is counted."

"I know, but I was tired. Like it said, it was a long night. All I wanna do is sleep," Marcus threw himself across the bed.

"So I take it that because you're so tired you won't be coming with me to pick up the wedding souvenir packages?" Billy asked.

Marcus popped his head up. "Can't we do it another day?"

"Marcus, the wedding rehearsal and dinner is tomorrow and we're getting married the next day. There won't be time to pick them up."

"A'ight then can you just take care of it?"

"Sure, why not? I've been doing everything else. For all this I might as well be marrying myself because there hasn't been a lot of involvement on your part."

Marcus sat up. "What the fuck is that supposed to mean?"

"It means, just what I said. This is our wedding not mine and I'm going to need you to get more involved," Billy told him.

"I am involved. I'm gonna show up aren't I?"

Billy grabbed a stick of deodorant off the dresser and threw it at him. "Don't be a dick, Marcus. I'm showing up too so don't act like

259

you're doing me no favors. It was your idea to rush and get married, but I can't get you to pitch in on shit."

Marcus was tired and irritated so he lashed out. "I'm paying for the whole damn thing! How much more pitching in do you need?" No sooner than the words left his mouth, he regretted them.

"Oh, so that's what this is all about, money?"

"Billy, I didn't mean it like that," Marcus said apologetically.

"Yes-the-fuck you did. I offered to help pay for it, but you told me you had it so I didn't stress it. Had I known that you were going to spend the money just to throw it back in my face then I would've never let you shoulder the whole load. I know better now, so when I get my income tax money I'll pay your petty ass back for half of everything you spent." The whole time Billy had to fight to keep her voice from trembling. Marcus had really hurt her feelings.

"Billy, let me holla at you for a minute," Marcus reached for her, but Billy jerked away.

"Fuck you, Marcus," she snapped. She was about to say something else when she heard the doorbell ring. She'd nearly forgotten that she'd invited Reese and Yoshi over. "This conversation isn't over by a long shot," she told him and stormed out of the bedroom.

Marcus breathed a sigh of relief when Billy left the room to get the door. He knew she was gearing up for a drag out argument and truth be told; she was well within her rights. He knew he was wrong for what he had said to Billy. The wedding was putting a great deal of strain on his pockets, but everything else going on was putting a strain on his sanity. He sat on the edge of the bed and placed his head in his hands. Marcus was already having a hard time dealing with the things going on around him and Trap making him an accessory to murder didn't make things any easier. He had always known that Trap was cold-hearted, but he hadn't realized how cold until he was forced to help him and Moochie get rid of Tammy's body.

*

After getting Tammy's corpse into Trap's trunk, Marcus jumped in his car and followed the Porsche to what was to be Tammy's final resting place. They rode north on the I-95 and pulled off on a country road near Waterbury, and followed it to a wooded area about three miles out. Moochie pulled Tammy's body out and slung her over her shoulder like she was a sack of laundry and led them deeper into the woods.

"Everything is going to be gravy," Trap assured Marcus as they hiked out into the middle of nowhere. Marcus wanted to believe him, but found it hard considering Trap was carrying a can of gasoline and a long fire axe.

They stopped in a thicket of woods, where Moochie dropped Tammy's body to the dirt. "I guess this is as good a spot as any," she dusted her hands off.

"So what now, do we bury her?" Marcus asked looking around nervously. It was completely dark save for the beam of light coming from Moochie's cell phone flashlight.

261

"Nah, that ain't nothing but a trail of breadcrumbs. In Florida, we usually let the gators take care of the evidence, but since y'all short on predators 'round these parts we gotta improvise," Trap held the axe out for Marcus.

"What am I supposed to do with that?" Marcus asked.

"Since you baked this cake," Trap motioned towards Tammy, "only right you get the first slice. No pun intended."

"Trap, I was down to ride out here with you to dump the body, but dismemberment falls outside my skill set," Marcus told him.

"Then you better look at this as on the job training," Trap shoved the axe into Marcus's chest. "I'm not asking."

"Blood on us…Blood on you," Moochie added.

Marcus looked back and forth between Moochie and Trap, who was waiting for him to make a decision. He knew without question that if he didn't choose wisely, he'd likely share in Tammy's fate. Trap was his friend, but he was also a killer backed into a corner. "Fuck it." Marcus took the hatchet and went to stand over Tammy's body. His hands were sweating so bad that he had trouble getting a good grip on the fire axe. Marcus resisted the urge to look down at Tammy's body and raised the axe.

"It's just like golf, swing with your hips!" Moochie called out.

Marcus could hear Moochie and Trap behind him laughing. To them this was a joke, but for Marcus he was about to add a black mark to his soul that he'd never be able to wash off and he'd brought it all on himself. Tammy was a good girl, but extremely fragile, and Marcus had broken her in the name of a cheap thrill. She deserved help, not being left in some unmarked stretch of woods for the

animals and worms to pick over. Marcus might not have done right
by her in life, but he would play no part in further disrespecting her
in death. "I can't do it," he tossed the axe down.

"Fuck you mean?" Moochie got in Marcus's face. "This bitch's
death is on you, and you're gonna touch some dirt one way or
another." The look on her face said she was ready to go all the way,
but the look Marcus shot back said he was ready to take the ride.

"Yeah, her death is on me and I gotta live with that. But hacking
her up like a side of beef," Marcus shook his head, "I ain't with it. So
do what you gotta do, Moochie," he stepped back and spread his
arms.

Moochie looked to Trap to see how he wanted to play it. Trap
weighed it for a few moments before giving her the signal to back
off.

Trap approached Marcus with his hands folded behind his back
and looked him squarely in the eyes. "I know I ain't gotta tell you
how bad this can end up for all of us if it ever comes back."

"Trap, you know me better than that. If it ever comes back it
won't be because of anything I said," Marcus assured him.

"Fair enough," Trap nodded. He scooped the fire axe from the
ground and spun it around in his hand to get familiar with the
weight. He looked from Tammy's lifeless body to his sister, who was
staring at Marcus in disgust. "Everything ain't for everybody," he
shrugged before bringing the axe blade down across Tammy's neck.

After Trap cut Tammy's body into pieces, Moochie poured a
generous amount of gasoline onto the remains and set the body on
fire. Marcus was made to sit out in that field for hours while the

263

remains of his mistress were charred to a crisp, then stomped to pulp, and then burned again. They'd kept Tammy's severed head along with her hands and feet in a separate garbage bag, which was filled with bricks and tossed into the river. If the police happened upon whatever remained of Tammy, they still wouldn't be able to identify her.

The whole ride back to New York Trap and Moochie carried on as if nothing had ever happened, but Marcus was numb. He was still in shock over what he'd just participated in. Marcus had done some heinous things in his life, but Tammy trumped them all. It would be a long time, if ever, before he would fully recover from that. They drove Marcus to the parking lot near Shooters so he could pick up his car and that was where the accomplices would part company. Before leaving, Trap had reminded Marcus never to speak of what had happened, but he didn't need to. Even if he wanted to, there was no way Marcus would ever be able to put into words the horrors he had witnessed. Trap had successfully dragged him to the very bowels of hell and shown him the Devil's face.

*

Marcus's phone ringing brought him back from the dark place. He looked at the caller ID screen and saw the words Bad News flash across the screen. He ignored the call. A few seconds later, the phone rang again from the same number. Marcus reasoned if he didn't answer, that they would keep blowing his phone up until he did.

"What you want now, Trap?" Marcus answered in a hostile voice.

"Rise and shine," Trap sang on the other end of the phone. "You know the early bird gets the worm."

"Fuck is you talking about? I ain't even been to sleep yet!"

"Don't change the fact that it's a new day and new days mean new opportunities. Now get up and out, I need to holla at you."

Marcus sighed. "Can't it wait?"

"No, it can't. I need to get with you about something ASAP. It's important," Trap told him.

"Okay, give me an hour or so. I'll meet you at Shooters."

"No need to go through the trouble. I'm outside your house," Trap informed him.

This bit of news shocked Marcus. "How do you know where I live?"

"Marcus you know better than to ask questions you really don't want the answers to. Now bring your ass on before I start leaning on this horn and make your wife mad," Trap joked and hung up.

*

"Wait a damn second," Billy shouted as she moved to answer the door. One of her friends thought it would be funny to keep hitting the bell, not knowing that Billy was in already in war mode. She snatched the door open and found Reese on the other side by herself. "Why the fuck are you ringing my bell like you don't have any sense?"

"Well hello to you too, sour ass," Reese came inside.

"How did you manage to get upstairs without security announcing you?" Billy asked.

Reese waved her off. "Girl, you know the security guard is sweet on me. Why are you so damn bitter this morning?"

"Man trouble," Billy said and flopped on the couch.

"If only I were lucky enough to have those kinds of problems." Reese sat next to her.

"Well you can take this petty ass nigga with you when you go," Billy fumed. "Check what he did." Billy went on to give Reese the short version of their argument, omitting the part about the money. She knew she could tell Reese anything without fear of judgment, but some things were best kept between her and her fiancé.

"Pay him no mind; it's just pre-wedding day jitters," Reese said.

"If he keeps talking slick there won't be no damn wedding. And where the hell is Yoshi? I thought y'all were coming together?"

"She called me earlier and said she would meet me here. She had to make a move first," Reese told her.

"Probably means she's caught up with that nigga. What do you know about her new little friend?" Billy asked.

Reese shrugged. "You know she ain't gonna tell me too much about who she's fucking."

"You're right about that," Billy said, remembering the misunderstanding over Gary. "Well she needs to hurry up. I wanna get out of here before I end up killing Marcus."

As soon as she said his name, Marcus came out of the bedroom. He was fully dressed and had his car keys in his hand.

NO SHADE: A Hood Rat Novel

Billy gave him a stink look. "I thought you were too tired to go out today?"

"I gotta take care of something right quick," Marcus told her.

"Like what?" Billy wanted to know.

He gave her a look. "Something, that's all."

"Hey Marcus," Reese spoke.

"What up, Reese?"

"Not too much. Is everything okay at the club? I heard they were shooting last night."

Marcus's face turned white as a ghost at the mention of a shooting. Did Reese know what he had done? If so, who else could've potentially placed him at the scene of the crime?

"Shooting? Marcus you didn't tell me anything about a shooting." Billy looked to him for an answer.

"I...uh..." he stuttered.

"Yeah, I heard some niggas tried to get at Shai Clark and his people when they were leaving," Reese elaborated.

"Oh that," Marcus breathed a sigh of relief. "I was gone by then but Bear told me about it. The police are looking into it," Marcus lied. He was relieved that his dirty deed hadn't gotten out, but someone having tried to off Shai at his club could present a problem. Though he nor his people were behind it, the fact that it happened at his club, where he was supposed to ensure the safety of his guests, could've looked bad on him. The last thing he wanted was people feeling like Shooters was an unsafe environment, or worse, Shai holding him accountable. It was a problem that he would have to address later. Right then, he had to get Trap the hell away from his building before Billy spotted him. "I gotta go. I'll be back in a few to finish our talk," he told Billy. He tried to kiss her on the lips but she turned her face away, and it landed on her cheek. "Whatever, man."

When Marcus went to slip on his coat, Billy noticed a gun peeking out the back of his pants. "What's that all about?"

Marcus adjusted his shirt. "Nothing, babe."

"Marcus, is everything okay?" she asked in a concerned tone. She knew Marcus well enough to pick up on when something was wrong.

"Yes, love. We'll finish our talk when I get back. I promise," Marcus told her and left.

"Is everything okay?" Reese asked noticing the worried look on Billy's face.

"I don't know, but I plan to find out." Billy walked over to the living room window, which overlooked the parking lot below. She saw Marcus come out of the building, but instead of getting into his car, he climbed into the passenger side of a blue Porsche truck. Something about the vehicle nagged at her then Billy realized it was the same make, model, and color as the one she had seen Yoshi getting out of. It could've been a coincidence, but Billy's gut told her that it wasn't. Something was going on and she was determined to find out what. She rushed back into the living room and grabbed her car keys from the table. "You feel like taking a ride?" she asked Reese.

"I thought we were waiting on Yoshi?" Reese was confused.

"We can call her on the way and have her meet us," Billy said, getting her purse and her gun.

"Billy, where are we going?" Reese followed her to the door.

"I won't know until we get there. Now bring your ass on."

CHAPTER 29

Marcus came out of his building wearing a scowl. It was bad enough that Trap had him caught up in a bunch of bullshit, but now he had violated by popping up at Marcus's house unannounced. Where Marcus and his lady lay their heads was sacred ground and he didn't take kindly to it being desecrated by the pop up visit.

Trap was sitting behind the wheel while Moochie occupied the seat in the back, which was unusual. Moochie usually did the driving because Trap was always drunk or high. There was something about the way that she was glaring at Marcus through the rear window that unnerved him.

"What the fuck is this all about?" Marcus asked, keeping a safe distance from the truck.

"Pardon the early morning pop up, but I got something to holla at you about that couldn't wait," Trap explained. His voice lacked the playful edge Marcus had become accustomed to.

"Okay, so holla," Marcus said.

"Get in and I'll fill you in on the way," Trap leaned over and opened the passenger side door.

"Trap, Billy is upstairs waiting for me. We got some shit we need to take care of for the wedding so I really don't have time to ride around with you today," Marcus lied. The whole set up felt wrong.

"It won't take but an hour or so and I'll have you right back," Trap promised.

"I really can't, Trap. It's not a good time," Marcus insisted.

Trap's face became serious. "Marcus, are you really going to make me have Moochie get out and drag your ass in the whip like an unruly child? Get in the car and stop bullshitting, man."

Marcus looked in the back at Moochie who looked like she couldn't wait for the opportunity to lay hands on him. "A'ight, Trap." He reluctantly got in.

"What's with you today, Marcus?" Trap asked after they had pulled away from Marcus's complex.

"Nothing, I'm just tired and got a lot on my mind. I'm sure you can understand," Marcus said sarcastically.

"What, you still tripping off that broad? Marcus, don't beat yourself up about it, dawg. It was us or her…it had to be done. Don't sweat it."

"Some of us aren't as comfortable with murder as others," Marcus said.

"The first few times are always hard, but after a while it becomes as easy as tying your shoes. Ain't that right, Moochie?" Trap asked from behind the wheel.

"Sho nuff," Moochie agreed.

"So what it is that you needed to talk to me about, Trap?" Marcus cut to the chase.

"Life, living it, and enjoying it," Trap said. "Marcus, how long have we known each other?"

"For quite a few years," Marcus answered.

"Right," Trap nodded. "You know since we been kicking it I've come to have more love for you than some niggas who I've known for twice as long. I look at you like family. Family is something that

271

a man like me takes very seriously. In times of need, I know I can depend on my family and my family can depend on me, especially when our backs are against the wall. Would you say I can depend on you, Marcus?"

"I'd have thought you'd know that by now, Trap," Marcus said.

"I do, but sometimes it's good to hear it again. There's power in words, Marcus. Depending on how words are used, they can either uplift you or tear everything down that you've worked so hard to build. Seeing how both of us have so much on the line right now, I'm sure you can appreciate that philosophy, Marcus."

"I can," Marcus agreed. He looked out the window and noticed that they were now in Brooklyn. Marcus recognized the BQE overhead as they rode down Park Avenue towards Bedstuy.

"Marcus," Trap continued, "I know since I've blown into town I've put you in some very compromising positions. Most people would've told me to go fuck myself, but not you. You rose to the occasion and helped your boy out. I appreciate you for that...I appreciate our friendship."

"I appreciate our friendship too, Trap," Marcus said sincerely.

"That's good to hear," Trap said and turned his attention back to the road. They pulled up to Marcy projects where Trap parked the truck. "Last stop. Everybody out."

"Trap, what are we doing here?" Marcus asked, looking up at the looming brown buildings. He was suddenly so nervous that his armpits began to sweat and his mouth dried. He looked through the rearview and could see Moochie staring daggers at him. She was doing something with her hands, but at that angle, he couldn't tell what.

"I can show you better than I can tell you," Trap got out of the car.

Marcus sat there for a few seconds, not really sure what to do. Moochie remained seated behind him, waiting for him to move. Marcus wished he'd put his gun in the front of his pants instead of the back. It'd be easier to reach should he happen to need it. With little other choice, Marcus got out of the car and followed Trap into the projects.

As they entered one of the buildings, Trap paused to give dap to a few of the young hustlers who were loitering out front. Marcus had no idea Trap knew people in Brooklyn, but the Miami native was proving to be full of surprises. Marcus just hoped that Trap didn't have any more surprises up his sleeve that day.

The ride up on the elevator was a tense one. Trap leaned against one of the walls, whistling a happy tune, while Moochie continued to stare at Marcus menacingly. When the elevator stopped on the fifth floor, Trap got off and motioned for Marcus to follow. He led them down the hall with Marcus in the middle and Moochie bringing up the rear. The closer they got to their destination, the more nervous Marcus got. He was like a man walking the last mile to the waiting electric chair. Marcus stopped short like he had to tie his shoe, allowing Moochie to pass him. When he was sure nobody was looking, he removed his gun from the back of his pants and slipped it into his jacket pocket. If he was going to go down it wouldn't be without a fight.

Their journey ended at an apartment door at the far end of the hall where Trap paused as if for dramatic effect. He gave Marcus a look like he had a secret that he couldn't wait to tell.

"What are we doing here, Trap?" Marcus asked nervously. His hand was tucked in his pocket, wrapped around the butt of his gun.

"If I told you, it'd ruin the surprise," Trap smirked. He dug in his pocket and pulled out a key, which he inserted into the lock. "I promise that when it's all said and done you'll finally realize just what kind of nigga you're dealing with."

Unfortunately, for Marcus, he already knew what kind of nigga he was dealing with. In the back of his mind, he kept hearing Shooter's warning and wished that he'd listened.

Trap entered first, followed by Moochie who held the door for Marcus. From his vantage point, he could see the inside of the apartment was dark, but he thought he saw a shadow cut across the shaded window. Marcus thought about running, but he would likely be a dead man before he made it to the staircase at the other end of the hall. There was no turning back. He took out his gun and let it hang inconspicuously at his side. If this was to be the end for him, he was going to go out in a blaze.

"Fuck it," Marcus said and stepped into the apartment, ready to meet his final reward. Just as Marcus was about to bring his gun up and blast Moochie, the lights flicked on in the apartment.

"Surprise!" he heard people yell in unison.

Marcus stood there in wide-eyed shock when he saw Wayne, and several other familiar faces standing amongst about half a dozen scantily clad women. Sitting on a folding table near the window was a cake that stood at least four feet tall with the word Congratulations written along the side. "What is this?" he asked, still dumbfounded.

"Your bachelor party!" Trap threw his arm around Marcus. "What did you think it was?"

"I…uh…" Marcus was at a loss for words.

Trap looked down and for the first time noticed the gun in Marcus's hand. "What? Did you think I was bringing you out here to whack you?" he sounded genuinely hurt by the notion. "I guess genuine friends are harder to come by than I thought. I'm disappointed in you, Marcus."

"Trap, I'm sorry. I thought when…"

"Save it," Trap cut him off. "This is your day and I ain't gonna ruin it by pointing out how foul you are for this shit," he said and walked off.

Moochie spared Marcus a last glance and shook her head before following her brother, leaving Marcus standing there feeling like shit.

*

"What the hell could they possibly doing in the projects?" Reese asked from the passenger side of Billy's car.

"How the fuck am I supposed to know when I'm here with you?" Billy snapped. They had followed Trap's truck into Brooklyn. They'd almost lost them when they got caught at a red light, but Billy spotted the blue Porsche as they were riding up and down Park Avenue trying to find them again. By the time they arrived, Marcus and whoever he was with were no longer in the truck, but they had to be in one of the buildings. Billy just wasn't sure which. They had been sitting and watching the truck for over an hour.

"So what now? Are we supposed to just wait here until they come out from wherever they disappeared to?" Reese asked.

"Unless you've got a better idea, yes," Billy said. "And where the hell is Yoshi? I called and hit her with the address forty minutes ago and she still ain't here."

"Maybe she got held up in traffic," Reese suggested.

As if on cue, a livery cab pulled up with Yoshi in the backseat. She paid the driver then got out and looked around for her friends. She spotted Billy's car and jumped into the backseat. "What kind of Secret Squirrel shit are you bitches on now?" she asked. Billy had been vague on the phone, only telling Yoshi she needed her to meet her at that address.

"Following Marcus," Reese told her.

"Again?" Yoshi shook her head in disappointment. "Billy didn't you learn your lesson after the last time you called yourself following Marcus?"

"I seriously doubt if this is another meeting with the jeweler in the middle of the projects," Billy said, continuing to watch the buildings.

"So, where are you just coming from? Seeing your guy friend again?" Reese asked Yoshi.

"No, for your information I was out shopping for Billy's wedding gift." Yoshi rolled her eyes.

"I told you that you guys didn't have to buy me anything. Y'all being here is present enough," Billy said.

"That might've been cool for this cheap bitch," Yoshi nodded at Reese, "but not for me. I had to make sure I got my girl something special."

"I hope you didn't spend a lot on it, Reese. You know I'm not materialistic like that," Billy reminded her.

"Actually, I didn't spend a dime on it. My new friend knew I wanted to get you something nice so he fronted me the money," Yoshi said proudly.

"And what did you have to give him in return?" Reese asked jokingly.

"None of your damn business," Yoshi stuck her tongue out, and Reese playfully tried to grab it.

"Things seem to be moving pretty fast between you and this new mystery man," Billy said.

"Not really, we're just having fun," Yoshi downplayed it. In truth, she was starting to develop feeling for Trap and she felt like it was mutual. Still, after all she had been through with men she knew better than to put all her cards on the table at once.

"So when are we gonna meet this mystery man of yours?" Reese asked.

"Soon enough. I was going to bring him to the wedding dinner tomorrow. He might even come to the wedding with me as my date, if that's okay with you, Billy?"

"Yoshi, if he makes you happy I'm fine with that. Just make sure he knows that if he breaks your heart I'm going to put the beats on him," Billy threatened.

"Well aren't you at least going to tell us his name?" Reese asked.

"If you must know, his name is —"

"Holy shit," Billy blurted out, cutting Yoshi off. All their attention turned in the direction Billy was looking in. There were three girls getting out of the van, pulling roll-ons behind them, and heading into the projects. Billy recognized one of them as a girl who danced at Shooters.

"Who are those bitches?" Yoshi asked.

"The trail of breadcrumbs that are going to lead us to Marcus," Billy said and got out of the car.

*

Marcus was sitting on a couch in the living room, taking a bottle of champagne to the face and trying to enjoy himself, but he couldn't. He felt horrible about the way he had carried Trap. He tried to talk to Trap several times during the party, but he brushed him off. He was still in his feelings. Marcus had thought Trap meant him harm, but it was the opposite. All he was trying to do was what none of his other friends had taken the time to, which was throw him a bachelor party. And Marcus had spat in his face for his efforts.

"Man, why are you sitting here looking like you just lost your best friend instead of enjoying your last moments as a free man?"

Wayne asked. He was sitting next to Marcus with a big booty stripper on his lap.

"I did some dumb shit, Wayne," Marcus admitted.

"I told you that the minute you told me that you proposed to Billy," Wayne joked, but Marcus didn't laugh. "C'mon man, whatever it was couldn't have been that serious."

"That all depends on who you ask," Marcus replied. "How the hell did you guys manage to pull this together anyhow?"

"I can't take credit for anything except putting into the calls for the girls. Trap paid for all this and secured the venue," Wayne admitted.

That made Marcus feel even worse. "He's a resourceful bastard, isn't he? But why do it in a project apartment?"

Wayne laughed. "You have no idea where you are, do you? Look around and let me know when it hits you."

For the first time, Marcus took a good look at the apartment. With everything going on when he first walked in, he hadn't noticed until then that it was very tastefully decorated for a project apartment. There was a big screen television, plush couches, and nice pieces of art hanging on the walls. Marcus had missed it on his first sweep, but hanging above them was what looked like a platinum plaque with a familiar name on it.

"Wait, does this place belong to one of the Big Dawg niggas?" Marcus asked with realization starting to set in.

"Not just any old Big Dawg nigga, thee big Dawg nigga," Wayne said. "This is one of Don B's spots."

Marcus was totally surprised. "You mean to tell me that with all the paper that dude has he still lives in the hood?"

Wayne shook his head at his friend's ignorance. "Hell no. This is the apartment Don B. was living in when he wrote his first platinum hit. The way I hear it he doesn't come here much, but he still holds on to the place for nostalgic reasons."

"Well how the fuck did Trap get access to it?" Marcus asked.

Wayne shrugged. "Beats the hell out of me. But fuck all that. I need you to get into the swing of things and at least act like you're having some fun," he removed the girl from his lap and pushed her off on Marcus.

"Baby, I'm good," Marcus tried to tell her, but Wayne wasn't trying to hear it.

"The hell you are," Wayne pulled a brick of singles from his pants pocket. "Baby, I want you to show the groom-to-be a good time. Don't stop popping that ass until he blows his load or this money is gone," he started showering her with money.

After a few blunts and another bottle of champagne, Marcus had loosened up enough to halfway enjoy himself. He knew a few of the girls who were dancing at the party, but there was some that he didn't. One in particular was a green-eyed Puerto Rican stallion with ass and hips for days. She currently occupied a spot on Marcus's lap, while he plied her with singles and whispered sweet nothings in her ear about why she should come to work for him at Shooters.

There was a knock at the door and Wayne jumped to his feet to go answer it. "That must be the other bitches," he sang. He walked to the door rubbing his hands together in anticipation.

NO SHADE: A Hood Rat Novel

"You got more joints coming?" Marcus's face lit up. "Man, y'all are gonna fuck around and have Billy kill me," he joked then went back to whispering to the Puerto Rican girl. She had big supple breasts and he had to fight the urge to put one in his mouth.

"Say Marcus," Wayne called from the door.

"What up my nigga?" Marcus asked, with eyes still fixed on the girl's breasts.

"You might wanna break out that black suit."

Marcus craned around the girl to see what Wayne was talking about and his heart stopped in his chest. Standing in the foyer were Wayne and three more strippers. Directly behind them, was his very angry fiancé, Billy.

*

Billy and her crew boarded the elevator with the strippers and tried their best not to act like weren't about to lead a commando strike. One of the girls on the elevator seemed to be paying a bit too much attention for Yoshi's tastes, so she called her on it.

"Something I can help you with?" Yoshi asked.

"I didn't mean to stare, but you just look so familiar," the girl said apologetically. "Which club do you dance at?"

"I don't dance," Yoshi told her. More accurately would've been to say that she didn't dance anymore.

The girl looked her up and down and shook her head. "That's a shame, because you've definitely got the body for it."

K'WAN

They girls listened for the rest of the ride up as the strippers chattered on about the bachelor party they were headed to and all the money that was promised to be in the room. Billy had to keep herself from snuffing the girl she recognized from Shooters when she heard her tell her friend that she was ready to put that pussy on her boss. Whipping her out would've been sweet, but it would've only been winning a battle while Billy was out to win the war.

Billy wasn't mad at the fact that Marcus was having a bachelor party, what had her hot was the fact that he had lied about it. When she'd tried to encourage him to have one he claimed that he didn't want to and she took him at his word. Because Marcus was going to forgo a bachelor party, she told her girls not to throw her a bachelorette party. Her making the sacrifice was her way of showing solidarity with her man. If he was doing it behind her back then that had to mean he was up to no good. Billy was going to give him the benefit of the doubt but if she caught Marcus wrong, his ass would be dead and so was the wedding.

Then there was the issue of the blue Porsche she kept seeing and how it connected Marcus and Yoshi. You didn't see many powder blue Cayenne trucks around the city so she knew it had to be the same one. If she had been thinking clearly she would've just asked Yoshi who the car belonged to, but her mind was focused on catching Marcus with his hand in the cookie jar.

When the strippers got off the elevator on the fifth floor, so did Billy and company. She could hear the sounds of loud music coming from the apartment at the end of the hall. The door to the apartment at the end of the hall was open, so the sound of loud music flooded the hallway. One of the girls knocked on the door, while Billy and her crew hung back and tried to blend in. As she heard the locks on the door coming undone she was reminded of that scene in 'Gladiator' when Russell Crowe and the slaves were about to go into the arena for the first time. She braced herself, having no idea what she was about to walk into. No matter what happened she would keep her cool, or at least try to.

Marcus's best friend Wayne opened the door wearing a shit-eating grin at the sight of the strippers. The smile on his face quickly faded when he saw Billy and her crew standing behind them. "Yo Marcus!"

"What up my nigga?" she heard Marcus call from somewhere out of her line of vision.

"You might wanna bust out that black suit."

"Yep, because he's damn sure gonna need something nice to be buried in," Billy shoved her way past Wayne and into the house. It felt like somebody stabbed her I in the chest when she saw the big booty Puerto Rican girl on Marcus's lap, and his face damn near buried in her chest. "What the fuck is this?"

"Billy, this isn't what it looks like," Marcus said. He was so shocked that he had completely forgotten the girl on his lap.

"It looks like a bitch is about to get her ass whipped," Billy said, taking her earrings off. She made to charge Marcus and the Puerto Rican, but Wayne grabbed her around the waist.

"Chill out, Billy," Wayne said, trying to restrain her.

"Get the fuck off me!" Billy struggled to get free.

"You heard her," Yoshi clocked Wayne on the back of the head. Reese joined in too and they started thumping Wayne.

"Marcus, come get these broads off me!" Wayne yelled trying to protect his face and restrain Billy at the same time.

"Who invited the hood rats?" the Puerto Rican girl asked.

"Shut up," Marcus tossed her off his lap and onto the floor while he went to try and help Wayne. "Billy, calm down," he pulled her free from Wayne.

"I catch you with a bitch trying to fuck you through your jeans and you're talking about calm down?" Billy was enraged to the point where she did something she thought she never would; laid hands on Marcus.

Marcus heard the slap before he actually felt it. It was like someone had set off a firecracker next to his ear before the intense stinging set in. The whole room got quiet and all eyes turned to Marcus. He was embarrassed and angry. "Word?" was all he could manage to say.

"Word," Billy spat. She didn't mean to hit him, but she was angry and it was too late to take it back. "Marcus, since when did we start lying to each other?"

"I haven't lied to you about anything. You in here acting an ass over nothing…again," Marcus said through clenched teeth.

"So what, is that bitch here to sell you some jewelry too? Marcus, I asked you if you were having a bachelor party and you said no. The fact you snuck and had one anyway leads me to believe there was some shit about to go on here that you didn't want me to know about," Billy accused.

NO SHADE: A Hood Rat Novel

"I'm not having a bachelor party...I mean I wasn't. Billy can we just go in the hallway and talk about this?" Marcus asked as calm as he could.

"Don't look like it's much to talk about to me," Reese added.

"Yo, mind your fucking business. This is between me and my girl," Marcus snapped.

"Don't get mad at her because I caught you dirty," Billy defended her friend. "This shit you pulled it petty and beneath you. We're supposed to be bigger than that, or at least I thought we were. How can I spend the rest of my life with a man I can't trust?"

"I'm afraid this is my fault because I orchestrated it," Trap stepped forward.

Billy's eyes narrowed to slits when she saw Trap. She knew who he was and what part of Marcus's life he represented. "Now it all makes sense. You been sneaking around and acting all jittery because this nigga was in town and you didn't want me to know. Marcus, I told you that if I found out you were back in the streets that I wasn't fucking with you anymore."

"Billy, it's not like that. I just need you to listen to me for a minute," Marcus pleaded with her.

"I'm done listening. You know what I went through with the last dope boy I dated and I can't allow you or anybody else to put me through that again."

"Is somebody gonna tell me who this dude is?" Reese asked, looking at the short dude with the bald fade and heavy jewelry.

"His name is Trap," Billy and Yoshi said simultaneously.

Billy gave Yoshi a quizzical look. "Wait, do you mean to tell me this is the guy you've been spending all your time with lately?" The pieces were starting to fall into place: Her seeing Yoshi and Marcus in and out of the same vehicle...Marcus's odd behavior. Trap was the link to it all.

Yoshi shrugged.

"Trap, I know damn well Yoshi isn't the Ms. California you've been going on and on about?" Marcus was equally surprised.

"The one and only," Trap said.

Billy looked from Yoshi to Trap and shook her head. "Could this shit get any crazier?"

No sooner than the worlds left her mouth, the top of the cake burst open, and out popped a naked woman. "Congratulations!"

CHAPTER 30

Turk had some hours to kill before he was supposed to pick Baby Doc up and meet the mysterious G, so he decided to go for a drive. He rode low in the seat, with his hand resting lazily on the wheel. The car was only a loaner and he'd have to return it to Swann, but for the time being, he was going to savor the feeling of importance the whip gave him. It felt good to ride in a luxury car and not be cursed to the backseat.

He rode slowly through Harlem with no particular destination, but somehow he found himself back at the scene of the crime; the projects where he'd met Rocky for the first time. It was a nice night so there were people out on the avenue, but none of them looked familiar…none of them were Rocky. He felt like a stalker being in her hood uninvited, but his curiosity about her no-show wouldn't let him rest. She didn't have to go out with him, but at the very least, she was going to tell him why he'd been stood up.

After a while, he began to feel foolish about the whole thing. He and Rocky had hit it off, but it hardly qualified them as a couple so she owed him no explanation. Turk had nobody to blame but himself for it. He should've known better than to get that invested in any female Holiday set him up with. Turk was about to peel when he saw Claudette walking down the street. Turk slowed the car down to match Claudette's pace. "Yo," he called out the window.

Claudette looked startled at first but when she saw the handsome face staring at her from behind the wheel of the pretty black Lexus she stopped. "Who that?" she asked, not recognizing him at first.

"The Turk," he replied.

"Oh hey," Rocky stepped into the street.

"What's good wit' you?" Turk asked.

"Nothing, trying to find something to get into," Claudette said suggestively. "What you doing around here, looking for Rocky?" she asked, hoping he said no.

"Not really, but kinda," Turk said to Claudette's disappointment. "We were supposed to hook up later tonight but I haven't been able to reach her since this morning. I ain't sweating her or nothing; I just wanted to make sure she was okay."

"Yeah, her shook ass has been hiding in the house all day," Claudette said in disgust.

This struck Turk as odd. "Why would she be hiding?"

"Over what happened this morning." Claudette went onto tell him about the shooting in front of their building.

"Damn, is she good?" Turk asked in a concerned tone. He remembered the first time he'd seen someone killed and how it had affected him, so he could've only imagined what Rocky, as a civilian, must've been going through.

"She's good, just a little shaken up," Claudette said as if it was nothing. "I feel bad for her, but I can't understand why she's taking it so hard. Niggas die in the hood every day; it's just a part of life down here. She didn't even know Bernie like that to be mourning him."

"Do you think I can see her?" Turk asked, ignoring Claudette's crass comment.

"Knock yourself out. She lives in 6G," Claudette freely gave out Rocky's information.

"A'ight, but I'm gonna need you to go upstairs with me," Turk said.

"For what? I ain't got nothing to do with what y'all got going on," Claudette said with an attitude. She was hoping that she would've been able to sway Turk into hanging out with her, but he was still caught up on Rocky.

"Claudette, I don't wanna seem like some stalker ass nigga by just popping up at Rocky's place. If I go up with you it doesn't seem as weird."

"Well, I was about to go meet somebody to pick up some bread and I'm gonna end up missing them. So…"

Turk already knew what time it was. "I got you," he agreed.

*

Rocky sat in the living room, staring out the window as she had been for the majority of the day. She was dead tired, but afraid to try and take a nap. Every time she closed her eyes, she saw visions of blood and death. As it turned out, Boots had survived, but was in critical condition and Happy had escaped with a flesh wound to his ass cheek. Bernie turned out to be the only casualty of the love-triangle.

After the shooting, the police had questioned Rocky and Claudette at length about what they saw. Of course, Claudette was belligerent and refused to cooperate, but Rocky was as forthcoming as she could be. The detectives asked her the same questions one hundred different times and worded it one hundred different ways, but Rocky's story never changed. Claudette hadn't been happy with her for cooperating, but Rocky didn't care. It wasn't like she was snitching because Bernie was dead and there was no one to be prosecuted for the crime. The detectives warned Rocky not to leave town in case they needed to ask her additional questions, but that wouldn't be a problem. Rocky wasn't sure if she'd be able leave the house again; let alone the city. She just wanted to hide away in her apartment for the rest of her life.

There was a knock at her front door, which scared the shit out of Rocky. She had been on pins and needles the whole day. She tiptoed to the door and eased the peephole to the side just enough for her to peer through the crack. Claudette stood on the other side of the door with her arms folded, tapping her foot impatiently while she waited for Rocky to let her in. Rocky started to ignore her, but she knew if she did that, Claudette would just keep coming back so she opened the door. To her surprise, Claudette wasn't alone.

"What is this?" Rocky asked looking from Claudette to Turk.

"Well, I've done my good deed for the day. Later y'all," Claudette said and abruptly left, leaving Turk and Rocky standing there in awkward silence.

"Ah…" Turk began. "I know how strange this must seem with me popping up on you like this. It's just that when I hadn't heard from you I got a little worried and wanted to make sure you were okay. I'll understand if you want me to leave." When Rocky didn't answer, Turk took it as a hint and started back down the hall.

"No, don't leave," Rocky called after him. "Come in," she opened the door wider for him to enter. When Turk crossed her threshold, she closed the door and applied every lock before slipping the door-chain into place too. "That was my fault; I should've called you back. I apologize for that."

"You don't owe me any apologies, Rocky. I know a lot has happened today," Turk told her.

"Claudette told you?"

"Yeah, she put me on. Are you okay?"

Rocky sighed. "Not really, but I'll be fine. My nerves are just shot out right now."

"I've got something that might be able to help with that." Turk pulled a bag of weed and a cigar out of his shirt pocket. "Do you burn?"

"Yeah, have a seat and roll up," Rocky directed him to the couch. "I would offer you something to drink, but I haven't felt much like going out to buy anything. I think all I've got is a flat Pepsi and some water."

"Water is cool," Turk sat on the couch. He began the task of rolling the weed up while Rocky went into the kitchen to get him some water. He looked around at the pictures hanging on the walls of Rocky's living room and spotted her degree hanging proudly over the dining room table. "You got a degree?" he was surprised.

"A Bachelors, but I was hoping to one day go back and get my Masters," she said as she sat a glass of water on the table for Turk

291

and took the seat beside him. "What, project bitches can't get educations?" she asked sarcastically.

"Cut it out, Rocky," he sipped the water then went back to sealing the ends of the blunt. "I wasn't trying to clown you or nothing. I was just a little surprised because I remember you saying you were having trouble finding another job. I always thought a degree put you on Easy Street."

"I wish! You know sometimes college graduates have it harder than dropouts," Rocky told him.

"How do you figure that?" Turk was curious.

"Well for starters, once we graduate we're automatically in debt because we have to pay back all the loans we took out to pay for school. Grants and scholarships pay for some of the stuff like classes and books, but we still have to eat and live. This means we have to work part time between classes and even with a job, it sometimes doesn't cover everything. This is how they gas us into applying for those high interest rate credit cards to float the rest. By the time I left school my credit score was shot to hell."

"Damn, sounds like that college shit is for the birds. I'm glad I skipped it," Turk said, lighting the weed. The time he spent away at prep school felt like mental torture and college was likely twice as hard. Why anyone would want to subject themselves to four more years of school after the first twelve was beyond him. The only reason he had stayed long enough to get his diploma was because he didn't want to disappoint his aunt. After high school, he was done with the classrooms and furthered his education on the streets.

"No, I'm not saying that. Education is extremely important. I might be struggling now, but one day the four years I busted my ass for will pay off," Rocky told him.

"If you say so," Turk handed her the blunt.

"Thanks, because I can sure use this right about now." Rocky accepted the blunt. She lit it and the minute she tasted the weed she knew it was high grade. Rocky held the smoke in her lungs and let its calming effects wash over her. "This hit the spot. Thanks Turk."

"It's all good, ma. You looked like you could use a stress reliever. Murder is never an easy thing to digest, especially when you ain't from that lifestyle," Turk said like he was an authority on the subject.

"I guess in your line of work you see dead bodies all the time, huh?" Rocky asked.

Turk laughed. "And what exactly is my line of work, Rocky?"

Rocky thought on the question. "You're one of Shai's crew, aren't you? The way Holiday was bragging I thought you guys ran the city."

"Holiday tends to exaggerate, lil' mama. I work for Shai, but technically I'm not part of his crew…at least not yet, but my time is coming," Turk said confidently.

"Okay, so what exactly is it that you do?" Rocky asked.

Turk measured his words. "I do what nobody else is willing to."

"I'm not even sure if I want you to elaborate on that one," Rocky said.

"Probably not," Turk chuckled.

K'WAN

After Rocky and Turk finished the blunt, he rolled another one. The munchies kicked in so they ordered some Chinese food and decided to pop in a movie. Rocky had an extensive collection, including one of Turk's favorites 'Jason's Lyric.' As it turned out it was one of her favorites too. Halfway through the movie Rocky fell asleep with her head resting on Turk's lap. He gently removed her glasses and sat them on the coffee table. He studied her face for a while, thinking how different she looked without her glasses.

Rocky wasn't the baddest chick he'd kept time with, but she was beautiful in her own way. Having a chick all on him like that was out of character for Turk, unless they were fucking, but it was different with Rocky. Of course, he wanted to sleep with her, but that wasn't all he wanted. Rocky was someone he felt like he wanted to get to know on more than just a physical level. He'd slept with plenty of women, but never had a real girlfriend and wondered if over time that was a step he could take with Rocky.

Turk's moment of reflection was interrupted when the text message alert went off on his phone. Without disturbing Rocky's sleep, he pulled it out of his pocket and looked at the screen. Baby Doc was hitting him up. It was 11:30 pm and almost game time. He could've stayed on that couch watching Rocky sleep all night, but he had business to handle.

"Wake up, ma," Turk nudged her.

Rocky's eyes fluttered open and looked up at Turk. When she realized she was laying on his lap she sat up. "I'm sorry."

"No need to be. I would've let you sleep, but I got something to do and didn't want to sneak out like a thief in the night." Turk got up.

"Okay, let me walk you out," Rocky said following him to the door. "Thank you for coming by to check on me. It meant a lot."

"I was happy to do it, even though you stood me up," Turk joked.

"You're never gonna let me live that down, are you?"

"Of course not," Turk winked.

"I wish you didn't have to go," Rocky said.

"Me too, but I've gotta handle something that demands my attention," Turk said.

Rocky suddenly felt a chill run down her back. For reasons she couldn't understand, she felt like she was saying her final goodbyes to a man who she still had so much to learn about. "Turk, promise this isn't the last night we spend together."

"Rocky, I can't promise you anything, but if it's God's will, I'll be back. I kinda dig you, Ms. Raquel."

"I kinda dig you too…a little," Rocky blushed.

Turk surprised Rocky by leaning in and kissing her softly on the lips. "Until we meet again," he slipped out of the apartment.

"Until we meet again," Rocky said to the empty doorway.

CHAPTER 31

"So, when were you going to tell me that Trap was in town?" Billy asked. She and Marcus were riding in her car on the way back to his condo. After she had busted up his little party, everyone went their separate ways. Trap dropped the girls off and Billy rode back with Marcus in her car so they could have some time to talk.

"You want an honest answer, or the politically correct one?" Marcus asked.

Billy looked over at him. "Boy, please don't make me pull this car over and put my hands on you."

"You mean again?" Marcus asked sarcastically.

"Marcus, I already apologized to you about that, but don't act like you didn't have it coming. How did you think I was going to react when I came in and saw that nasty bitch all on your lap?"

"So that's what you're mad about? A lap dance?"

"No, I'm mad because you felt the need to lie to me. In all the time we've been together, we've always kept it funky with each other. No lies and no bullshit, that's what our relationship was built on."

"Billy I didn't lie to you," Marcus reiterated. "I didn't know Trap was throwing me a bachelor party until I got there."

"Which brings me back to my original question; when were you going to tell me he was in New York?"

"I wasn't," Marcus said honestly. "I know how you feel about Trap, and being that he was only going to be here a few days I figured why upset you for nothing?"

"Marcus, it's never nothing when Trap is in town. He's a killer and a dope peddler!" Billy raised her voice.

"He's also my friend," Marcus countered.

"The same friend who gets you into some shit whenever he's around," Billy shot back. "Trap is a walking, breathing, open case."

"He can't be that bad if your bestie is fucking him."

"Just because they went on a few dates doesn't mean Yoshi is fucking him," Billy defended her.

Marcus gave her as a look.

"Okay, maybe she is fucking him," Billy conceded, "but Yoshi is grown. And this ain't about what Yoshi is doing with Trap; it's about why you're creeping around with him. What's the lick, Marcus?"

"Ain't no lick, Billy," Marcus said.

"So you wanna go two-for-two with this lying shit, huh?" Billy knew better.

"Okay, he needed me to help him out of a small bind." Marcus went on to give her the short version of the why Trap had come and the favor he asked.

"Marcus I can't believe you gambled everything you worked to build for a nigga like Trap," Billy was furious.

"I owed him, Billy," Marcus said in a defeated tone. "I didn't want to tell you, but I ran into some financial trouble a while back and Trap helped me to get back on my feet."

"So you are back in the streets?"

"No, baby. I just made a few moves to flip some paper. I never touched any drugs or a pistol," Marcus assured her.

"Marcus, you should've just told me we were hurting for money. We could've just gotten married at City Hall. I didn't need a big wedding."

"It isn't about what you needed, Billy. It's about what you deserved. Ma, you've had my back through the good times and the bad. You've never asked me for anything, except for this wedding. When it looked like I wouldn't be able to give you the wedding of your dreams, I did what I had to do to make it happen. I know what I risked, but honestly, if I had it to do all over again, I would in a heartbeat. You're my soul and I would move heaven and earth to make your dreams come true."

Billy tried to fight back the tears, but she couldn't. For as dumb as what he did was, she knew that his heart was in the right place. Not many men would've gone through what he had just to please his lady, but Marcus wasn't many men; he was one of a kind...he was hers.

"Marcus, I don't agree with what you did, but I understand. Just promise me that there's nothing else you're keeping from me. I can't take anymore secrets."

Marcus thought back on the vacant expression on Tammy's dead face when they dismembered her in the woods. "Nah, baby. No more secrets," he lied.

*

"I can't believe you know my best friend's man and didn't tell me," Yoshi was pacing back and forth in her hotel room. They dropped Reese off first then Moochie had left Trap and Yoshi at her hotel.

"How was I supposed to know that Billy was your home girl? You weren't very forthcoming about your personal life and who your friends were." Trap was sitting on the edge of her bed rolling a blunt. "I don't see why it's such a big deal. What do Billy and Marcus have to do with what we got going on?"

"Everything and nothing," Yoshi said. "Billy is my best friend in the whole world and it's important to me that she approves of anybody I'm seeing."

"Oh, so we're seeing each other now?" Trap raised an eyebrow.

Yoshi stopped her pacing and gave him a dirty look.

"Take it easy, Yoshi. I was only kidding." Trap put the blunt in his mouth and prepared to light it but Yoshi snatched it away.

"This is a non-smoking room," she tossed the blunt on the dresser.

"Well then let's go outside and smoke it. It's obvious that you need something to calm your nerves. Or maybe instead of the L," he grabbed Yoshi by the arm and pulled her to him, "you need the D."

"Trap, how can you be thinking about sex when I'm in the middle of a crisis?"

"Yoshi, this is hardly a crisis. More like a coincidence. Okay, so our friends know each other. This can be a good thing. At least now, we don't have to go on one of those awkward double dates while our friends feel us out. The ice has already been broken."

"I'm glad you can see the upside in all this, because I can't. Billy didn't seem to be too thrilled when she saw you. What'd you do to her?" Yoshi asked.

"I've never done anything to her. I've only met Billy a few times. She's more pissed about the fact that me and Marcus are running tight again. We've kind of got history," Trap told her.

"And how exactly do you know Marcus?" Yoshi asked.

"We made some not so legal moves back in the days, and Marcus got caught up in some shit. She's always blamed me for it, like I put a gun to his head and made him do dirt. She probably thinks I'm trying to get him back in the game," Trap said honestly.

"Well are you?" Yoshi asked seriously.

"Hell no," Trap declared. "Yoshi I ain't never claimed to be no angel, but I'm not ashamed of who I am either. I know Marcus is a square now, and I respect that. I'm trying to fly straight myself, which is why I came to see him. My business with Marcus this trip is all about my push to go legit." It wasn't the complete truth, but close enough to it.

"And what kind of business is it that you've got with Marcus?"

"No disrespect, but that really ain't none of your concern. Just know that I ain't trying to put him or me in harm's way," Trap told her.

"Sounds like bullshit to me," Yoshi said and started pacing again.

Trap stood up and took her in his arms. She tried to pull away, but he held tight. "Yoshi, I don't care what it sounds like; I can only tell you what it is. Now for as much as I respect you wanting your home girl to approve of me and all, I'm more worried about what you think of me than anybody else. I'm the same person now that I was before you found out I knew Marcus."

"And who is that person, Trap?"

"A man who has fallen head over heels for a woman he barely knows," Trap kissed her passionately. Yoshi resisted at first, but gave in and kissed him back. Trap steered her towards the bed and laid her flat on her back.

"What do you think you're doing?" Yoshi asked, looking down at him easing her pants down.

"I can show you better than I can tell you," Trap tossed her jeans into the corner and slid her panties to the side.

Yoshi had been falling down drunk the first time she had sex with Trap, but now that she was sober, she could appreciate his skill and his girth. For a short man, Trap was very well hung. He took his time easing the head of his dick inside Yoshi and teasing her with it. "Damn," she hissed.

"You like that, baby?" Trap eased deeper inside of her.

"Yes," she panted.

Trap pumped slowly at first, building up the moisture in Yoshi's box. When she was good and wet, he started plowing her a little faster. Yoshi's pussy felt like heaven had folded around the shaft of his dick and all the nerves in his body came alive at once. If he stroked any faster, he was sure he would cum prematurely, so he buried his dick all the way inside her and held his position. "Throw it back," he commanded.

Yoshi locked her legs behind Trap's and pushed her hips off the bed, plunging him deeper inside her. She could feel him swelling as the blood rushed to his thick dick and filled every inch of her cave. "Right there, baby…right there."

Trap and Yoshi's lovemaking session lasted for about an hour, including the ten-minute intermission before their second round. They did it in just about every position imaginable and a few that Yoshi had never thought of. When it was over, Trap went into the bathroom and came back out with a soapy rag, which he used to clean her up. A man hadn't done that for her since Jah, and she found herself overcome with emotions.

"Are you okay? Did I do something wrong?" Trap asked, noticing that she was crying.

"No, you did everything right," she wiped her tears with the palms of her hands. "Come lay with me," she pulled him down on the bed with her. Trap snuggled against her from behind, running his fingers through her hair. "Where are we going with this?"

Trap sat up on his elbow. "Wherever you wanna go with it, baby."

"Don't tell me what you think I wanna hear so I'll keep giving you the pussy, keep it one hundred." Yoshi rolled over so that she could see his eyes.

"To be honest, I don't know. I didn't get into this putting any expectations on it. I know that I like you and I'm feel like you're digging me, I'd say that's a pretty good starting point. I ain't trying to run with it if just yet if that's what you're asking, but I'm down to slow walk it with you and see where we end up."

302

"I respect your honesty, Trap. And as long as you're always honest with me, I'll respect you." Yoshi ran her hand down the back of his bald-fade.

"In my world, respect it is more precious than gold," Trap planted a kiss on her cheek. "Dig though; I know things are kinda tense between me and your peeps right now so if you want me to sit the rehearsal and dinner out tomorrow I'll understand."

Yoshi thought about it for a few seconds. "Trap for this thing…whatever it is, to have a fair chance we can't build it on the past. Whatever beef Billy has with you over your relationship with Marcus really doesn't have anything to do with me. Billy is a big part of my life and it's important to me that you guys get along, but it's also important that our relationship isn't influenced by how somebody else feels. Trap, I'm still not sure if you've come into my life for a reason or a season, but I'd really like to find out."

CHAPTER 32

Turk and Baby Doc pulled up in front of the bar about ten minutes early and found G was already standing outside waiting for them. He always seemed to be one step ahead of them and Turk didn't like it. The whole set up had felt wrong to him from the beginning, but Andrew had to die and G was their best shot.

"Punctuality is a rare thing in young men these days. I'm impressed," G greeted them.

"Save ya compliments and let's get down to business. You got that information we need?" Turk said in a harsh tone. He could've been enjoying the company of a pretty girl and a good movie, yet he was dragged out into the streets to do his boss's bidding. He wasn't happy about it and had a hard time hiding it.

"Did Shai agree to my terms?" G asked.

"Yeah, he's gonna personally give you what you got coming," Baby Doc said. Shai had been livid when they relayed G's demands about payment. Baby Doc thought that he would blow a gasket and have them tell G to fuck off, but to his surprise, Shai finally agreed. Andrew's betrayal had him so mad that he was willing to do whatever it took to see him dead, even if it meant getting his own hands dirty.

"Then as agreed," G said and made a move to climb in the back of the Lexus, but Baby Doc stopped him.

"Nah, you ride up front with Turk. I'll play the backseat," Baby Doc held the passenger door open for him.

NO SHADE: A Hood Rat Novel

"That paranoid attitude of yours will ensure you have a long life in this game, shorty," G told Baby Doc before getting into the passenger seat.

G directed them to the Gun Hill section of the Bronx where they parked across the street from a rundown motel that was right on the strip. Turk was familiar with it from his days of hand to hand hustling up in that area; back before he met Baby Doc and Nickels. It was a notorious hang out for prostitutes and drug addicts. Under the dingy green awning, a woman was doing the dope fiend lean. Her body twisted at a near impossible angle and looked like she would fall over at any moment. Just before she made contact with the ground, she popped up and repeated the process. According to G, that's where they would find Andrew.

"You sure he's held up in there?" Turk asked suspiciously. To his knowledge, Andrew didn't get high and there couldn't have possibly been a sober soul in that whole building.

"As of an hour ago, yes," G said. "I've had one of my people laying on him all day and according to them he hasn't left. You'll find him in room 509."

"You ain't coming with us?" Baby Doc asked.

"That ain't in my job description. You wanted to know where to find Andrew and I've shown you," G told him.

"How do we know we're not walking into a set up?" Turk asked.

"Homie, you ain't high enough on the totem pole for anyone to care enough to pay to get you back and your head ain't worth enough to feed my drug habit for a week. You can either take my word as good or go back to Shai and tell him it was a dead end. Your choice," G reclined in the passenger seat.

"Fuck it. Let's just go see what's good," Baby Doc said to Turk from the backseat.

Turk nodded in agreement. He opened the driver's door to get out, but as an afterthought, took the key out of the ignition.

"C'mon man, at least let me hear the radio while I'm waiting," G protested him taking the key.

"My nigga, if your information doesn't pan out the only thing you're gonna hear is my pistol bust when I split your wig," Turk said seriously and got out of the car.

G watched from the passenger seat as Turk and Baby Doc crossed the street and entered the motel. "Check," he laughed to himself.

*

Turk and Baby Doc drew pulled their hoodies on before walking into the motel lobby. They kept their heads down and walked towards the stairs as if they knew where they were going. Passing the front desk the man sitting behind the glass opened his mouth to question them about their destination, but a cold look from Turk silenced him. He knew the shadow of death when he saw it.

Turk led the way, taking the stairs two at a time. He knew as soon as they were out of sight the man behind the glass would be on the phone with the police so they didn't have a lot of time. They prodded on booted feet down the hallway on the fifth floor, checking the room numbers. A base head was passed out on the floor outside an open room door, where inside a woman who looked like death warmed over was giving an overweight white man a blowjob. Turk ignored the urge to throw up in his mouth at the sight and pressed on.

Room 509 was located at the far end of the hall, right next to the fire stair, which was a good thing in case they needed to make a speedy exit. Turk pulled the .22 from his pocket and screwed the suppressor onto the barrel. He would've liked to give Andrew the business end of his cleaver, but they had to get in and out and guns would be quicker. He looked to Baby Doc to see if he was ready and found his friend hesitant.

"You good, B.D.?" Turk asked.

"Yeah, I'm cool." Baby Doc's voice was confident, but his body language wasn't. The gun in his hand shook visibly.

"If you want you can cover the door and I'll take care of Andrew," Turk offered.

"No, I'm not sitting this one out. We win together or we lose together," Baby Doc said.

"So be it," Turk raised his booted foot and kicked the door.

*

Andrew was sprawled out on a sheet-less mattress in and out of a nod. He was more lucid than he had been in the last few hours, but still sluggish from the regular heroin shots. His shirt was sweated down and his pants reeked from him pissing himself several times during his captivity. Andrew's hands and feet were no longer bound, but they didn't have to be because he was so doped up that he could barely stand let alone escape.

In a wooden chair in the corner sat a white woman who looked like she had seen better days. Andrew didn't know her, but he remembered hearing his captor call her Maxine. She was someone his captor had called on to help him in his scheme. Her job was a simple one, to sit with Andrew and every time he seemed to be coming around, shoot him up again. Luckily, she was so caught in the throes of her own nod that she had slipped and missed giving him his last shot. If Andrew had any hope of escape, it would have to be then.

Andrew collected himself to try and get up. His legs were still shaky, but he was able to stand up without falling on his face. Getting across the room seemed to be a slightly more complicated task. His legs ached with every step and the ground felt uneven beneath his feet. It was like trying to walk on a balloon. "One foot after the other," Andrew repeated to himself as he inched towards the door. He had just laid his hand on the knob, when the door came crashing in, knocking him to the floor. He looked up through the haze of pain and his dope induced haze and was able to make out two hooded figures. His brain screamed danger, but his body wouldn't react accordingly to the threat. All he could do was sit there on the floor with a dazed expression on his face.

"Get yo' bitch ass up," Turk grabbed him by the front of his soiled shirt and yanked him to his feet.

Andrew recognized the voice. "Turk?"

"No, Santa Clause," Turk slapped him viciously across the face, sending Andrew spilling to the bed. "There's some people that ain't too happy with you right now, Andrew."

"Turk, I been set up, I swear that wasn't on me," Andrew slurred. He was having trouble getting his mouth to work in tandem with his brain.

"Save it, homie. Shai has already passed sentence on you," Turk raised his gun.

"C'mon, don't do me like this. At least give me a chance to explain myself to Shai," Andrew pleaded.

"Shai don't wanna hear nothing you gotta say. You were a bitch in life, at least have the decency to die like a man," Turk said in disgust.

Andrew turned his teary eyes to Baby Doc. "B.D., help me out. You know me, man. We been thick as thieves since I started working for the Clarks. Don't let him do me like this."

What Andrew said was true. He and Baby Doc had developed a friendship and it was breaking his heart to see Andrew like that, but orders were orders. "I'm sorry, Andrew. You should've thought about that before you double-crossed the big homie." He turned his back.

Just about then, Maxine came out of her nod. When she saw the two armed men standing over Andrew she knew what time it was. G had paid her to keep Andrew doped up, not to die with him. She leapt to her feet and bolted towards the door, screaming her head off. It was a long shot but maybe someone would hear her screams and send help.

"Shut that bitch up, Baby Doc!" Turk ordered.

"Relax," Baby Doc grabbed her by the waist and tried to restrain her. Maxine was surprisingly stronger than Baby Doc thought and he was having trouble. "Shorty, you're only going to make things worse. Please stop fighting," he urged, but Maxine kept at it. She was fighting for dear life. Her struggling finally stopped when her head exploded, spraying Baby Doc with skull particles, and her blood. In wide-eyed shock, he looked over at Turk who was holding a smoking gun.

"I told you to quiet that bitch," Turk snarled. He turned his attention back to Andrew so they could finish the job and get out, but found himself the recipient of a sucker punch. Andrew had caught him square in the jaw. There wasn't enough force behind the blow to hurt Turk, but it shocked him enough to give Andrew a chance to try and flee. He had almost made it to the door, before three slugs to the back put him down. Turk put one more slug in his head for good measure, and ended Andrew.

In the distance, they could hear police sirens.

"Let's get the fuck out of here!" Baby Doc said nervously.

"In a minute." Turk rolled Andrew over onto his back and straddled his corpse. From beneath his hoodie, he produced his trusty cleaver.

"Turk what the fuck are you doing?"

"Stepping out of my father's shadow," Turk told him before bringing the cleaver down across Andrew's wrist.

CHAPTER 33

It had been a rough night for Billy, but promised to be a better day. In less than twenty-four hours, she would be Mrs. Marcus Manning and she couldn't wait.

The wedding rehearsal was to be held at the actual wedding location in Brooklyn. It would be the first time anybody beside Billy and Marcus would see the venue. It was a mansion that had been converted into a bed and breakfast, which rested in the heart of Bedford Stuyvesant, Brooklyn. Billy and Marcus had rented out the entire spot the wedding day and that night. Certain members of the wedding party would be given complementary rooms for the night and be there to have a special breakfast with the new bride and groom before they left for their honeymoon. It was going to be an event of epic proportions.

Though it was only the rehearsal, Billy still found herself extremely nervous. Marcus was deep in conversation with the pastor while he explained where he and his groomsmen would line up. Her best friends since the sandbox were milling about helping the florists with prep work to make sure each arrangement was placed perfectly. Even Sharon's lazy ass pitched in. She had gotten there earlier than any of them to receive the furniture delivery and tended to whatever Billy needed throughout the day. Sharon was still rough around the edges, but it looked like she was trying to finally grow up. Seeing all the people she loved gathered in one place for one cause made it all real to Billy. She was really about to get married.

"You good?" Kat crept up beside Billy. She was wearing tight black leggings, high heels, and had her weave ratted up into a high mound on top.

"Trying to be. I just can't believe the day is almost here," Billy said.

"Well believe it because it is. You and my brother are about to take the ultimate leap of faith."

"I just hope I live up to his expectations. I've never been anyone's wife," Billy said with uncertainty in her voice.

"Well to my knowledge he's never been anyone's husband, so you two can make it up as you go along," Kat winked. "But on a serious note; I'm proud of you guys. You know how protective I am of my brother, and at times, I had my doubts but I can honestly say you're a good girl, Billy. You're good people and good for my brother. I'm going to be proud to have you as a sister," Kat hugged her.

"Thanks, Kat. That means a lot coming from you," Billy hugged her back.

"Don't try and sample the bride's goodies before the groom. You can get next," Marcus joked. He came over and draped his arm around Billy, kissing her on the cheek. "You ready to become Mrs. Manning?"

"If I'm not, bet I'll be ready by tomorrow," Billy laughed. "I've been preparing for this moment my whole life, but I never dreamed it would actually come."

"I told you that it's my sole purpose in life to make all your dreams come true," Marcus told her.

"Aww, young love is so sweet," Reese said sarcastically. She and Yoshi had just gotten done helping the florist with the set up.

"Shut up, heifer," Billy capped.

"Nah, she's right," Yoshi added. "You and Marcus have been through a lot and you deserve this moment. I should only hope to be lucky enough to have you and Reese see me walk down the aisle before I'm old and gray."

"With the way Trap has been all up your ass, you may have your moment sooner than later," Marcus joked.

"Trap is cool, but I don't know if he's husband material. We haven't even reached the boyfriend and girlfriend stage so don't go trying to marry me off so quickly," Yoshi smirked. "Billy I wanted to thank you again for being keeping an open mind about Trap being here."

"He's okay...I guess," Billy looked over at Trap who was having a deep conversation with Shooter and the pastor about only God knew what, but whatever it was, he seemed to be engrossed in it.

Accepting Trap and Yoshi's relationship hadn't been an easy thing. It was hard for her to look beyond his past with Marcus and see his potential future with Yoshi, but for the sake of her best friend, she agreed to at least try. Billy had found her happiness and it was only fair to allow Yoshi to have a shot at her own. She just made sure that Trap knew if he hurt Yoshi he wouldn't be given another pass.

"Is everyone ready?" the pastor asked.

K'WAN

He separated them into two groups with guys on one side and girls on the other. Shooter would have the honor of giving Billy away. When she'd asked the old timer to stand up in place her father she could've sworn he got misty eyed. He deserved the honor. Shooter had been there through thick and thin with both Marcus and Billy. As usual, cousin Mud was drunk of his ass, but managed to hold his standing position just behind the best man. Trap became the last minute alternate groom's man when Shooter was asked to give Billy away. He seemed genuinely happy to be standing up for Marcus. There was still a bit of lingering tension between them over what had happened at the bachelor party, but it would pass, and Marcus would do what he had to do in order to make sure it did. In spite of all Trap's flaws, he proved to be a genuine friend when it really counted.

All the guys were in position, but things got a bit awkward when it was the ladies' turn to line up. The wedding was the next day and Billy was still without a Maid of Honor.

"Billy, I already told you that I was okay with Yoshi being the Maid of Honor," Reese conceded.

"Nah, it should go to you, Reese," Yoshi argued. The two of them went back and forth for nearly five minutes before Billy surprised them both.

"Neither one of you will be my Maid of Honor," Billy announced to everyone's shock. "Maid of Honor is an important position and should go to the woman who I can count on through thick and thin. The both of you are my best friends and it'd be an unfair decision to have to choose between you so I've decided the honor will go to Kat."

"Me?" Kat was shocked.

"Yes," Billy told her. "Kat, you've helped me through some pretty dark times. There are things I've shared with you that I wouldn't tell another soul, and you've never betrayed my trust. Even before your brother offered me his last name, I've always looked at you like my sister. I could think of no better choice to stand with me on my wedding day."

"Billy...I don't know what to say." Kat was teary-eyed.

"Say yes, so we can get through this rehearsal and go to dinner. I'm starving!" Wayne said.

"Are we finally ready to continue?" the pastor asked, looking at his watch.

Billy looked to Kat, who came to stand next to her. "Yes, we're ready."

*

Rocky's freedom pass had finally expired and it was time for her to go pick up her kid. She didn't mind though. After the couple of days of excitement she'd had she was more than ready to go back to her quiet life as a single mother.

She hadn't spoken to Turk that day, but they had been texting back and forth. There was no doubt in Rocky's mind that she was falling for him. Turk was a gangster and hardly her normal type, but sometimes opposites attracted. She would never totally agree with his lifestyle, but was willing to accept him as he was. So long as his other life didn't overlap hers, Rocky was okay with it.

Rocky's mother lived all the way in Brooklyn and she would have to get there by subway. She didn't want to take the long ride by herself so she enlisted Claudette. She promised to buy her a bottle if she took the trip and Claudette was all for it. The whole ride to Brooklyn Claudette questioned Rocky about Turk and how far she planned on going with him. Rocky let Claudette in on the fact that she liked him and they planned to see where things went, but nothing more than that. She knew better than to tell another woman too much about anyone she was seeing, especially a woman like Claudette. Sometimes the lonely souls got big ideas. She didn't think Turk would ever do anything with Claudette, but there was no sense in tempting fate.

It took Claudette and Rocky and hour to reach Rocky's mom's house in Brooklyn, but Rocky was in and out in less than ten minutes. She knew her mother would have a million and one questions about what she had been up to on her few days of freedom and Rocky hated lying to her mother. She thanked her for babysitting, kissed her on the cheek, and got out of there.

It was about a two block walk from Rocky's mother's building back to the C train on Nostrand. They were cutting down McDonough when they noticed a crowd of people just inside the gate of the big mansion on the corner. It looked as if they were having some kind of party. Upon closer inspection, Rocky spotted the two girls Claudette had gotten into it with at the welfare office.

316

Rocky was about to suggest that they go the other way so Claudette didn't see them, but it was too late.

"Ain't that them bitches that tried to pop off on me?" Claudette asked heatedly.

"Claudette, I've got my kid with me. Leave it for another time," Rocky pleaded. The last thing she wanted was for her son to see her fighting in the streets like a common hood rat.

"Nah, don't even worry about it. You and little man go ahead to the train and I'll see you back on the block." Claudette whipped out her phone and started pacing while she was waiting for the person on the other end to pick up.

"Who are you calling?" Rocky asked.

"My posse."

*

The rehearsal went off without a hitch. Everyone played their positions accordingly, including cousin Mud, though he almost got knocked out by Trap for trying to grope Yoshi. Outside of that, it was painless.

The group filed out of the mansion courtyard and onto the cub in front of the place. Billy and Marcus were walking arm and arm, both swooning like schoolchildren.

"I know this was only the rehearsal, but it felt so real," Billy said excitedly.

"Word, I almost broke down crying a couple of times." Marcus wiped the fake tears from his eyes.

317

"Well tomorrow is the big dance. After dinner I suggest we all go home and get some rest. It's gonna be a long day," Shooter said.

Billy cupped Marcus's face in her hands and kissed him on the lips. "Thank you, baby. I couldn't ask for a more perfect day."

"What's that?" Reese asked, noticing a cubed delivery truck backing up to a stop in front of the mansion.

"Billy, you expecting anymore deliveries?" Marcus asked.

"No, everything except the food is here already and that doesn't arrive until tomorrow morning," Billy told him.

"Well if it's not a delivery, what is it?" Marcus wondered out loud.

Just then, the back of the truck slid up and revealed about a half dozen girls in the back. They were all wearing shower caps and pajama pants. Leading the pack was the girl Reese and Sharon had beat up at the welfare office.

"Remember me bitches?" Claudette bellowed before she and the Shower Cap Posse swarmed the wedding party.

NO SHADE: A Hood Rat Novel

EPILOGUE

As it turned out, the only thing epic about Billy's wedding was the brawl that had broken out after the rehearsal. The dirty girls in the shower cap showed up expecting to win the day by having numbers on their side, but little did they know everybody who was a part of the wedding party were battle tested street veterans. Even old Shooter got down when the fighting started. They had to call in units from two different precincts to break the scuffle up. Those who didn't find themselves in the emergency room wound up in jail.

They locked Billy and her crew up in one cell and the girls from the Shower Cap Posse in another. During the fight, Billy didn't know or care what it had started over, she just saw that her girls were getting jumped and rushed to defend them. When she found out that it had all started over something Reese and Sharon did, she was livid. The whole time they were in the cage, Reese kept trying to apologize, but Billy didn't want to hear it.

It took several hours for the police to sort out what had happened. Most of the wedding party was released and given court dates to reappear, but they kept Shooter on a five year old child support warrant for a ten year old boy that he had apparently fathered. Claudette was also kept because she had two other open cases in addition to that one. After she was taken downtown to be arraigned she would be transferred to the Rose M. Singer building on Riker's Island. A part of Billy prayed they'd release the girl soon so she could whip her ass for ruining her wedding.

For as happy as Billy and Marcus were to be free, their wedding plans were still shot. Because of the fight at the mansion, they could no longer have their wedding there. In fact, the owner was suing them for damages. They still had the food and the wedding cake, which were both scheduled to be delivered the next day, but no venue.

"I can't believe this shit." Billy stood in front of the precinct in tears. She and the girls had just been released and were waiting for Marcus, Trap, and Wayne.

"It's going to be okay, sis." Kat tried to console her.

"How Kat? We paid thousands on the catering that we can't get back, not to mention there are two hundred people who are going to show up tomorrow expecting a wedding. Where are we supposed to get married now that we've lost the mansion?" Billy fumed.

"Maybe we can get another venue," Reese suggested.

"Another venue? Do you know how many months in advance I had to book this one? Where the fuck am I supposed to get another wedding venue with less than twenty-four hours' notice?" Billy snapped. She hadn't meant to be so harsh on Reese. She understood that it wasn't Reese's fault that the girls had attacked them, but she couldn't help but to think that if Reese and Sharon hadn't been fighting at the welfare office then none of it would've happened. All it took was a split second wrong decision and Billy's perfect day was ruined.

"I might have a solution," Yoshi took out her phone and punched in a number.

NO SHADE: A Hood Rat Novel

*

When Boo got the call from Yoshi and heard her plight, he was more than happy to help. Instead of having the food delivered to the mansion as scheduled, it was diverted to their new wedding location. The after-hours spot hardly compared to the mansion, but at the end the day it wasn't about where they got married, it was about the union they were entering into. There, in the shadow of D.J. booth, Billy and Marcus exchanged their wedding vows in front of their closest friends and loved ones. Billy cried like a baby when the pastor announced them Mr. and Mrs. Marcus Manning. Even gangster ass Trap got misty eyed. They had literally gone through hell to get to that day, but in the end it had all been worth it for Billy and Marcus to spend the rest of their lives together.

*

Turk and Baby Doc pulled up next to the basketball court on West 4th street where Shai had told them to meet him. He had picked such an open area so that he could spot any funny business before it happened. You would think that after all Turk had gone through for Shai he'd be a little more trusting, but the king was not. He even had Angelo and Swann pat Turk and Baby Doc down before allowing them into the park. Shai stood under the basketball hoop with Holiday, his cousin Nickels, and a few others at his side.

"What's that?" Shai motioned to the shoebox Turk was carrying under his arm.

321

"A tribute to my king," Turk mock bowed and handed him the box.

Shai looked at the box suspiciously and gave it a little shake trying to determine what was inside. "This ain't a bomb is it?"

"No, it's me showing you how committed I am to your family," Turk said.

"Then you open it," Shai gave him the box and took a cautious step back.

Turk opened the box and one by one began removing the objects. "If a man raises a hand against my king, I bring you that hand," he removed Andrew's left hand from the box. "If a man allows another to speak ill of my king, I'll bring you the ears he used to listen," he pulled out one of Andrew's ears. "And if a man speaks out against my king, I bring you his tongue," he pulled out Andrew's tongue and held it between his fingers, "so that he may never speak again."

Shai didn't know what to make of Turk's display so for a while he just stood there with a his mouth agape.

"You are one sick fuck," Swann kicked the box away. "What kind of dude brings a box full of body parts to someone as a gift?"

"A dedicated one," Shai said. "Turk, though I agree with Swann and you could've picked a less graphic way to prove the task was done, but I admire your creativity. You've more than proved yourself. Later on I'll have Holiday drop a little something on you to show my appreciation."

"With all due respect, Shai, I don't want your money. All I want is what you promised me," Turk told him.

"Well, my word is my word. Very well, young Turk. From this day forward you're no longer a soldier. I'm making you a full ranking Capo. You'll pick your own crew and answer only to me," Shai agreed.

"Can I pick anybody I want?" Turk asked.

"Sure, as long as it's not one of my personal guards," Shai told him.

"Fine, I'll take Baby Doc and Nickels to start with," Turk informed him.

Shai frowned. "Baby Doc you can have, but not Nickels."

"Come on, Shai. Don't act like that," Nickels pleaded. He had been watching his older cousin for years and felt like he was ready to step up. Besides, he was the son of a reputed killer.

"Nickels you're my cousin Gator's only heir, and I gave my word when you came to me that I would look after you. Besides, you're just a boy," Shai told him.

"Boys eventually grow to be men," Turk interjected. "Begging your pardon Shai, but if you think Nickels is still that bookworm orphan you took in then you haven't been paying attention. I've seen him operate. He's no killer, but he's got a brilliant mind. I don't want him with me as a solider, I want him with me because he's one of my best friends. You have my word that I'll look after him and teach him the game the right way, same as you would."

Shai weighed it. He knew that even if he denied Nickels chances are he'd just sneak around with Baby Doc and Turk like he'd been doing. Shai often had his hands so full that he couldn't keep track of what Nickels was into. Maybe if he let him study under Turk and Baby Doc, who were his peers, it would help keep Nickels out of harm's way. "Okay," Shai relented. "But I don't want Nickels in no shit. If he wants to hang around, cool, but under no circumstances are you to allow him to partake of the family business. When and if the time comes for him to step up, it'll be a decision that I make."

"Fair enough," Turk agreed.

"The three of you look more like a boy's club than a street crew," Angelo laughed.

"That's Billionaire Boys Club," Baby Doc corrected him.

Shai looked to Turk for clarification.

"It's just something we called ourselves when we were getting into trouble at boarding school," Turk explained.

"Billionaire Boys Club," Shai let the name roll around. "I like it. A billionaire is something you three knuckleheads should aspire to be. Now there's the matter of payment to the snitch who pointed you to Andrew. Where is this brazen muthafucka who demands an audience with me in person?"

"He's waiting in the car. I'll go get him," Baby Doc jogged off.

Shai and the others watched as he said something to the man in the backseat before opening the door for him. When G stepped out, Shai couldn't help but feel like he knew the man from somewhere. As he neared Shai, his features became more familiar. He looked slightly different with the beard obscuring most of his face, and he now walked with a bit of a limp, but Shai would know him anywhere.

"Somebody tell me that I'm not the only one seeing this," Swann blinked to make sure his eyes weren't playing tricks on him.

"Nope, you ain't the only one," Angelo said, equally shocked.

"It can't be," Shai gasped. Even when G was standing right in front of him, Shai refused to believe what his eyes were telling him.

"You guys know each other?" Turk looked from Shai to G.

"I'm sorry, youngster. There's a bit of information that I withheld from you when we met. I figured it make for a better surprise when you reunited me with my cousin," G said.

"Cousin?" Turk didn't understand.

"First cousins at that, but you wouldn't know it the way Shai left me for dead," G sneered showing off his jagged gold teeth. "In case you haven't figured it out yet, the G in my name stands for *Gator*."

This came as a shock to all of them, but none more so than young Nickels. "Dad?" he gasped.

*

Later that night Billy and Marcus would return to their condo instead of spending the night at the mansion, but it was okay by them. The next morning they were flying into Puerto Rico to board a cruise ship that would take them all through the Southern Caribbean for the next seven days. They were walking from the parking lot to their building when Billy saw two men in off the rack suits standing outside the entrance. As she got closer, she realized that she knew them from watching them chase Jah, Tech, and eventually Animal around for so many years. Whenever Detectives Brown and Alvarez were around, trouble always followed.

"Marcus Manning?" the brown-skinned detective asked, flashing his badge.

"Something I can help you with?" Marcus asked suspiciously. His heart thudded rapidly in his chest.

"We just need to ask you a few questions," the Hispanic detective chimed in.

"Look, I've had a long day and I've got a plane to catch in a few hours. I'm going on my honeymoon. Any questions you have for me you can direct to my lawyer," Marcus took Billy by the hand and brushed past them.

"It's about Tamara Jones," Detective Brown announced.

At the mention of Tammy's name, Marcus stopped dead in his tracks.

"Thought that would get your attention," Detective Brown said smugly.

"What about her?" Marcus asked, trying to keep his cool.

"Her roommate has reported her missing and according to her, the last time she saw Tammy she was distraught and on her way to your club," Detective Alvarez told him. "Now you can spare us five minutes to tell us what happened the last time you saw Ms. Jones or you we can get a warrant to bring you in and that honeymoon of yours will be delayed indefinitely. Pick your poison."

Marcus looked at Billy who had a million and one questions dancing behind her eyes...questions he wasn't sure he could answer. There was a saying that Shooter always used about chickens coming home to roost and Marcus now found himself in a hen house.

Animal IV: Last Rites

The Fix Series:

The Fix

The Fix 2

The Fix 3

Shorts/Anthologies/Novellas:

The Game

Flirt

Flexin & Sexin (Vol 1)

From The Streets to the Sheets

From Harlem With Love

Love & Gunplay (Animal Story)

The Leak (Animal Story)

Purple Reign (Vol 1: Purple City Tales)

Little Nikki Grind (Vol 2: Purple City Tales)

The Life & Times of Slim Goodie (Season 1)

First & Fifteenth (A Hood Rat Short)

Black Lotus

Venus vs Mars

Ashanti

Made in the USA
Middletown, DE
22 October 2015